In Old Kentucky

Edward Marshall

and Charles T. Dazey

Contents

IN OLD KENTUCKY

BY

Edward Marshall and Charles T. Dazey

CHAPTER I.

She was coming, singing, down the side of Nebo Mountain--"Old Nebo"--mounted on an ox. Sun-kissed and rich her coloring; her flowing hair was like spun light; her arms, bare to the elbows and above, might have been the models to drive a sculptor to despair, as their muscles played like pulsing liquid beneath the tinted, velvet skin of wrists and forearms; her short skirt bared her shapely legs above the ankles half-way to the knees; her feet, never pinched by shoes and now quite bare, slender, graceful, patrician in their modelling, in strong contrast to the linsey-woolsey of her gown and rough surroundings, were as dainty as a dancing girl's in ancient Athens.

The ox, less stolid than is common with his kind, doubtless because of ease of life, swung down the rocky path at a good gait, now and then swaying his head from side to side to nip the tender shoots of freshly leaving laurel. She sang:

"Woodpecker pecked as a woodpecker will,
 Jim thought 'twas a knock on the door of the still,
He grabbed up his gun, and he went for to see,
The woodpecker laughed as he said: 'Jest me!'"

She laughed, now, not at the song, which was purely automatic, but in sheer joy of living on that wonderful June day in those marvellous Kentucky mountains. Their loneliness did not depress her; indeed, to her, they were not lonely, but peopled by a host of lifelong friends who had greeted her at birth, and would, she had every reason to suppose, speed her when her end came. Their majesty did not overwhelm her, although she felt it keenly, and respected it and loved it with a certain dear, familiar awe. And everywhere about her was the Spring. Laurel blossomed at the trail's sides, filling the whole air with fragrance; the tardier blueberry bushes crowding low about it had begun to show the light green of their bursting buds; young ferns were pushing through the coverlet of last autumn's leaves which had kept them snug against the winter's cold, and were beginning to uncurl their delicate and wondrous spirals; maple and beech were showing their new leaves. The air was full of bird-notes--the plaintively pleading or exultantly triumphant cries of the mating season's joy and passion. Filmy clouds, like scattered, snowy ostrich plumes, floated, far, far up above her on a sea of richest blue; a fainter blue of springtime haze dimmed the depths of the great valley which a wide pass gave her vision of off to the left--and she was rather glad of this, for the haze, while, certainly, it hid from her much beauty, also hid the ugly scars which man was making there on nature's face, the cuts and gashes with which the builders of the new railway were marring the rich pasture lands.

She turned from this to pleasanter and wilder prospects, close at hand, as her path narrowed, and began to sing again in sheer joyousness of spirit.

"Mr. Woodpecker laughed as a woodpecker will,   As Jim stood lookin' out of the door of the still,   'Mr. Jim,' he remarked, 'I have come for to ax   *Ef* you'd give me a worm for my revenue tax'!"

The placid ox, plodding slowly down the trail, did not swerve when the bushes parted suddenly at one side, as she finished this verse of her song, but Madge Brierly looked about with a quick alertness. The sound of the rustling leaves and crackling twigs might mean a friend's approach, they might mean the coming of one of the very enemies whom the song had hinted at so lightly, but against whom all the people of the mountains keep perpetual watch, they might even mean a panther, hungry after his short rations of the winter and recklessly determined on a meal at any cost.

But it was Joe Lorey's face which greeted her as she abruptly turned to see. His coon-skin cap, his jerkin and trousers of faded blue-jeans, his high, rusty boots matched perfectly with his primitive environments. As he appeared only the old-fashioned Winchester, which he carried cradled in his crooked elbow, spoke of the Nineteenth century. His face, though handsome in a crudely modelled way, had been weather-beaten into a rough, semi-fierceness by the storms through which he had watched the mountain-passes during the long winter for the raiders who were ever on his trail. The slightly reddened lids of his dark, restless eyes, told of long nights during which the rising fumes of moonshine whisky stealthily brewing in his furtive still, cave-hidden, had made them smart and sting. Even as, smilingly, he came up to the strangely mounted maid, there was on his face the strong trace of that hunted look which furtive consciousness of continual and unrelenting pursuit gives to the lawbreaker--even to the lawbreaker who believes the laws he breaks are wrong and to be violated without sin and righteously.

"That you, Joe?" said the girl. "You skeered me."

"Did I?" he replied, grinning broadly. "Didn't plan to."

From far below there came the crash of bursting powder. Quick and lithe as a panther the man whirled, ready with his rifle. The girl laughed.

"Nothin' but the railroad blastin' down there in the valley," she said with amusement. "Ain't you uset to that, yet?"

"No," said he, "I ain't--an' never will be."

His tone was definitely bitter. Never were the "sounds of progress more ungraciously received than there among the mountains by the folk who had, hedged in by their fastnesses, become almost a race apart, ignorant of the outside world's progressions and distrustful and suspicious of them.

"Where you goin', Madge?" he asked, plodding on beside the lurching ox.

"I ain't tellin'," she said briefly. "But you can go part ways--you can go fur as th' pasture bars."

"Why can't I go as fur as you go?"

"Because," said she, and laughed. "I reckon maybe that th' water's started to warm up down in the pool, ain't it?" she cried, and laughed again.

"Oh!" said he, a bit abashed, and evidently understanding.

They did not pursue the subject.

"What you got there?" he inquired, a few moments later, as they were approaching the old pasture. He pointed to a package carefully wrapped in a clean apron, which she hugged beneath her arm.

"Spellin' book," said Madge, as, just before the bars she slid down from her perch upon the ox. "I'm learnin'."

His lip curled with the mountaineer's contempt for books and all they have to teach.

"What you want to **learn** for?"

He had gently shouldered her aside as she had stooped to raise the bars back to position, and, with a certain crude gallantry, had done the task himself.

"Bleeged," she said briefly, and then, standing with one brown and rounded arm upon the topmost rail, paused in consideration of an answer to his question.

The ox stopped, dully, close within the closed gap in the rough fence. She went closer to him and patted his side kindly. "Go on, old Buck," she said. "I'm through with you for quite a while. Go on and have some fun or rest, whichever you like best. You certainly can stand a lot of rest! And here is new spring grass, Buck. I should think you would be crazy to git at it."

As if he understood, the old ox turned away, and, slowly, with careful searching for the newest and the tenderest of the forage blades which had pushed up to meet the pleasant sunshine, showed he was well fed at all times.

"What do I want to learn for?" the girl repeated, returning to Joe's question. "Why--why--I don't know, exactly. There's a longin' stirrin' in me.

"While you was over yon" (she waved her hand in a broad sweep to indicate the mountain's other side). "I had to go down into town after--after quite a lot of things." She looked at him somewhat furtively, as if she feared this statement might give rise to some unwelcome questioning, but it did not. "I saw what queer things they are doin'--th' men that work there on that railroad buildin'. Wonderful things, lots of 'em, and the bed-rock of 'em all was learnin'. I watched a gang of 'em for near plum half a day. There wasn't a thing they did that they didn't first read from a sheet of paper about. If they hadn't had them sheets and if they couldn't read what had been written on 'em, why, they couldn't never **build** no railroad. And not only that--they got all kinds of comfort out of it. They have their books that tell 'em what other men have done before 'em, they have their newspapers that tell 'em-- **every-day**, Joe--what other men are doin', everywhere, fur as th' earth is spread.

"They **know** things, them men do, and they're heaps happier because of it." She paused, leaning on the old worn fence.

"An' their wimmen knows things," she went on. "I'm goin' to, too. It's th' greatest comfort that they've got. I'm goin' to **have** that comfort, Joe!"

She patted the new spelling book as if it were a precious thing.

"I'm goin' to have that comfort," she continued. "I'm goin' to know th' ins an' outs o' readin' an'" (she sighed and paused a second, as if this next seemed more appalling) "an' of writin'. Dellaw! That's hard! All sorts of curves an' twists an' ups an' downs an' things, an' ev'ry one means somethin'!"

Joe looked at her, half in admiration, half in apprehension. "You goin' to git too good fer these here mountings?" he inquired.

She gazed about her with a little intake of the breath, a little sign of ecstasy, of her appreciation of the wondrous view.

"Too good for these here mountings?" she said thoughtfully. "Learnin' couldn't make me that! It might show me how to love 'em more. Nothin' in th' world, Joe, could make me love 'em less!"

He became more definite, a bit insistent. It had been plain, for long, that it had required some self-control for him to walk as he had walked, close by her side, without some demonstration of his admiration for her, to stand there with her at the bars without some sign that in her presence he found happiness much greater than he had ever known, could ever know, elsewhere.

"You goin' to git too good fer--me?" he asked.

She turned toward him impulsively. Great friendship shone frankly in her fine eyes. On her face was that expression of complete and understanding comradery which one child chum may show another. Almost she said as much of him as she had said of the surrounding mountains, but there was that upon his face which stopped her. It was too plain that friendship was not what he wanted, would not satisfy him. There was a hungry yearning in his eyes, mute, respectful, worshipful, not for comradery, but for a closer tie. She had watched this grow in him within the recent months, with worry and regret. It seemed to her a tragedy that their old friendship should ever prove inadequate.

"No," she answered gently, "I shall never get too good for you, Joe--for any of my friends."

He looked, almost with aversion, at the book she held so closely. He distrusted books. Instinctively he felt them to be enemies.

"If you get them there ideas about learnin', an' all that, you will!" he gruffly said. "Leastways you'll be goin' off, some day an' leavin' us--me, the mountings an'--an' all yer friends up here."

An expression of great earnestness, of almost fierce intensity grew in his face.

"Madge," he said, "Madge Brierly, you're makin' a mistake! You're plannin' things to take you off from here; you're plannin' things to make you suffer, later on. You're gettin' bluegrass notions, an' bluegrass notions never did no mounting-born no good." He stepped closer to her.

The latent fires in his approaching eyes were warning for her and she stepped back hastily. "Joe Lorey, you behave yourself!" said she. "I--"

"Can't ye see I love ye, Madge?" he asked, and then the fires died down, leaving in his eyes the pleading, worried look alone. "Why, Madge, I--"

She tried to make a joke of it. "Joe Lorey," she said, laughing, "I reckon you're *plum* crazy. An' you ain't givin' me a chance to do what 'twas that I come down for."

"But--"

"I ain't goin' to listen to another word, to-day," said she, and waved him off.

He went obediently, but slowly and unhappily, his rifle snuggling in the crook of his left elbow, his heavy boots finding firm footing in the rough and rocky trail as if by instinct of their own, without assistance from his brain. A "revenuer," coming up, just then, to bother him about his still and its unlawful product of raw whisky, would have met small mercy at his hands. He would have been a bad man, then, to quarrel with. His temper would have flared at slightest provocation. He would not let it flare at her; but, unseeing any of the beauties which so vividly appealed to her, the bitter foretaste of defeat was in his heart; and in his soul was fierce revolt and disappointment. He had not the slightest thought, however, of accepting this defeat as final.

Madge watched him go with a look of keen distress upon her fresh and beautiful young face. She must not let him say what he had almost said, for she shrank from the thought of wounding him with the answer she felt in her heart that she would have to make. He had slouched off, half-way down the trail and out of sight, before she put the thoughts of the unpleasant situation from her mind and turned again to the great matter which had brought her there, that day.

With a last glance at the gap in the rail fence, to make sure that it had been carefully replaced, so that there could be no danger of finding her ox gone when she returned, she started down the mountain, by a path different from that which Joe had taken.

She had not gone very far, when, from a clump of bunch-grass just in front of her, only partly, yet, renewed by the new season, a hare hopped awkwardly, endeavoring to make off. Its progress was one-sided, difficult.

Instantly she saw that it was wounded and with a little cry she ran toward it and caught it. Instinctively the tiny animal seemed to recognize her as a friend and ceased to struggle. One of its fore legs had been broken, as she quickly saw.

With a little exclamation of compassion, she sat down upon a hummock, tore from her skirt a bit of cloth, found, on the ground, two twigs, made of these crude materials rude splints and bandages, bound the wounded creature, and sent it on its painful way again. She sighed as, after having watched it for a moment, she arose.

"Pears like us human bein's always was a-hurtin' somethin'," she soliloquized, distressed. "Thar some chap has left that rabbit in misery behind him, and here I've sent Joe Lorey down the mountain with a worse hurt than it's got." She sighed. "It certain air a funny world!" she said.

The subject of the wounded rabbit did not leave her mind until she had clambered down the rocky path half-way to the small stream which she sought below. She was ever ready with compassion for the suffering, especially for dumb and helpless suffering animals, and, besides, the episode had puzzled her. Who was there in those mountains who would *wound* a rabbit? Joe might have shot one, as might any other of the mountain dwellers who chanced to take a sudden fancy for a rabbit stew for supper, but Joe nor any of the other natives would have left it wounded and in suffering behind him. Too sure their markmanship, too careful their use of ammunition, for such a happening as that. Trained in the logic of the woods, the presence of the little suffering animal was a proof to her that strangers were about. The people of the mountains regard all strangers with suspicion. Half-a-dozen times she stopped to listen, half-a-dozen times she started on again without having heard an alien sound. Once, from the far distance, she did catch a faint metallic clinking, as of the striking of a hammer against rock, but it occurred once only, and she finally attributed it to the mysterious doings of the railroad people in the valley.

Down the path she sped, now, rapidly and eagerly. It was plain that something which she planned to do when she reached her destination filled her with anticipation of delight, for her red lips parted in a smile of expectation as charming as a little child's, her breath came in eager pantings not due wholly to the mere exertion of the rapid downward climb. When, beyond a sudden turn in the rude trail, she suddenly saw spread before her the smooth waters of a pool, formed by the creek in a hill-pocket, she cried aloud with pleasure.

"Ah," said she. "Ah! Now here we be!"

But it was not at this first pool she stopped. Leaving the path she skirted its soft edge, instead, and, after having passed down stream some twenty yards or more, pushed her skilled way between the little trees of a dense thicket and into a dim, shadowy woods chamber on beyond, where lay another pool, velvety, en-dusked, save for the flicker of the sunlight through dense foliage.

Here her delight was boundless. She ran forward with the eagerness of a thirsty bird, and, leaning on the bank, supported by bent arms, bent down and drank with keenest relish of the cool spring waters gathered in the "cove," then dabbled her brown slender fingers in the shining depths, watching, with a smile, concentric, widening ripples as they hurried out across the glassy surface, to the ferned bank beyond. A few yards away a hidden cascade murmured musically. Through the sparse and tender foliage of spring above her, the sunlight flickered in bright, moving patches of golden brilliance, falling on the breast of her rough, homespun gown, like decorations given by a fairy queen. Around the water's edges budding plants and deep-hued mosses made a border lovely everywhere, and for long spaces deep and soft as velvet pile. A thrush called softly from the forest depths behind her. From the other side his mate replied in a soft twittering that told of love and confidence and comfort. A squirrel scampered up the trunk of a young beech, near by, and sat in the first crotch to look down at her, chattering. A light breeze sighed among the branches, swaying them in languorous rhythm, rustling them in soft and ceaseless whisperings.

All these familiar, pleasant sights and sounds delighted her. During the long winter she had been shut away from this, her favorite spot among the many lovely bits of wilderness about her, and now its every detail filled her with a fresh and keen delight. She looked and listened greedily, as happy as a city child, seated, for the first time in a space of months, before a brightly lighted stage to watch a pantomime. A dozen times she ran with little, bird-like cries to bend above some opening wild-flower, a space she spent in watching two intently busy king-birds, already fashioning their nest. Another squirrel charmed her beyond measure by sitting, for a moment, on a limb to gaze at her in bright-eyed curiosity, and then, with a swift run down the trunk, quite near to her, as if entirely satisfied that he saw in her a certain friend, scuttling to the water's edge for drink. She had never seen a squirrel drink before--few people have--and she stood, as motionless as might a maid of marble, watching him, until, having had his fill, he gave his tail a saucy flirt and darted back to his beech fortress, to sit again upon his limb and chatter gossip at her.

After he had gone back to his tree she looked carefully about her. It now became apparent that she had come there to the pool for some especial purpose and that she wished to be quite sure of privacy before she put it into execution, for she went first to the path by which she had descended, there to listen long, intently, then, with a lithe spring where the brook narrowed at the pool's mouth, to the other side, where, at some distance in the forest, by another woods-path's edge, she stood again, intent and harkening.

Apparently quite satisfied that so far as human beings went her solitude was quite complete, she returned, now, to the pool's edge and stood gazing down upon its polished surface. Soon she dipped the toe of one brown, slender foot into it, evidently prepared to draw back hastily in case of too low temperature, but tempted, when she found the water warm, she gently thrust the whole foot in, and then, gathering her skirt daintily up to her knees, actually stepped into the water, wading with little shrill screams of delight.

For a moment she stood poised there, both hands busy with her skirt, which was pulled back tight against her knees. Then, after another hasty glance around, she sprang out upon the bank with a quick gesture of determination, and, close by the thicket's edge, disrobed entirely and came back to the water as lovely as the dream of any ancient sculptor, as alluring as the finest fancy of the greatest painter who has ever touched a brush.

Slim, graceful, sinuous, utterly unconscious of her loveliness, but palpitating with the sensuous joy of living, she might have been a wood nymph, issuing vivid, vital, from the fancy of a mediaeval poet. The sunlight flecked her beautiful young body with fluttering patches as of palpitant gold leaf. The crystal water splashed in answer to the play of her lithe limbs and fell about her as in showers of diamonds. Flowers and ferns upon the pool's edge, caught by the little waves of overflow, her sport sent shoreward, bowed to her as in a merry homage to her grace, her fitness for the spot and for the sport to which she now abandoned herself utterly, plunging gaily into the deepest waters of the basin. From side to side of its narrow depths she sped rapidly, the blue-white of the spring water showing her lithe limbs in perfect grace of motion made mystically indefinite and shimmering by refraction through the little rippling waves her progress raised. She raced and strained, from the pure love of effort, as if a stake of magnitude depended on her speed.

Then, suddenly, this fever for fast movement left her and she slowed to languorous movement, no less lovely.

The trout, which had been frightened into hiding by the splashing of her early progress, came timidly, again, from their dim lurking places, to eye this new companion of the bath with less distrust, more curiosity. With sinuous stroke, so slow it scarcely made a ripple, so strong it sent her steadily and firmly on her zig-zag way, she swam, now, back and forth, around about, from side to side and end to end in the deep pool, with keen enjoyment, each movement a new loveliness, each second bringing to her fascinating face some new expression of delight and satisfaction. Behind her streamed her flowing hair, unbound and free to ripple, fan-like, on the water; before her dainty chin a little wave progressed, unbreaking, running back on either hand beside her, V-shaped. Her hands rose in the water, caught it in cupped palms and pushed it down and backward with the splashless pulsing thrust of the truly expert swimmer.

Only the warm blood of perfect health could have endured the temperature of that shaded mountain pool so long, and soon even she felt its chill gripping her young muscles, and, as unconscious of her wholly revealed loveliness as any nymph of old mythology, scrambled from the water to the bank and stood there where a shaft of comfortable sunshine found its welcome way through rifted foliage above. To this she turned first one bare shoulder, then the other, with as evident a sensuous delight as she had shown when the cool water first closed over her. Then, throwing back her head, she stood full in the brilliance, and, inhaling deeply, let the sunlight fall upon the loveliness of her young chest. The delight of this was far too great for voiceless pleasure, and her deep, rich laughter rippled out as liquid and as musical as the tones of the tiny waterfall above the pool. She raised a knee and then the other to let the vitalizing sunlight fall upon them; then, with head drooped forward on her breast, stood with her sturdy but delicious shoulders in its shining path. Her happiness was perfect and she smiled continually, even when she was not giving vent to audible expressions of enjoyment.

Suddenly, however, this idyllic scene was interrupted. In the woods she heard the crashing of an awkward footstep and a muttered word or two in a strange voice, as might come from a lowlander whose face has suffered from the sting of a back-snapping branch.

For an instant she poised, frightened, on the bank. The intruder's crashing progress was bringing him, as her ears plainly told her, steadily in her direction. Panic-stricken, for a moment, she crouched, hugging her bare limbs in an ecstasy of fear. To get her clothes and put them on before he reached the pool would be impossible, a hasty glance about her showed no cover thick enough to flee to.

One concealment only offered perfect hiding--the very pool from which she had so recently emerged. She poised to slip again into the water noiselessly and then caught sight of her disordered clothing on the bank. To leave it there would as certainly reveal her presence as to remain on the bank herself! Hastily she gathered it and the new spelling book into her arms, and, with not ten seconds of spare time to find the cover which she so desperately needed, endeavored to slip quietly into the pool again.

Her certainty of movement failed her, this time, though, and one foot slipped. Into the pool she went, half-falling, and with a splash which, she was certain, would be audible a hundred yards away. Terrified anew by this, she dived quickly to the bottom of the pool and with all a trout's agility and fearlessness, her clothing and beloved book clasped tight against her bosom by her crooked left arm, her right arm sending her with rapid strokes, when she was quite submerged, the full length of the pool to its far end. There a fallen tree, relic of some woodland tempest of years gone by, extended quite from bank to bank, moss-covered, half hidden by small rushes and a little group of other water-plants. She dived beneath this log with the last atom of endurance she possessed and rose, perforce, upon the other side, stifling her gasps, but drawing in the air in long, luxurious breathings. With her mouth not more than half-an-inch above the water and her feet upon hard bottom, she crouched there, watching through the screen of plants, her clothes and book still pressed against her breast.

As she peered across the log between the rushes, she saw the stranger, with a wary step, break through the undergrowth about the pool--cautiously, expectantly. The water heaved a bit about her chin, for her hidden chest was palpitating with the short, sharp intakes of a chuckling laughter.

"Thought I were a b'ar, most likely!" she thought merrily, quite certain of the safety of her hiding place. "Some furriner." All strangers, in the mountains, are spoken of as "foreigners" and regarded with a hundred times the wonder and distrust shown in cities to the native of far lands, remote.

Her guess was shrewd. The stranger had plainly been attracted by the sounds of her delighted splashing and had hurried up with rifle ready for a shot at some big game. Now he stood upon the granite edges of the pool, disappointed even in his instinctive search for footprints, with only the slowly widening circles left upon the surface by her hurried flight to show him that he had not wholly been mistaken in his thought that something most unusual had recently occurred there in the "cove." Eagerly his disappointed glance roved around the circling thicket--nowhere did it see a sign. When it neared the place of her concealment the hidden girl ducked, softly, making no undue commotion in the swiftly running water at the pool's outlet, and the searching glance passed on, quite unsuspecting, before her breath failed and her head emerged again.

"Confound it!" the deeply disappointed youth exclaimed. "I was dead certain I heard something. I *did* hear something, too." He sighed. "But it is gone, now."

At length he turned away in a bad temper, and presently she heard him crashing awkwardly through brush and brake, departing.

Shivering from her long submersion in the gelid waters of the mountain stream, she cautiously emerged, struggling between light-hearted laughter at the comedy of her escape and rueful worry about the fact that she was not only deeply chilled but had no clothes which were not wet. Her soaked spelling-book, also, gave her much concern. Before she spread her clothing out in the sparse sunlight, she took the dripping volume to the warmest little patch of brilliance on any of the rocks surrounding, and, as she opened its leaves to catch the sunshine, examined it with loving solicitude to find how badly it was damaged.

"Fast color," she said happily, looking at the mighty letters of its coarse black print. "Ain't faded none, nor run, a mite." This plainly give her great relief. Deftly she turned each leaf, using the extremest care to avoid tearing them, handling them with loving touch. Between them she laid little pine cones, so that air might circulate among them and assist the process of their drying. Then, having wrung her clothing till her strong, brown, slender wrists ached, she spread that out in turn, but on less favored rocks, and, as her feeling of security increased, fell into an unconscious dance, born of the necessity of warmth from exercise, but so full of grace, abandon, joy, that a poet might have fancied her a river-nymph, tripping to the reed-born music of the goat-hoofed Pan.

When, later, she had slowly dressed, and was kneeling at the pool's edge, using the now placid surface of the water as a mirror to assist her in rough-fashioning her hair into a graceful knot, she heard again, from a great distance, a metallic "tink, tink-tink," which had caught her ear when she had first stood on the pool's edge. It came, she knew, from far, however, and so did not rouse her apprehension, but, mildly, it aroused her curiosity.

"Hull kentry's 'full o' furriners," she mused. "That railroad buildin' business in the valley brings 'em. Woods ain't private no more." Again the tink, tink-tink. "Sounds like hammerin' on rocks," she thought. "It's nearer than th' railroad builders, too. I wonder what--but then, them furriners are wonderful for findin' out concernin' ev'rythin'."

She hugged her pulpy spelling book against her breast with a little shiver of determination. "*I'm* goin' to l'arn, too," she said with firm decision as she scrambled up the rough and rocky mountain path.

For a time, as she progressed, her thoughts remained afield, wandering in wonder of what that "furriner" might be up to with the tink-tink of his hammer upon rocks. This soon passed, however, and they dwelt again on the pool episode.

She had never seen a man dressed as the stranger had been. A carefully made shooting-jacket had covered broad and well-poised shoulders which were free of that unlovely stoop which comes so early to the mountaineer's. A peaked cap of similar material had shaded slightly a broad brow with skin as white as hers and whiter. Beneath it, eyes, which, although they were engaged in anxious search when she had seen them, she knew could, upon occasion, twinkle merrily, had gazed, clear, calm, and brown. A carefully trimmed mustache had hidden the man's upper lip, but his chin, again a contrast to the mountaineers' whom she had spent her life among, showed blue from constant and close shaving. Yet, different as he was from her people of the mountains, as she recalled that face she could not hate him or distrust him.

She had never in her life seen any one in knickerbockers and leggins before, and the memory of his amused her somewhat, yet she admitted to herself that they had seemed quite "peart" as she peered at them through the reeds.

But it was the modern up-to-date Winchester which he had held, all poised to fly up to the ready shoulder should he find the splashing animal which had attracted his attention by its noise, which, next to his handsome, clean-cut face, had most aroused her admiration.

"Lordy! Joe'd give his eyes to hev a gun like that," she said.

And then she made a pun, unconscious of what the outer world calls such things, but quite conscious of its humor. "Thought I was a b'ar," she chuckled. "Well, I certainly *was* b'ar!"

Feeling no further fear of any one, defiant, now that she was fully clothed, of "furriners," rather hoping, as a matter of fact that she might sometime meet this one again, she let her laugh ring out unrestrained. A cat-bird answered it with a harsh cry; a blue-jay answered him with a still harsher note. But then a brown thrush burst into unaccustomed post-meridian song. Even his throbbing trills and thrilling, liquid quaverings, had not more melody in them, however, than had her ringing laughter.

CHAPTER II

Her laugh, too, roused more than vagrant birds into attention. She had emerged from the abrupt little valley and was entering upon a plateau which had been left comparatively open by the removal of great trees, sacrificed to furnish ties for the new railroad building in the lowlands. The place was littered with the discarded tops of pines and other woodland rubbish and seemed forlorn and wrecked. She swept her eyes about with the glance of a proprietor, for Madge Brierly owned all of this as well as most of the land through which the brook which deepened into the pool of her adventure flowed. Indeed the girl was counted rich among her fellows and owned, also, land down in the valley on which she would not live, but which she rented for an annual sum to her significant, although it would not have kept a lowland belle in caramels.

In the center of the disordered clearing just before her, was the person who, like the birds, had been roused to keen attention by the maiden's ringing laugh. She saw him first while he was peering here and there, astonished, to learn whence the sound had come, and, with the instinctive caution of the mountain-bred, she quickly stepped behind a clump of laurel, through which she peered at him.

He was a man of sixty years, or thereabouts, wiry, tough and well preserved. His hair, of grizzled grey, was longer than most men wore theirs, even among the mountains, where there are few conventionalities in male attire. He was dressed in the ordinary garb of the Kentucky planter of the better class--broad soft hat, flowing necktie, long frock-coat, which formed a striking contrast to the coarse high-boots into the tops of which his trousers had been tucked--and yet he hardly seemed to her to belong to the class of gentlemen to which his dress apparently assigned him. His face was coarse and hard, his eyes, as he peered about in search of her, were "shifty," she assured herself. His hands were large and crudely fashioned.

"'Pears like 'most ev'ry one is roamin' 'round my land to-day," she thought. "I wonder what *this* one is up to, thar?"

For fully fifteen minutes her curiosity remained unsatisfied, for, startled by the ringing laugh, the stranger spent at least a quarter of an hour in furtive peering, here and there, about the clearing, plainly searching for the laughter. At no time, however, did he approach her hiding place near enough to see her, and, finally, apparently satisfied that his ears had fooled him, or that whoever it had been who had disturbed him with the merry peal had gone away, he went back to his work.

Just what this work could be was what she waited curiously to see. She felt not the least resentment of the trespass it involved, for the land was wild, and on it, as elsewhere in the mountains, any one was free to come and go who did not commit the foolishness of neglecting camp fires, likely to start forests into blaze, or the supreme treachery of giving information to the revenue officials about hidden stills. Her eager curiosity was aroused, more by the mysterious nature of the stranger's operations than by the fact that they were conducted on her land.

Having satisfied himself that no one, now, was near, and, therefore, that he was not watched, the unpleasantly mysterious old man went back to the work which evidently had brought him hither. With utmost care he moved about the place, scrutinizing outcropping rocks, and this, as they were everywhere, meant a minute examination of the land. In his hand he carried a small hammer, and, with this, now and then, after a careful visual examination of a rock, he knicked it, here and there, investigating carefully and even eagerly the scars he made, the bits of rock which were clipped off, now and then even looking at the latter through a magnifying glass, which he took for the purpose from a pocket of his vest.

She had watched these operations, fascinated, for, possibly, a full half hour, despite the discomfort of damp clothing, which had begun to chill her, when she saw signs of violent excitement on the old man's face and in his actions, after he had chipped a rock, from which he first had had to scrape a thin superstratum of light soil.

Like a miner who has found the gold for which, for years, he has been searching, he arose, with the tiny fragments in his hand, to look at them with greedy eyes, in a more comfortable, upright posture. His face had very plainly paled and in his eyes was an expression of such avaricious eagerness and satisfaction as she had never seen before upon a human countenance.

Before he made a sound she knew that he had found that thing for which he had been seeking. His grizzled countenance, intent as any alchemist's of old upon his search, and, as its absorption grew, continually less a pleasant face to contemplate, now twisted, suddenly, into an expression of incredulous joy. He took the fragment he had been examining in both his hands and held it close before his eyes. Then he made a minute search of it with his little magnifying glass. Then he fell upon his knees, and, with his clawlike fingers, scraped more earth from the rock whence he had chipped it.

Satisfied by what he saw there, after he had done this, he rose with a new expression on his face--so crafty, so exultant, and, withal, so evil, that Madge involuntarily shrank back to better screening in her leafy hiding place.

The old man, with sweeping movements of his heavily booted feet, swept the thin earth he had scraped from the rock's surface back into its place, thrust the fragments deep into his pocket, and started hurriedly away, plainly greatly pleased, along the trail which led into the valley. She watched him with a beating heart, much puzzled.

What could it be that he had found, there, on her land? Visions of gold mines and of diamonds, rose within her mind, crude, unformed, childish, based on the imperfect knowledge she had gained of such things from the story-tellers of the mountains. As mountain people go she was, already, a rich woman, but now dreams of mightier wealth swept through her brain tumultuously. Ah, she would buy happiness for all her friends when she had, later on, unearthed the secret treasures of her backwoods clearing! Maybe she would, sometime, have a ***real silk dress***!

She hurried forward in a stooping run to make examination of the place, as soon as the old man had vanished down the mountain side, to see (she thoroughly expected it) the glitter of bright gems or yellow gold beneath the sand which he had with such care spread back upon the little scar which he had made there in the earth. With trembling fingers she pushed back the yellow earth, and found-- nothing but black rock, uncouth, and unattractive.

She sat there on the ground in her damp skirts, too disappointed, for a moment, to make an exclamation. In many ways the girl, although well past her sixteenth year, was but a child. The reaction from the mighty dreams of fortune she had built almost unnerved her.

It was her native humor which now saved her. Instead of weeping she burst into sudden laughter.

"Dellaw!" said she, aloud. "Ain't I a fool? The man was just a crazy!"

For some time she sat there in the rocky clearing amidst the litter of pine-tops and small undergrowth, contemplating her own silliness with keen amusement.

"Why, he had me that stirred up," said she, "that I reckoned I was rich a'ready!"

But she put the joke aside, to be told upon herself when the first chance came. Her long hiding in the thicket while she watched the queer proceedings of the stranger had chilled her through and through.

Close to the black rock which had so excited him and which she had uncovered after he had gone, a little forked stick stood upright, and in its fork, with one end slanted to the ground, a twig of green witch-hazel still reposed. Beneath the twig a tiny spiral of arizing smoke showed that here, with these primitive appliances, the treasure seeker had prepared his dinner, later carefully covering his fire.

"No matter how queer he was dressed, or what queer things he did," she told herself, "he sure was mountain-born. This here's a mountain fireplace, sartin sure."

She broke dead branches from a pine-top, not far away, but still far enough so that, with reasonable watching, it would not be endangered by a fire built on this spot (the old man plainly had considered this when he made the fire, for the place was almost the only one in all the clearing free enough from dry pine branches to make fire building safe) and laid them on the coals which he had buried, but which she now had carefully uncovered. She would, she had decided, dry her clothes before she started on the long, cool, woods-road climb up to her cabin.

Kneeling by the coals and blowing on them, skillfully adjusting splinters so that they would catch the draft, she soon had started a small flame. Fed carefully, this grew rapidly. Within five minutes there was burning on the site of the old man's little cooking-fire a cheerful blaze of size. Its rushing warmth was very grateful to her, and she held her hands out to it, then her feet, one after the other, with skirts lifted daintily, so that her chilled limbs might catch the warmth.

Invigorated by the pleasant heat, she once more yielded to the urgings of the bounding spirit of rich youth within her. Even as she had sported in the water ere the interloper came to interrupt her sylvan bath, now she sported there about the fire in an impromptu dance, never for a second uncouth, despite the fact that she was quite untrained; scarcely less graceful than her merrymaking in the water, although then she had not been, as now, hampered in her grace of movement by the unlovely draperies of homespun linsey-woolsey. As she had been a water-nymph, so, now, she might have been some Druid maid dancing by an altar fire. The roughness of the ground did not annoy her--her feet had not known dancing upon polished waxen wood; the lack of spectators did not deter her--those whom she had learned to know and love, the mountains, trees, the squirrels, and birds, were there.

In the very midst of the abandon of this rustic symphony of movement, the thought came to her that the precious spelling-book was lying on the rock, near by, quite soaked, neglected. She sped to it and took it to the fire's edge, where, opening its pages one by one, so that each would get the warmth, she held it as close as she opined was safe. Having dried it until she no longer feared the wetting it had had would seriously harm its usefulness (the lovely smoothness of its magic leaves was gone, alas! beyond recall) she paused there for a moment, herself still far from dry, with a bare foot held out to the blaze, and studied curiously one of the book's pages.

Thereon the letters of the alphabet, large, ominous, suggestive to her mind of nothing in the world but curlycues, loomed, mystifying. For the first time it occurred to her that in securing the small volume she had not, as she had thought to do, solved the problem of an education. The characters, she saw to her dismay, meant nothing to her. In the absence of a teacher she could not learn from them!

Alas, alas! The matter was a tragedy to her. How could she have been so stupid as to fail to think of this at first? She stood there with flushed face, despairing, looking at the mystic symbols with slowly sinking heart.

Suddenly, though the crackling of the fire filled her ears, she was aware, by some subtle sense, that she was now not wholly solitary there. Without a sound to tell her, she was conscious that some other person had within the moment come into the clearing. Hastily she looked about. To her amazement, and, for a moment, to her great dismay, she saw, standing on the clearing's edge, the young man who had, not long before, unknowingly invaded her seclusion at the pool.

Instantly her body became fiercely conscious. Prickling thrills, not due to bon-fire heat, shot over it. Shame sent the blood in mantling blushes to her cheeks, although she tried to stop it. Why should she blush at sight of him? True, she had been there in the water, bare as any new-born babe, when he had reached the pool's edge--but he had not seen her. To him she, quite undoubtedly, was a mere strange mountain maid, unrecognized. Self-consciousness then was quite absurd.

And this man was a stranger and was on her land. She must not forget her mountain courtesy and fail to make him welcome.

"Howdy," she said briefly.

"Howdy, little girl?" said he, and looked at her and smiled.

This form of address much amused her. She was not far beyond sixteen, but sixteen is counted womanhood, there in the mountains, and often is an age for wife--and motherhood as well. "Little girl," to her, seemed laughable. But then she suddenly remembered that to stop their flapping, when they were all soaked, against her ankles, she had pinned her skirts up--and she was not tall. The mistake, perhaps, was natural.

"Got a fire here?" he inquired, inanely, for the fire was very much in evidence.

"Looks like it, don't it?" she said somewhat saucily, but robbed the comment of offense by smiling somewhat shyly at him as he stood there.

He was better looking, she reflected, now that she had an unobstructed view of him, even than he had appeared when she had peered at him from her concealment behind the log and barricade of rushes. Of course he was a "foreigner," and, therefore, a mere weakling, not to be considered seriously as a specimen of sturdy manhood (how often had she heard the mountain men speak of the lowlands men with scorn as weaklings?) but, none the less, he interested and attracted her, even if he did not inspire her with respect.

He laughed. "It does," said he, "looks very much like it. Been burning brush?"

"No," she replied, "jest warmin' up a little."

"Why, it's not cold."

"I--I was wet."

" **Wet?**" said he, astonished.

She saw her slip, and flushed. "Fell in the crik," she answered briefly, hastily and falsely.

"Why, that's too bad," said he, with ready sympathy, unfeigned and real.

All the time the girl was eying him through often-lowered lashes, and the more she looked at him the more she felt that he was not, like many "foreigners," to be distrusted and be held aloof. His clothes did not suggest to her the "revenuer," although they certainly were different from any she had ever seen before on man or beast (his knee breeches gave her some amusement), and he was totally unarmed, having laid his rifle down and left it at a distance, leaning against a stump.

His hands and face were not sunburned--indeed, his hands were delicately fashioned and much whiter than any she had ever seen before on man or woman. His appearance certainly did not, to her, convey the thought of strength--and manhood, there among the mountains, is thought to find its first and last expression through its muscle; yet, for some reason, although her first glance made her think he was a puny creature, she neither scorned nor pitied him. He was, perhaps, too smoothly dressed, too carefully shaved; the gun he had laid down so carelessly had too much "bright work" on it--but on the whole, she liked him. A city maiden might have well been dazzled by the really handsome chap. This simple country girl was not--but, on the whole, she liked him.

Her hand which held the spelling-book dropped, unconsciously, so that the open pages of the volume were revealed, upside down, against her knee.

"Studying your lessons?" he inquired, quite casually, good-naturedly, coming nearer.

Again her disappointment rushed upon her. Impulsively she told him of it.

"Oh," said she, "I don't know how! I bought me this yere book down in th' settlement, an' thought I'd learn things outen it. But how'm I goin' to learn? I can't make nothin' out of it to get a start with."

Instantly the pathos of this situation, not its humor, made appeal to him.

"Isn't there a school here?" he inquired.

"Nearest school is twenty mile acrost, over on Turkey Creek," she said briefly. "Oncet there was a nearer one, but teacher was a Hatfield, and McCoys got him, of course. This was McCoy kentry 'fore they all got so killed off. He ought to 'a' knowed better than come over here to teach."

This casual reference to a famous feud--news of whose infamy had spread far,

far beyond the mountains which had hatched it--from the lips of one so young and lovely (for he had long ago admitted to himself that as she stood there she was lovelier than any being he had ever seen before) appalled Frank Layson, son of level regions, graduate of Harvard, casual sportsman, amateur mountaineer, who had come to look over his patrimony and the country round about.

"Ah--yes," said he, and frowned. And then: "It leaves you in hard luck, though, doesn't it, if you want to learn and can't," said he.

"It sartin does, for--oh, I *do* hanker powerful to learn!"

"May I stay here by the fire with you a while and get warm, too," he asked. (The unaccustomed exercise of tramping through the mountains had kept him in a fever heat all day.)

"An' welcome," she said cordially, moving aside a bit, so that he could approach without the circumnavigation of a mighty stump.

He could not tell whether or not she had made note of many sweat-beads on his brow and wondered at them on a chilly man.

"Perhaps," said he, "I might, in a few minutes, show you a little about what you want to know. I've been lucky. I have had a chance to learn."

She liked the way he said it. There was no hint of superiority about it. He was not "stuck up," in his claim of knowledge. He "had had a chance," and took no credit to himself for it. This pleased her, won her confidence--if, already, that had not been done by his frank face, in spite of his fancy clothes and her assumption that he was a namby-pamby weakling.

"Oh--if you would!" she said, so eagerly that it seemed to him most pitiful.

So, five minutes later, when all her clothing save her heavy outer skirt, had been quite dried there by the fire, and that same fire's abounding warmth had sent his temperature up to high discomfort mark, they sat down, side by side, upon a log, the spelling-book between them, and he began the pleasant task of teaching her her A, B, Cs.

"'A,'" said he, "is this one at the very start."

"The peaked one," said she.

"Yes, that one.

"And 'B,'" he went on, much amused, but with a perfectly grave face, "is this one with two loops fastened, so, to a straight stalk."

"I know where thar *is* a bee-tree," she remarked, irrelevantly.

"It will help recall this in your mind," said he, maintaining perfect gravity, "imagine it with two big loops of rope fastened to one side of it--"

"Rope wouldn't stick out that-a-way," said she, "it would just droop. They'd have to be of somethin' stiffen"

"Well--" said he, and tried to think of something.

"You could use that railroad-iron that I saw 'em heat red-hot an' bend, down in the valley," she suggested.

"That's it," said he. "Two loops of railroad-iron fastened to a bee-tree" (he pointed) "just as these loops, here, are fastened to the straight black stem. That's 'B.'"

"I won't forget," said she, her beautiful young brow puckered earnestly as she stored the knowledge in her brain.

"And this is 'C,'" said he.

"'C,' 'C'" said she. "Jest take off one of th' loops an' use it by itself."

"That's so," said he. "And here is 'D'"

"Cut off th' top th' tree," said she. "Just cut it plumb off, loop an' all."

He laughed. It was clear that she would be an earnest and quick-thinking pupil to whomever had the task of giving her her education.

As he looked at her, now, he for the first time fully realized her beauty. He had known, from the first, that she was most attractive, most unusual for a mountain maid; but now, laughing, although her head was still bent to the book, her big eyes, sparkling with her merriment, raised frankly to his face, were revelations to him. He had not seen such eyes before, and all the old-time similes for deep-brown orbs sprang instantly to mind. "Fathomless pools," "translucent amber"--no simile would really describe them. Late hours had never dimmed them, illness had never made them heavy, he was sure a lie had never made them shift from their straight gaze for one short second. He had not seen such eyes in cities!

And from careful contemplation of the eyes, he kept on with a careful contemplation of the other beauties of his fair and unexpected pupil. Her homespun gown, always ill-shaped and now unusually protuberant in spots, unusually tight in others, because of its late wetting and impromptu, partial drying, could not hide the sylvan grave of her small-boned and lissome figure, just budding into womanhood. Her feet, crossed on the ground, were as patrician in their nakedness as any bluegrass belle's in satin slippers. Her ankles, scratched by casual thorns and already beginning to blush brown from the June sun's ardent kisses, were as delicate as any he had ever seen enmeshed in silken hose. Her hands, long, slender, taper-fingered, actually dainty, although brown and roughened by hard labor, were, it seemed to him, better fitted for the fingering of a piano's keys than for the coarse and heavy tasks to which he knew they must be well accustomed. He gazed at her in veritable wonder. How had she blossomed, thus, here in this wilderness?

"Where do you live?" he asked, interrupting their scholastic efforts.

"Up thar," she pointed, and, above, he could just see the top of a mud-and-stick chimney rise above a crag between the trees.

"Have you brothers or sisters?"

"Ain't got nobody," she answered, and to her face there came a look of keen resentment rather than of sorrow or of resignation. "I'm all th' feud left," she said simply. She looked at Layson quickly, wondering if he would be surprised that she should not have fought and also died. "Girl cain't fight alone, much," she went on, in hurried explanation, or, rather, quick excuse. "I might take a shot if I should git a chanst, but I ain't had none, an', besides, I guess it air plum wrong to kill, even if there's blood scores to be settled up. I toted 'round a rifle with me till last fall, but then I give it up. They won't git me--but maybe you don't know what feuds are in the mountings, here."

He was looking at her with new interest. All his life he had heard much about the dreadful mountain feuds. As the bogey-man is used in Eastern nurseries, so are the mountaineers used in the nurseries of old Kentucky and of Tennessee to frighten children with. Their family fights, not less persistent or less deadly than the enmities between the warring barons of the Rhine in middle ages, form a magnificent foundation for dire tales.

"Yes," said he, "I know about the feuds, of course. But you--"

It did not seem possible to him, even after her frank statements, that this bright and joyous creature could in any way be joined to such a bloody history as he knew the histories of some of these long feuds to be.

"It's been thirty years an' better," said the girl, "since the Brierlys and Lindsays had some trouble about a claybank filly an' took to shootin' one another--shootin' straight an' shootin' often an' to kill. For years th' fight went on. They fired on sight, an' sometimes 'twas a Lindsay went an' sometimes 'twas a Brierly. Bimeby there was just two men left--my pappy an' Lem Lindsay.

"One day Lem sent word to my pappy to meet him without no weepons an' shake han's an' make it up."

Her face took on a look of bitterness and hate which almost made her hearer shiver, so foreign was it to the fresh, young brightness he had watched till now.

"My daddy come, at th' ap'inted time," she went on slowly, "but dad--he knowed Lem Lindsay, an' never for a minute trusted him. He ast a friend of his, Ben Lorey, to be a hidden witness. Ben hid behind a rock to watch. 'Twas right near here--just over thar." She pointed.

"Soon Lem, he come along, a-smilin' like a Judast, an', after some fine speakin', as daddy offered him his hand, Lem whipped out a knife, an'--an' struck it into my daddy's heart."

The girl's recital had been tense, dramatic, not because she had tried or thought to make it so--she had never learned not to be genuine--but because of the real and tragic drama in the tale she told, the matter-of-course way in which she told it.

It made Layson shudder. What sort of people were these mountaineers who went armed to friendly meetings and struck down the men whose hands they offered to clasp? Where was the other man while his friend's enemy was at this dreadful work?

"But Lorey," said her fascinated listener, "the man who was in hiding as a witness, made him pay for his outrageous act!"

"No," said the girl, with drooping head. "He stepped out from behind the rock where he was hidin', an' he pulled the trigger of his rifle. But luck was dead against us that day. Wet powder--somethin'--nobody knows what. The gun did not go off. Before he got it well down from his shoulder so's to find out what it was that ailed it, Lem Lindsay was upon him like a mountain lion--an' he laid him thar beside my daddy. He didn't mean that there should be no witnesses."

She paused so long that Layson was about to speak, feeling the silence troublesome and painful, but before he had decided what to say in comment on a tale so dreadful, she went on:

"He didn't mean there should be no witnesses, Lem Lindsay didn't, but as it happened there was two. My mother, me clasped in her arms, had stole after my daddy, fearin' that somethin' wicked would come out o' that there meetin' with his old-time enemy. She spoke up sudden, an' surprised th' murderer, standin' there by th' two poor men he'd killed. At first it scared him. I can't remember everythin' about that awful day, but I can see Lem Lindsay's face as she screamed at him, just as plain this minute as I seed it then. I'll never forget that look if I live a thousand years!

"At first he was struck dumb, but then that passed. He give a yell of rage an' started toward us on th' run. She jumped, with me a-hinderin' her. Like a mountain deer she run, in spite of that. She was lighter on her feet than he was upon his, an' soon outdistanced him. He hadn't stopped to pick his rifle up--he only had th' knife he'd done th' killin' with, so he couldn't do what he'd 'a' liked to done--shoot down a woman an' a baby!

"We lived where I live now, alone, an' then, as now, there was a little bridge that took th' footpath over th' deep gully. Them days was wicked ones in these here mountains, an' daddy'd had that foot-bridge fixed so it would raise. My mother just had time to pull it up, when we had crossed, before Lem Lindsay reached there. He stopped, to keep from fallin' in the gully, but stood there, shakin' his bare fist an' swearin' that he'd kill us yet. But that he couldn't do. Folks was mightily roused, and he had to leave th' mountings, then an' thar, an' ain't been in 'em since, so far as anybody knows."

Her brows drew down upon her eyes. Her sweet mouth hardened. "He'd better **never** come!" she added, grimly.

After a moment's pause she went on, slowly: "So, now, here we be--Joe Lorey, Ben's son, an' me. My mother died, you see, not very many years after Lindsay'd killed my daddy. Seein' of it done, that way, had been too much for her. I reckon seein' it would have killed me, too, if I'd been more'n a baby, but I wasn't, an' lived through it. Ben's lived here, workin' his little mounting farm, an'--an'--"

She hesitated, evidently ill at ease, strangely stammering over an apparently simple and unimportant statement of the condition of her fellow orphan. She changed color slightly. Layson, watching her, decided that the son of the one victim must be the sweetheart of the daughter of the other, and would have smiled had not the very thought, to his surprise, annoyed him unaccountably. Whether that was what had caused her stammering, he could not quite decide, although he gave the matter an absurd amount of thought. She went on quickly:

"He's lived here, workin' of his little mounting farm an'--an'--an' doin' jobs aroun', an' such, an' I've lived here, a-workin' mine, a little, but not much. After my mother died there was some folks down in th' valley took keer of me for a while, but then they moved away, an' I was old enough to want things bad, an' what I wanted was to come back here, where I could see th' place where mother an' my daddy had both loved me an' been happy. I've got some land down in th' valley-- fifty acres o' fine pasture--but I never cared to live down there. Th' rent I get for that land makes me rich--I ain't never wanted for a single thing but just th' love an' carin' that my daddy an' my mother would 'a' give me if that wicked man hadn't killed 'em both. For he **did** kill my mother, just as much as he killed daddy. She died o' that an' that alone."

Again she fell into a silence for a time, looking out at the tremendous prospect spread before them, quite unseeing.

"Oh," she went on, at length, her face again darkened by a frown, her small hands clenched, every muscle of her lithe young body drawn as taut as a wild animal's before a spring. "I sometimes feel as if I'd like to do as other mountain women have been known to do when killin' of that sort has blackened all their lives--I sometimes feel as if I'd like to take a rifle in my elbow an' go lookin' for that man- -go lookin' for him in th' mountings, in th' lowlands, anywhere--even if I had to cross th' oceans that they tell about, in order to come up with him!"

Her voice had been intensely vibrant with strong passion as she said this, and her quivering form told even plainer how deep-seated was the hate that gave birth to her words. But soon she put all this excitement from her and dropped her hands in a loose gesture of hopeless relaxation.

"But I know such thoughts are foolish," she said drearily. "He got away. A girl can't carry on a feud alone, nohow. There's nothin' I can do."

Again, now, with a passing thought, her features lighted as another maiden's, whose young life had been cast by fate in gentler places might have lighted at the thought of some great pleasure pending in the future.

"There is a chance, though," she said, with a fierce joy, "that Lem Lindsay, if he is alive, 'll git th' bullet that he earned that day. Joe Lorey's livin'--that's Ben's son- -an' he--well, maybe, some time--ah, he can shoot as straight as anybody in these mountings!"

The look of a young tigress was on her face.

It made the young man who was listening to her shudder--the look upon her face, the voice with which she said "And he can shoot as straight as anybody in these mountings!" For a second it revolted him. Then, getting a fairer point of view, he smiled at her with a deep sympathy, and waited.

He had not to wait long before a gentler mood held dominance. It came, indeed, almost at once.

"No," she said slowly, "a girl can't carry on a feud alone, nohow.... And, somehow, when I think of it most times, I really don't want to. It's only now an' then I get stirred up, like this. Most times I'd rather learn than--go on fightin' like we-all always have.... I'd rather learn, somehow.... An'--an'--an' that's been mighty hard--*is* mighty hard"

"You--haven't had much chance," said he, looking at her pityingly.

She gave him a quick glance. Had she really thought he pitied her she would have bitterly resented it.

"Had th' same chance other mounting girls have," she said quickly, defending, not herself, but her country and her people.

She stood, now, at a distance from the fire, for it was blazing merrily, but her face was flushed by its radiant heat, its lurid blaze made a fine background for the supple, swaying beauty of her slim young body. She raised her arms high, high above her head, with that same genuineness of gesture, graceful and appealing, which he had seen in all her movements from the first and then clasped them at her breast.

"But oh," said she, "somehow, I want to learn, now, terrible!"

"Let me help you while I'm in the mountains," he replied, impulsively. "I'll be glad to help you every day."

"Would you?" she said. "I would be powerful thankful!" Her bright eyes expressed the gratitude she felt.

While they had talked a strange paradox had come about there by the fire without their notice. The long, black outcropping of rock against which they had brought the old man's blaze to life, had, instead of keeping the fire from spreading to the undergrowth, strangely permitted it to pass.

It was the girl who first discovered this. She sprang up from her place with a startled exclamation.

"Oh," said she, "th' fire is spreadin'!"

He rose quickly to his feet.

CHAPTER III

They were appalled by the predicament in which they found themselves. The thing seemed quite mysterious.

The rock against which the fire had been built was all aglow, as if it had been heated in a furnace till red hot--strange circumstance; one that would have fascinated Layson into elaborate investigation had he had the time to think about it--and, beyond it, evidently communicated through it as a link, the rustling leaves of the past autumn, their surface layers sun-dried, were bursting into glittering little points of flame all about the narrow ledge of rock on which they were standing. As they gazed, before Layson could rush forward to stamp out these sparkling perils, the fire had spread, as the girl, wise in the direful ways of brush-fires, had known at once that it would spread, to the encircling pine-tops, left in a tinder barricade about the clearing by the sawyers and the axemen.

"Oh," she said, distressed, "we're ketched!"

Layson, less conscious of their peril because less well informed as to the almost explosive inflammability of dry pine-tops, took the matter less seriously. "We'll get out, all right," said he. "Don't worry."

"There's times *to* worry," said the girl, "an' this, I reckon--well, it's one of 'em."

As if to prove the truth of what she said, with a burst almost like that of flame's leap along a powder-line, the fire caught one resinous pine-top after another with a crackling rush which was not only fearfully apparent to the eye, but also ominously audible. Within ten seconds the pair were ringed by sound like that of crackling musketry upon a battlefield, and by a pyrotechnic spectacle of terrifying magnitude. Layson had heard guns pop in untrained volleys at State Guard manoeuvres, and was instantly impressed by the amazing similarity of sound, but he had never in his life seen anything to be compared to the towering ring of flame-wall which almost instantly encircled them. He lost, perhaps, a minute, in astonished contemplation of the situation. Then realization of their peril burst upon him with a rush. To wait there, where they were, too evidently meant certain death. Not only would the pulsing heat from the pine-tops already burning soon become unendurable, but there was enough of tindrous litter strewn about the entire area of the little clearing to make it horribly apparent to him that, in a moment, it would all become a bed of glittering flame. He gazed at the menacing, encroaching fire, appalled.

Madge, understanding the desperation of their situation even better than he did, knowing, too, that a stranger could, indeed, scarce conceive the deadly peril of it, was, at first, the cooler of the two. Her life there in the mountains, where any man she knew might meet, and her own father had met, death stalking with a rifle in his bended elbow, or a knife clutched in his clenched hand, had given her a certain poise in time of peril, an admirable self-control, quick wits, firm nerves. She felt that there was small chance of escape, yet she was not visibly terrified, and made no outcry.

Had she been caught, thus, with a mountaineer (which scarcely could have happened) she would have felt small apprehension. Learned in the perils of the woods, heavy-booted, sturdy-legged, a native, like Joe Lorey, for example, would, she felt quite certain, have been able to effect her rescue. But the chances, she decided, were practically nil, with this untrained "foreigner" as her companion. She had been told that "bluegrass folks" were lacking in strong nerves and prone to panic if real danger threatened. Barefooted as she was, there was little she, herself, could do. She knew that she would quickly fall unconscious from intolerable pain if she so much as tried to make a dash for safety. That she was badly frightened she would have readily admitted, that she was panic-stricken none who looked at her could, for a moment, dream.

She glanced at Layson with a curiosity which was almost calm, as, for a moment quite bewildered, he ran from side to side of their rapidly narrowing space of safety, endeavoring to find a weak spot in the wall of flames through which they might escape, but failing everywhere. For a moment she thought that he had lost his head, and thus proved all too true those tales which she had heard of "foreigners." It was almost as one race gazing at another suffering ordeal in test, that she observed his every movement, each detail of his facial play. While they had sat there on the log, intent upon their work above her spelling-book, she had wondered if the harsh, uncharitable mountain judgment of the "foreigners" had not been too merciless. Now she felt that she began to see its justification. The man, undoubtedly, she thought, showed an unmanly panic.

"No use tryin' to get out that-a-way," she said calmly. "You'd better--"

Even as she spoke, and before her words could possibly have influenced him, she saw a change come over him. The signs of fear, which had so displeased her, faded from his actions and his facial play. Placed in unusual, unexpected circumstances, for a second he had been bewildered, but, as soon as opportunity had come for gathering of wits, he found composure, coolness, nerve. She did not even finish out her sentence. Instead, her thoughts turned to that acme of breeding, nerve, endurance and high spirit dear to all Kentuckians, the race horse. "He's found his feet!" she thought.

The man impressed her, now, even more than when, with courtesy, such as she had never known, tact which had maintained her comfort when she might have felt humiliated, learning which to her seemed marvellous, he had offered her the key to learning's mysteries upon the log. She saw that he had quickly won a mighty victory over self. She thought of tales which she had heard by mountain fireplaces about "bad men," who, when they first had heard a bullet's song, had dodged and whitened, only to recover quickly and be nerved to peril evermore thereafter. Her doubt of Layson fell away completely. Instead of thinking of him as of one whose manhood is inferior to that of the rough mountaineers she knew, perforce she saw in him superiorities. There was not the least sign of bragadocio, of counterfeit, about his new-found calm. It was, she recognized at once, entirely genuine. "Rattled for a minute," she thought, wisely, again amending her first judgment, "but cooler, now, than cucumbers."

She looked gravely at him as he moved about investigating, not excitedly, alertly, full of the necessary business of escape. "Looks bad, don't it?" she said gravely. "Like powder, them thar pine-tops."

"Oh, we'll get out all right," he answered, easily, and now she felt a comfort in the fact that he was intentionally minimizing danger to give confidence to the supposed weakness of her sex.

"Maybe so an' maybe not," said she, discovering, to her disgust, that it was hard, now that he was showing strength, to keep the panic tremolo from her own voice.

The fire had, by this time, encircled them completely, and from a hundred points was running in toward them on tinder lines of dry pine-needles and old leaves, flashing at them viciously along the crisp, dry surface of old moss and lichens on the rocks. A wind had suddenly arisen, born, no doubt, of the fire's own mighty draft. Bits of blazing light wood, small, burning branches, myriads of flaming oak leaves and pine-cones were swept up from the ring of fire about them, in the chimney of the blaze, to lose their impetus only at a mighty height, and then fall slowly, threateningly down within the burning ring. So plentiful were these little, vicious menaces, that, within another minute, they were dodging them continually.

He now took his place close by her side and gazed upon the spectacle, calm-eyed, as if he found it interesting rather more than terrifying.

"Oh, we'll get out, all right," said he, again.

And then he turned to her in frank and unexcited inquiry. To her increased disgust the sobs of growing fear convulsed her throat. She fought them back and listened to his question.

"You know more about woods-fires than I do," he said evenly. "Better tell me what to do, eh?"

This confession of his ignorance strengthened her growing confidence in him instead of weakening it. The fact that he could ask advice so calmly made her think that, probably, he would be calm in taking it if she could offer it. It steadied her and helped her think. And then she saw him spring, and, actually with a smile, strike in the air above her head, diverting from its downward path which would have landed it upon her, a flaming fragment of pine-top fully five feet long. He actually laughed.

"Like handball," he said cheerily. "Don't worry. I won't let anything fall on you. You just-- ***think!***"

Her panic, now, had vanished as by magic. Instantly she really *ceased* to worry. He would *not* let fire fall on her. He would get her out of that. She was certain of it. She *could* think--calmly and with care.

But she could not think of a way out--at least she could not think of a way out for her. Barefooted as she was, she scarcely could expect to find, even in her strong young body, strength enough to endure the pain of treading, as she would be forced to if she made a dash, on an almost unbroken bed of glowing coals and smouldering moss ten yards in width. He, with his heavy boots, might manage it. Therefore there was hope for him; but for her to try it would be madness.

Had he been a sturdy mountaineer, she wofully reflected--having found a detail of lowland inferiority which, she was quite certain, would not be dispelled as had some others--he might, in such a desperate case, have summoned strength to "tote" her through, although she scarcely thought Joe Lorey, the best man whom she knew, could really do it; still there would have been the possibility. But no weak-muscled "foreigner," pap-nurtured in the lowlands, could, she knew, of course, accomplish such a feat. It was fine to know things, as he did, but *muscle* was what counted now! In queer, impersonal reflection, born, doubtless, of a dumb hysteria, she reflected bitterly upon the healthy weight of her own mountain-nourished person.

"If I was only like them triflin' bluegrass gals Joe tells about," she thought, "made up of nothin' or a little less, it wouldn't be no trick to tote me outen this; but dellaw! I'm just as much as that there ox of mine feels right to carry when I got a couple bags o' grist on, back an' front."

She looked around the ring of fire, dull-eyed, disheartened. "Ain't no use," said she, aloud.

He seemed to almost lose his temper. "Use?" said he, "of course there's use! You tell me where the best chance is and we'll fight out, all right."

She did not even answer; the situation seemed to her so wholly hopeless.

He acted, then, without further question. Hastily throwing the loop of his gun over his shoulder, he crooked one arm beneath her much-astonished knees, clasped another tight about her waist, and started for the fire with a determined spring.

"No, no; not there!" she screamed, astonished, terrified, and yet, withal, delighted by the unexpected hardness of the muscles in the arms which held her, the unexpected spring in the apparently not overburdened limbs which bore them up, the unexpected nerve, determination of the man's initiative.

This "foreigner," it seemed, was not so weak, was not so namby-pamby as his class had been described to be. She did not struggle in the circling arms, she only made an explanation.

"That's hard wood, burnin' there," said she. "Burnin' hard wood's harder to break through an' hotter, too. Try some place where it's pine.... But you can't never do it!"

"Where?" said he. "Show me! You know, I don't."

"Well--over thar," she said, and indicated, with a pointing hand, the place in the encircling conflagration where passage seemed least hopeless.

At that moment fire blazed high there, but her knowing eye told her that it was largely flaring needles, brittle twigs, and easily dissipated cones which fed it.

A few great springs, such as she now felt that the quivering, eager limbs which held her, were possessed of the ability to make, might take them through this flimsiest spot in the terrible barricade. The crackling, burning branches of the dead pinetops would be likely to give way before them, not to trip them up, as oak would, to thrust them, falling, on the bed of glowing coals fast forming on the ground.

"Over thar," said she, again. "I reckon that's the best place--but you cain't--"

With the new respect the knowledge of his trained and ready muscles brought to her, arose in her a towering admiration of him. When she first had seen him, there beside the pool, she definitely had liked him; while they had delved into the mysteries of the alphabet upon the log his patient, willing, helpful kindness had increased her prepossession in his favor. It was only when, after disaster had so swiftly, so unexpectedly, descended on them and she had compared his body, made apparently more slender in comparison to the rude-limbed mountaineers she knew than it was really by tight-fitting knickerbockers and golf-stockings and its well-cut shooting-jacket, that she had lost confidence in him. But now his muscles, closing round her, seemed like thews of steel. She had never heard of athletes, she did not dream that muscle-building is a part of modern education--that alertness on the baseball, polo, football fields, count quite as much, at least in college popularity, as ready tongues and agile wits. The last fibres of destroyed respect for him rebuilt themselves upon the minute. Her confidence returned completely in a sudden flash--quicker than the magic leapings of the fire about them. She knew that he would take her through to safety.

A thought occurred to her, for, suddenly, with the new respect for him the knowledge of his trained and ready muscles gave her, arose a new consideration for him, almost motherly. He would be breasting dreadful peril in the passage of the flames--peril to his eyes and face and clinging, tight-clasped hands especially. And round her limbs there was the means of saving him, in part, from it.

"You let me down for just a minute," she said briefly. "Just a minute. Then I'll let you take me up an' carry me. An' you can *do* it, too! You're strong, ain't you?"

Wondering, he released his hold on her, and she slid to her feet. Then, with a quick movement, she unbuttoned the waistband of her outer skirt, and, letting it slip down to the ground, stepped out of it.

"Ain't it lucky I got wet?" said she, and smiled. "It ain't more'n half dry yet. The under one is wet, too, and both of 'em are wool--and that don't burn like cotton would.

"Now pick me up again an' I'll just fix this skirt--so--there--now--that's the way. Can you see, now? All right? Well, it'll keep th' fire from catchin' in our hair, an' it'll save your eyes."

He laughed. "That's fine!" said he, and, almost before she realized that they were under way, a mighty leap had taken them close to the blazing barrier, another one had landed them within its very midst, another one had carried them beyond its greatest menace, another had delivered them from actual peril, leaving them on ground where filmy grass, dead leaves, dry needles, had blazed quickly, with a consuming flash, and, utterly and almost instantly destroyed, had left behind them only thin, hot ash, devoid of peril, scarce to be considered.

But he did not let her feet touch ground again until they were even beyond this. Finally, when they reached a rocky "barren," where the little fire had found no fuel, she felt his tautened thews relax.

Instantly she slipped from his encircling arms, and he began to whip the flames in grass and little brush close to them with the dampened skirt. Even on the little isle of safety they found it necessary, still, to agilely avoid innumerable bits of floating "light-wood" brands, and, for a time, to beat, beat at the hungry little flames around them, but, at last, the danger was all over, and they stood there, looking at each other, with a sense of great relief. He smiled, breathing hard, but not exhausted.

"Tight work, eh?" he said cheerfully.

"Jest *wonderful*!" she answered, with a ready tribute.

Then the memory of his embracing arm, the fact that her own arms had been as tightly clasped about his neck, came to her with a rush, although, while they had raced across the burning strip she had not thought of these things. Shyness stirred in her almost as definitely as it had while she lay hidden at the pool's mouth, watching him and tingling with shamed thrills at thought of her amazing plight there. No man had ever had his arms about her in her life before.

But, even while she blushed and thrilled with this embarrassment, she fought to put it from her. He, evidently, had not thought of it at all, was, now, not thinking of it. What had been done had been a part of the day's work, a quick move, made in an emergency, when nothing else would serve. His attitude restored her own composure.

And gratitude welled in her. She struggled to find words for it.

"I--I'm much obleeged to you," were all she found, and she was conscious of their most complete inadequacy.

"No reason why you should be," he said gayly. "We got caught in a tight place, that's all, and we helped one another out of it."

She laughed derisively. "I helped *you* out a lot, now didn't I?" she asked.

Again she made a survey of him, standing where he had been when he had loosed his hold of her, unwearied, smiling, and she looked with actual wonder. Good clothes and careful speech were not, of a necessity, the outward signs of weaklings, it appeared!

Joe Lorey, in a dozen talks with her, had told her that they were. She did not understand that this had been a clumsy and short-sighted strategy, that, finding her more difficult than other mountain girls--the handsome, sturdy young hill-dweller had not been without his conquests among the maidens of his kind; only Madge had baffled him--he had feared that, now when the railroad building in the valley had brought so many "foreigners" into the neighborhood, one of them might fascinate her, and it had been to guard against this, as well as he was able, that he had spoken slightingly of the whole class. He had delighted in repeating to her tales belittling them, deriding them, and she, of course, had quite believed his stories.

But her experience with this one had not justified that point of view, and the matter largely occupied her thoughts as they walked slowly through the thickets of a bit of "second-growth" beyond the fire, which, stopped by the rocky "barrens," was dying out behind them. Her companion was, to her, an utterly new sort of being, not better trained in mind alone, but better trained in body than any mountaineer she knew; doubtless ignorant of many details of woods-life which would be known to any child there in the mountains, but, on the other hand, even more resourceful, daring, quick, than mountain men would have been, similarly placed, and, to her amazement, physically stronger, too! The fact that he had shown himself more thoughtful of and courteous to her than any other man had ever been before, made its impression, but a slighter one. Hers were the instincts of true wisdom, and she valued these things less than many of her city sisters might, although she valued them, of course. She looked slyly, wonderingly at him. He was a very pleasant, very admirable sort of creature--this visitor from the unknown, outside world. She quite decided that she did not even think his knickerbockers foolish, after all.

For a moment, even now, she thrilled unpleasantly with a mean suspicion that he might be a "revenuer," after all, and have done the good things he had done as a part of that infernal craft which revenuers sometimes showed when searching for the hidden stills where "moonshine" whisky is illegally produced among the mountains; but she put this thought out of her heart, indignantly, almost as quickly as it came to her. Instinctively she felt quite certain that duplicity did not form any portion of his nature. They had not been traitor's arms which had so bravely (and so firmly) clasped her for the quick and risky dash across that terrifying belt of fire!

"No," said she, determined to give him fullest measure of due credit, "I didn't help you none. I didn't help you none--an' you did what I don't believe any other man I ever knew could do. I'm--"

Again she paused, again at loss for words, again the quest failed wholly.

"I'm much obleeged," said she.

Then, suddenly, the thought came to her of that other and less prepossessing "foreigner" whom, that day, she had seen there in her mountains. She described him carefully to Layson, and asked if he could guess who he had been and what his business could have been. Descriptions are a sorry basis for the recognition of a person thought to be far miles away, a person unassociated in one's mind with the surroundings he has suddenly appeared in; and, therefore, Layson, who really knew the man and who, had he identified him with the unknown visitor, would have been surprised, intensely curious, and, possibly, suspicious, could offer her no clue to his identity.

CHAPTER IV

That same "foreigner," for a "foreigner," was acting strangely. Surely he was dressed in a garb hitherto almost unknown in the rough mountains, certainly none of the mountaineers whom he had met (and he had met, with plain unwillingness, a few, as he had climbed up to the rocky clearing where his fire had blossomed so remarkably) had recognized him. But, despite all this, it was quite plain that he was traveling through a country of which he found many details familiar. Now and then a little vista caught his view and held him for long minutes while he seemed to be comparing its reality with pictures of it stored within his memory; again he paused when he discovered that some whim of tramping mountaineers or roaming cattle, some landslide born of winter frosts; some blockade of trees storm-felled, had changed the course of an old path. Always, in a case like this, he investigated carefully before he definitely started on the new one.

When he had first come into the neighborhood he had made his way with caution, almost as if fearing to be seen, but now, after the bits of rocks which he had taken from Madge Brierly's clearing, had slipped into his pocket, he used double care in keeping from such routes as showed the marks of many recent footsteps, in sly investigations to make sure the paths he chose were clear of other wayfarers. His nerves evidently on keen edge, he seemed to fear surprise of some unpleasant sort. Each crackling twig, as he passed through the thickets, each rustling of a frightened rabbit as it scuttled from his path, each whir of startled grouse, or sudden call of nesting king-bird, made him pause cautiously until he had quite satisfied himself that it meant nothing to be feared. He was ever carefully alert for danger of some sort.

But not even his continual alarms, his constant watchfulness, could keep his mind away from the rough bits of rock which he had chipped from the outcropping in the clearing. More than once, as he found convenient and safe places--leafy nooks in rocky clefts, glades in dense, impenetrable thickets--he took out the little specimens, turned them over in his hands with loving touches, and gazed at them with an expression of picturesquely avaricious joy. Had any witnessed this procedure they would have found it vastly puzzling, for the specimens seemed merely small, black stones and valueless. But once, while looking at them lovingly, he burst into a harsh and hearty laugh as of great triumph, quite involuntarily; but hushed it quickly, looking, then, about him with an apprehensive glance. Each step he made was, in the main, a cautious one, each pause he made was plainly to look at some familiar, if some slightly altered, vista.

It was quite clear that with the finding of the little bits of rock he had achieved the errand which had brought him to the mountains, and that now he roamed to satisfy his memory's curiosity. Smiles of recognition constantly played upon his grim and grizzled face at sight of some old path, some distant, mist-enshrouded crag, even some mighty pine or oak which had for years withstood the buffeting of tempestuous storms; now and then a little puzzled frown, added its wrinkles to the many which already creased his brow, when, at some spot which he had thought to find as he had left it, long ago, he discovered that time's changes had been notable.

Once only did the man become confused among the woods-paths (where a stranger might have lost himself quite hopelessly in twenty minutes) and that was at a point not far from where Madge Brierly and Layson had, on their way up from the clearing, paused while she told her youthful escort of the grim but simple tragedy of her feud-darkened childhood. Before the old man reached this spot he had been traveling with puzzled caution, for a time, across a slope rough-scarred by some not ancient landslide which had changed the superficial contour of the mountain-side. When, suddenly, he debouched upon the rocky crag, hung, a rustic, natural platform above a gorgeous panorama of the valley, the view came to him, evidently, as a sharp, a startling, most unpleasant shock.

That the place was quite familiar to him none who watched him would have doubted, but no smiles of pleasant memories curved his thin, unpleasant lips as he surveyed it. He did not pause there, happily, communing with his memory in smiling reminiscence as he had at other points along the way. Instead, as the great view burst upon his gaze, he started back as if the outlook almost terrified him. He had been traveling astoop, partly because the burden of his years weighed heavy on his shoulders, partly as if his muscles had unconsciously reverted to the easy, slouching, climbing-stoop of the Kentucky mountaineer. But at sight of this especial spot his attitude changed utterly, the whole expression, not of his face, alone, but of his body, altered. His stoop became a crouch. His hands flew out before him as if, with them, he strove to ward away the charming scene. His feet paused in their tracks, as if struck helpless and immovable by what his eyes revealed to him.

For a full moment, almost without moving, he stood there, fascinated by some old association, plainly, for there was nothing in the prospect which, to an actual stranger, would have seemed more notable than details of a dozen other views which he had peered at through his half-closed, weather-beaten eyes within the hour. Here, clearly, was the arena of some great event in his past life--an arena which he gladly would have never seen again. His face went pale beneath its coat of tan, his shoulders trembled slightly as he tried to shrug them with indifference to brace his courage up. Twice he started from the spot, determined, evidently, to shut away the crowding and unpleasant recollections it recalled to him, twice he returned to it, to carefully, if with evident repugnance, make closer study of some detail of its rugged picturesqueness. More than once, as he lingered there against his will, his hands raised upward to his eyes as if to shut away from them some vivid memory-picture, but each time they fell, with strangely hopeless gesture. The picture which they strove to hide plainly was not before his eyes in the actual scene, but painted in the brain behind them and not to be shut out with screening, claw-curved fingers.

The effect of this especial spot on the old man, indeed, was most remarkable. His lips, as he stood gazing there, moved constantly as if with words unspoken, and, once or twice, the crowding sentences found actual but not articulate voice. Whenever this occurred he started, to look about behind him as if he feared that some one, who might overhear, had crept up upon him slyly. Finally, making absolutely certain that he had not been observed by any human being, and evidently yielding to an impulse almost irresistible, he went over the ground carefully, examining each foot of the little rocky platform with not a loving, but a fascinated observation.

When he finally left the spot a striking change had come upon his features. He had reached the place sly, cunning, and, withal, triumphant, as if he had accomplished, that day, through securing the small stones, some secret thing of a great import. His countenance, as, at length, he went away, was not triumphant but half terrified. It was as if some long-forgotten scene of horror had been brought before his gaze again, to terrify and astonish him.

His footsteps had been slow and leisurely, the footsteps of a contemplative, if a surreptitious sightseer, but now they quickened almost into running, and the intensely disagreeable effect of the mysterious episode had not left him wholly, when, twenty minutes afterward, he had mounted the rocky hill path by a precipitous climb and found himself within a little, cupped inclosure in the rocks, secluded enough and beautiful enough to be a fairies' dancing-floor. There, again, he seemed to recognize old landmarks, but with fewer of unpleasant memories connected with them. Plain curiosity glowed, now, in his narrow, crafty eyes.

"I wonder," he exclaimed, "if it's here yet."

As he spoke his glance flashed swiftly to the far side of the little glade, where, on the face of a dense thicket, a trained eye, such as his, might mark a spot where bushes had been often parted with extreme care not to do them injury and thus reveal the fact that through them lay a thoroughfare. Noting this with a wry smile of malicious satisfaction, he started slowly toward the spot.

The caution of his movements was redoubled, now. While he had worked, back in the clearing, cooking his simple noonday meal and chipping off the little specimens of rock, he had shown that he wished not to have his strange activities observed. On the mountain paths he had plainly been most anxious not to run across chance wayfarers who might ask questions, or (the possibility was most remote, but still a possibility) remember him of old. He had been merely cautious, though, not definitely fearful.

Now, however, actual and obsessive dread showed plainly on his face and in his movements. Such a fear would have induced most men to abandon any enterprise which was not fraught with compelling necessity; with him insistent curiosity seemed to counterbalance it. The man's face, rough, hard, cruel, was, withal, unusually expressive; its deep lines were more than ordinarily mobile, and every one of them, as he proceeded, soft-footed as a cat, amazingly lithe and supple for his years, as competent to find his way unseen through a woods country as an Indian, showed that irresistible and fiercely inquisitive impulse was offsetting in his mind a deadly apprehension.

In one way only, though, in spite of the accelleration of his eager curiosity, did he drop his guard, at all, and this was quite apparently the direct result of high excitement. That he had dropped it he was clearly quite unconscious, but when his lips moved, now, they more than once let fall articulate words.

"Ef th' old still's thar ..." they said at one time; then, after a long pause devoted to worming troublous way through tangled areas of windfall, they muttered, in completion of the sentence: "... it'll be th' son that's runnin' it." Another busy silence, and: "Thar was a girl ... th' daughter of...."

Either a spasmodic contraction of the throat at mere thought of the name--a grimace, almost of pain, which suddenly convulsed the old man's evil face might well have made a stranger think that his muscles had rebelled--or an unusually difficult struggle across a fallen tree-trunk prevented further speech, as, probably, it prevented for the time, consecutive further thought of old-time memories. His mind was tensely concentrated on the work of climbing through the tangle of dead trunks and branches, and, when he had accomplished the hard passage, was turned wholly from the things which he had been considering by a slight crackling, as of some one stepping on a brittle twig, at a distance in advance of him.

Instantly he was on his guard, showing signs quite unmistakable of deadly fear. He shrank back into the thicket with the speed and silence of a frightened animal.

The panic which had seized him soon had passed, however, for, within a few short seconds it was clear to him that the noise which he had heard had not been made by any one suspicious of his presence or a-search for him.

Peering cautiously between the slender boles of crooked mountain-laurel bushes, he soon found a vantage point from which he could see on beyond the densely woven foliage, and, to his astonishment, found, before he had thought, possible that he had progressed so far, that he had already reached the place he sought. Memory had made the way to it a longer one than it was really, and, in spite of the delays caused by his advancing age and awkward muscles, long unaccustomed to the work of threading mountain paths, he had traveled faster than he thought.

Not fifty feet away from him, separated from the thicket he was hiding in but by a narrow stretch of mountain sward, he saw, among the mountain side's disordered rocks, the carefully masked entrance to a cave.

An untrained eye would never have made note of the few signs which made it clear to him, at once, that this cave was, as it had been long years before when he had known it well, a place of frequent call for footsteps skilled in mountain cunning. No path was worn to its rough entrance, but, here and there, a broken grass-blade, in another place a pebble recently dislodged from its accustomed hollow, elsewhere a ragged bit of paper, torn from a tobacco-package, proved to him that, although hidden in the wilderness of old Mount Nebo's scarred and inaccessible sides, this spot was yet one often visited by many men.

A grim smile stirred the leathern folds of his old cheeks.

"Thar yet," he thought, "an' doin' business yet."

Again, after he had worked about to get a better view.

"Best-hidden still in these here mountings. Revenuers never *will* get run of it."

The place had a mighty fascination for him, as if it might have played a tremendous part in long-gone passages of his own life. As he stood gazing at it cautiously, the mountaineer seemed definitely to emerge from his low-country dress and superficial "bluegrass" manner, fastened on him by long years of usage. Old expressions of not only face but muscles came clearly to the front. Now, no person watching him, could ever for a moment doubt that he was mountain-born and mountain-bred, if they but knew the ear-marks of that people--almost a race apart. The sight of the old cave-mouth plainly stirred in him a horde of memories not wholly pleasant. Leathern as his face was, it none the less showed his emotions with remarkable lucidity now that he was off his guard. Now sly cunning dominated it, with, possibly, a touch left of the early fear to flavor it.

"I bet a hundred revenuers in these mountains have looked for that there still," he thought, "an' no one ever found it, yet. Forty years it's been thar--through three generations o' th' Loreys--damn 'em!--an' no one's ever squealed on 'em. I ... wonder...."

A look of vicious craft and malice wholly drove away the searching curiosity which had possessed the old man's features. For a time he plainly planned some work of bitter vengefulness. Then, with shaking head, he evidently abandoned the enticing thought.

"Too resky," he concluded, and edged a little nearer to the thicket's edge. "Might stir up old--"

He paused suddenly, alert and keenly listening. From another path than that by which he had approached the place there came the sound of voices raised in talk and laughter. He easily identified them, to his great surprise, as those of some young mountain-girl and some young bluegrass gentleman. Their tones and accents told this story plainly. Surprised and curious, he went farther, his head bent, with study of the voices, peering, meanwhile, through the thicket's tangle to get sight of them as soon as they appeared within the clearing. Suddenly he dropped his jaw in blank amazement.

"Frank Layson!" he exclaimed.

The girl's voice he did not recognize, but knew, of course, from its peculiar accent, that it was some mountain maiden's.

"Well!" he exclaimed beneath his breath in absolute astonishment. "I didn't think it of Frank Layson! What would Barbara--"

The pair emerged, now, from a gully by-path, and came into view. He tightly shut his jaws and watched them with a peering, eager curiosity.

A moment later, and by her wonderful resemblance to her dead mother, he recognized the girl.

She, above all people, must not know that he was there, even if she only thought him to be Horace Holton, newcomer among the bluegrass gentry in the valley. His plans had been laid carefully, and for her to find them out would almost certainly upset them all. He was far from anxious to meet Layson, there among the mountains, for it would mean awkward questioning, but he was doubly anxious to avoid a meeting with the girl, first because she owned the land on which he had secured the bits of rock then nestling in his pocket, and, second, because she was the daughter of--

His thoughts were interrupted, for, for a second, he thought they must have seen him, so definite was their approach straight toward the thicket where he hid. He crouched, frightened. It would be a very awkward matter to be found there by them, and, besides, he did not know who might be out of sight within the hidden still. It was quite possible that there might lurk a deadly enemy. He must worm back through the thicket with great caution, and, following the secluded ways which he had traversed in his coming, get back to the railroad camp, where was safety.

He stepped backward hastily, and, in so doing, trod upon a rotten branch. He had not been as cautious as he had intended, and this mis-step unbalanced him and sent him to the ground, with a tremendous crashing of the brittle twigs and dead-wood.

Springing to his feet while the young people, startled by the great disturbance, paused where they were standing, for an instant, he hurried back into the hidden, thicket-bordered path, now using all his recrudescent skill of silent woods-progression, and made complete escape, leaving them not sure that the disturbance had been caused by human blundering and not some vagrant beast's.

Madge held back, but Layson hurried to the thicket, with gun raised ready for a shot.

Just then, from the carefully concealed cave-entrance, came Joe Lorey, rifle poised for trouble, eyes gleaming fiercely, evidently keyed to meet a raid by revenuers.

It was plain enough that he believed the noise which had disturbed, alarmed him, had been made by this young sportsman. Indeed, as he who really had caused the uproar was, now, well on a cautious backward way along the path by which he had come up, and the girl and Layson were the only folk in sight, the young moonshiner's mistake was natural.

Madge, almost as much disturbed as Lorey was by the crashing in the thickets, was looking in the direction whence the noise had come, and, at first, did not see him. When she did she smiled at him, and called to him, but, absorbed in study of the bluegrass youth who had so suddenly appeared there in his secret place among the mountains in company with the girl whom he, himself, adored, Joe did not answer her, at first. When he did it was with nothing more than a curt nod. He was astonished and alarmed to see her in such company.

After that curt nod he waited for no explanation, but, like a shadow, slipped into a thicket, disappearing instantly. No Indian from Cooper's tales could have more instantly obliterated all trace of himself, could have more quickly, noiselessly, mysteriously disappeared amongst the greenery, than did this mountaineer. His movements, made with the instinctive cunning of the woodsman and with muscles trained not only by wild life there in the mountains to speed, endurance and exactitude, but by many an hour of stealthy stalking of the "revenuers" sent to search out his moonshine still, raid it, take him prisoner, were almost magically active, cautious, furtive and effective.

For an instant Madge herself, accustomed to the native's skill in woodcraft, as she was, gazed after him, astonished by the magic of his disappearance, and, at first, piqued not a little by his scanty courtesy. Then realizing that the mountaineer was, possibly, quite justified in feeling grave suspicions of the stranger who was with her--of any stranger coming thus, without a herald to the mountains--she turned again to Layson, and, with her hand lightly guiding him by touch as delicate, almost, as a wind-blown leaf's upon his sleeve, led him to the nearest mountain path and on, toward a point whence she could clearly point out to him the way to his own camp.

And, suddenly, her own heart throbbed with worry. Had she not done wrong in bringing this unknown and, therefore, this mysterious stranger so close upon the heart of Lorey's secret? She had chosen the path thoughtlessly. She realized that, now, and much regretted it. The man had wholly won her confidence, but had it been considerate or fair to Joe, her lifelong friend, or to the other people of the mountains who had things to hide from strangers, to be quite so frank with him in her revelation of the byways of the wilderness?

Between the mountain-dwellers and the people of the lowlands never could exist real confidence or friendship. From her babyhood she had been taught to feel suspicion of all strangers: that was, indeed, first article in the creed of all folk mountain-born. Why had she so freely dropped her mantle of reserve before *this* stranger? That he had saved her from the bush-fire was excuse for her own gratitude, but was it valid reason for exposing her best friends to danger at his hands, if they proved treacherous? The revenuers, she had been informed, were men of devilish craft, unscrupulous cunning. Might not this youth with the fine clothes, the splendid manner, the great learning, the soft voice, the quick resource and the undoubted bravery, very well be one of them?

She had once heard a mountain preacher draw a picture of the devil, which made him most attractive and in the same way that this youth was most attractive. Certain of the sympathies of his rough hearers, the man had painted Beelzebub with broad, rough, verbal strokes, as a bluegrass gentleman intent on the destruction of the honor, independence, liberty of mountaineers. The mountaineer has never and will never understand what right the government of state or nation has to interfere with whatsoe'er he does on his own land with his own corn in his own still. Just why he has no right to manufacture whiskey without paying taxes on the product he really fails to comprehend. He regards the "revenuer" as the representative of acute and cruel injustice and oppression. When he "draws a bead" on one he does it with no such thoughts as common murderers must know when they shoot down their enemies. He does not think such killings are crude murder, any more than he regards feud killings as assassinations.

With such ideas Madge had been, to some extent, imbued. With feud feeling she was quite in sympathy--had not she lost her loved ones through its awful work? Could she ever have revenge on those who had thus bereaved her through any means save similar assassination?

And certainly the revenuers were her enemies, for they were the foemen of her friends. If this young man should be a revenuer she might have done a harm incalculable by guiding him along the secret mountain byways which they had been travelling.

Her heart was in her throat from worry, for an instant. Had she, whose very soul was fiercely loyal to the mountains and their people, been the one to show an enemy the way into their citadel? Had she, bound especially to Joe Lorey, not only by the ties of lifelong friendship but by that other comradeship which had grown out of mutual wrongs and mutual hatred of Ben Lindsay (not dimmed, a whit, by the mere fact that, terrified, he had, years ago fled from the mountains), done Joe the greatest wrong of all by leading this fine stranger to the very entrance of his hidden still? *Was* he a revenuer in disguise?

The magnitude of her possible indiscretion filled her with alarm. That crashing in the bushes back of them might have been made by some associate of his, who had trailed them at a distance, ready to give assistance, if needs be, or, in case all things went right and the bolder man who had gone first and fallen into the great luck of an acquaintance with her had no need of help, to corroborate his observations, help him to scheme the way by which to make attack upon the still when the time for it should come.

As she considered all these possibilities, quite reasonable to her suspicious mind, she shuddered.

But then, as she went slowly down the mountain path beside the stranger she looked up and caught the frank calm glances of his eyes.

Surely there was nothing of cowardice such as would fool a trusting girl into betrayal of her friends, in them; surely there was not the low craft of a spy in them; surely their clear and unexcited gaze was not that of a keen hunter, unscrupulously on the trail of human game, who has just learned through the innocent indiscretion of a girl who trusted him, the secret of its covert.

As she looked at him she was convinced of two things, vastly comforting. One was that Layson had no knowledge of the still; that, untrained to mountain ways and unsuspicious, he had not even guessed at the secret of the little hidden place among the mountains. Another was--and this gave her, although she could have scarcely explained why, a greater comfort than the first had--that had he had that knowledge he would not have used it meanly.

She thrilled pleasantly with the complete conviction that the man whom she had liked so much at first sight, the man who had shown such pluck in saving her from fire, the man who had exhibited such thoughtfulness and helpfulness in starting her upon the rocky path toward education, was true and fair and fine--was, in the curt language of the mountains, "decent."

When she left him at the foot of the rough path which wound up to the cabin where she lived alone, she had quite recovered confidence in him. She eagerly assented to his suggestion that they meet again, the following day, for the continuation of her studies.

CHAPTER V

Their next lesson was in a new school-room. The clearing where they had had their first, was, now, charred and blackened, not attractive, after the small fire; so, after going to it, the following day to look it over with that interest with which the man who has escaped from peril seeks again, the scene of it in curiosity, they found another glade wherein to carry on their delving after knowledge of the ABC's.

There, beneath a canopy of arching branches and the sky, between rustling walls of greenery pillared by the mighty boles of forest trees, they had the second lesson of the course which was to open up to Madge the magic realm of books and of the learning hidden in them.

Nor did her investigations now, confine themselves, entirely to the things the small book taught. She questioned Layson about a thousand things less dry and matter-of-fact than shape of printed symbols and the manner of their combination in the printed word. Life, life--that was to her, as it has ever been to all of us, the most fascinating thing. Here was one who had come from far, mysterious realms which she had vaguely heard about in winter-evening gossip at the mountain-cabin firesides; realms where men were courteous to women, careful in their speech; where women did not work, but sat on silken chairs with black menials ready to their call to serve their slightest wish; where maidens were not clad as she was clad, and every woman she had ever known was clad, in calico or linsey-woolsey homespun, but richly, wondrously, in silks and satins, laces, beaded gew-gaws. In her imagination's picture, the maids and matrons of the bluegrass were as marvellous, as fascinating, as are the fairies and the sprites of Anderson and Grimm to girls more fortunately placed. No tale of elf born from a cleft rock, touched by magic wand, ever more completely fascinated any big-eyed city child, than did the tales which

Layson told her--commonplace and ordinary to his mind: mere casual account of routine life--about his family and friends down in the bluegrass, the enchanted region separated from them where they sat by a hundred miles or so of rugged hills and billowing forests. Her eager questions especially drew from him with a greed insatiable account of all the gayeties of that mysterious existence.

"And that aunt of yours--Muss Aluth--Aluth--"

"Miss Alathea Layson?" he inquired, and smiled.

"Yes; what queer names the women have, down there! Is she pretty? Does *she* dress in silks and satins, too, like the girls that go to them big dances?"

He laughed. "None of them are always dressed in silks and satins," he replied. "Perhaps I've given you a wrong idea. We work down there, as hard, perhaps, as you do here, but we have more things to work with. Don't get the notion, little girl, that all these things which I have told you of are magic things which surely will bring happiness! There is no more of that, I reckon, in the bluegrass than there is here in the mountains. Silks and satins don't make happiness, balls and garden-fetes don't make it. A girl who's sobbing in a ball gown can be quite as miserable as you would be, unhappy in your homespun."

She was impatient of his moralizing. "I know that," she said. "Dellaw, don't you suppose I've got some sense? But it ain't *quite* true, neither. Maybe if I was going to be unhappy I'd be just as much so in a silk dress as I would in this here cotton one that I've got on; but I guess there's times when I'd be happier in the silk than I *would* be in this. My, I wisht I had one!"

He looked at her appraisingly. She would, he thought, be wondrous beautiful if given the accessories which girls more fortunate had at their hand. Beautiful, she was, undoubtedly, without them; with them she would be--he almost caught his breath at thought of it--sensational!

Mentally he ran over all the girls he knew in a swift survey of memory. Not one of them, he thought, could really compare with her. Even Barbara Holton, with her haughty, big featured, strikingly handsome face, although she had attracted him in days passed, seemed singularly unattractive to him, now.

While he sat, musing thus, almost forgetful of the puzzling ABC, she gazed off across the valley dreamily, the ABC's as far from her. It was a lovely prospect of bare crag and wooded slope, green fields and low-hung clouds, with, at its center, here and there the silver of the stream which, back among the forest trees, supplied the water to the hidden pool where she had watched him, furtively, the first time she had ever seen him. But it was not of the fair prospect that the girl was thinking. The coming of the stranger had brought into her life a hundred new emotions, ten thousand puzzling guesses at the life which lay beyond and could produce such men as he. Were all men in the bluegrass like Frank Layson--courteous, considerate, and as strong and active as the best of mountaineers? If so--what a splendid place for women! She was sure that men like him were never brutal to their wives and daughters, sisters, mothers, as the mountaineers too often are; she was certain that they did not craze themselves with whisky and terrify and beat their families; she was sure that when one loved a girl the courtship must be all sweet gentleness and happiness and joy, not like the quick succession of mad love-making and fierce quarrels which had characterized the heart-affairs that she had watched, there in the mountains.

She, herself, had had no love-affairs. Instinctively she had held herself aloof from the ruck of the young mountain-men, neither she nor they knew why, unless it was because she owned the valley land and so was what the mountain folk called rich. Most of them had tried to pay her court, but none of them, save Joe, had in the least attracted her, and she had let them know this (strangely) without arousing too much anger.

Now she had one suitor, only, who was at all persistent--Joe. She had sometimes thought she loved him. Now she knew, quite certainly, that she did not, and, in a vague way, was sorry for him, for she was quite certain of his love for her. It never once occurred to her that she was rapidly falling in love with the young man by her side. She had not thought of him as being socially superior: the spirit of independence, of equality of men, is nowhere stronger, even in this land of independence and equality, than it is among the mountains of the Cumberland; but she knew he was most wise. Had not the puzzling symbols in the spelling-book been, to him, as simple matters? She knew that he was gentle-hearted, for the kindness of his acts proved that. She knew that he was, really, a gentleman, for his manner was so perfectly considerate, so ever kind. She did not realize that she was thinking of him as a lover; but she dreamed, there, of the girls down in the bluegrass and wondered how it must seem to them to have lovers such as he. She could but very vaguely speculate as to their emotions or appearance, but her speculations on both points, vague as they might be, made her suffer strangely and cast queer, furtive little side-glances at him. In her heart were stirrings of keen jealousy of these distant maidens, but this she did not realize.

She broke into his revery with: "Don't you know any women, down there, but your aunt?"

"Er--what?"

"Don't you know any women, down there, but your aunt?"

"Why, yes," said he, and laughed. "I know a lot of women, down there; lots and lots of women, certainly."

"All them that go to balls, and such?"

"Many of them."

"Do you like to dance with them?"

"Oh, yes; of course."

"Tell me--all about the things they wear." This was not quite the question she had started out to ask, but an answer to it might be very interesting.

She settled comfortably back upon the boulder she had chosen as a seat, her hands clasped about one knee, her face turned toward him eagerly, her eyes sparkling with keen zest.

But he looked at her, appalled. "Why," said he, "why--I don't believe I can. I know they always seem to be most charming in appearance, but just how they work the magic *I* don't know."

"Can't you tell me nothing?" Her voice showed bitter disappointment. She unclasped the hands about her knee and sat dejected on the boulder. She gave him not the slightest hint of it, but, suddenly, a plan had come into her mind.

He looked at her regretfully. "Perhaps you'd better question me," said he. "Maybe I can scare up details if you'll let me know just what you wish to hear about."

"How are their dresses made?" she asked.

"Oh, skirt, and waist, and so on," he airily replied.

She made a gesture of impatience. "Well, then, how is the skirt made? Tell me that. Tell me everything that you remember about skirts. Are they loose as mine, or tighter?" She rose and stood before him, in her scant drapery of homespun, turning slowly, so that he might see.

It was very clever. Instantly it brought to mind the last girls he had seen down in the lowlands at a lawn-party, with their wide and much beruffled skirts.

"Oh, they're looser," he said gravely. "Much, much looser. Why, they are as big around as that!" He made a sweeping, circular gesture with his arms.

"What for trimmings do they have?"

"Oh, all sorts of things--ruffles, frills, embroidery and laces."

"What's embroidery?"

He tried to tell her, but he did not make it very clear, and, realizing that he had done quite his best although he had not done so very well, she sighed and dropped that detail of the subject. But she knew what frills and ruffles were.

"And how about their waists?" said she. "Like mine, are they?"

He looked, appraisingly, at the loose basque, which, because of the budding beauty of her form rather than because of any merit of its own, had seemed to him most charming and attractive. Close examination did not show this to be the case. It was a crude garment, certainly, of crude material, crude cut, crude make. The beauty all was in the wearer's soft young curves and lissome grace.

"No," he answered, honestly, "they're not like that. In the summer, and for evenings--such as dances and the like--they are cut low at the neck. And they are tighter."

"I suppose," said she, "they wear them things that they call corsets, under 'em. I've heard of 'em--I saw one, once--but I ain't never had one. Maybe I had better get one."

He spoke hastily. At that moment, as he gazed at her slim grace, undulant, un-trammelled and as willowy as a spring sapling's, it seemed to him that it would be a sacrilege to confine it in the stiff rigidity of such artificialities as corsets. It seemed a bit indelicate, to him, to talk to her about such matters, but her guilelessness was so real and he was so assured of his own innocence, that he did what he could to make things clear to her. He descanted with some eloquence upon the wickedness of lacing, the ungracefulness of artificial forms and the beauty of her own wholly natural grace.

"I'm glad you think I'm pretty," she said frankly, plainly greatly pleased, "but I reckon I'd be prettier if I had one of them there corsets."

His protests to the contrary were not convincing, in the least.

So the lessons from the book did not go so very far that day.

"Furbelows have always interested females, I suppose," said he, "but I didn't really think you'd lose your interest in spelling-books because of them."

"I ain't lost interest in spelling-books," she said. "I ain't lost interest, at all. After I've studied good and hard I can read all about such things in the picture-papers that Mom Liza has down to the store. They've got all kinds of pictures in 'em--all of fancy gowns and hats and things like that. She showed one to me, once, but all I could make out was just the pictures, and she couldn't manage to make out much more. She can read the names on all the letters comin' to the post-office, for there's only three folks ever gets 'em, but she ain't what you'd really call a scholar."

He laughed heartily. "So, even in the mountains, here, they take the fashion papers, do they?"

"No; she don't pay for 'em," she gravely answered. "They're always marked with red ink, 'Sample Copy,' so she says; but they send 'em ev'ry once a while. If you're in th' post-office, you get a lot o' things, like that--all sorts o' picture-papers, an' cards, all printed up in pretty colors, to tell what medicines to take when you get sick."

"Ah, patent-medicine advertisements."

"Yes; that's what she calls 'em, an' she's read me some powerful amazin' stories out of 'em--them as was in short words--of folks that rose up almost from th' dead! They're wonderful!"

"They are, indeed!"

"But what I always liked th' best was them there papers tellin' about clo'es."

"Eternal feminine!"

"I don't know what you mean by that, but they are mighty peart, some o' them dresses pictured out in them there papers."

"I've not the least doubt of it."

"And I suppose they are th' kind th' girls you know, down in th' bluegrass, wear for ev'ry day!" she sighed.

He looked at her in quick compassion and in protest.

"Madge," he said, "please listen to me. It's not dress that makes the woman, any more than it is coats that make the man. You would like me just as well if I were dressed in homespun, wouldn't you?"

"That's different."

"It isn't; it's not, a bit."

"Laws, yes! It's--oh--heaps different!" She nodded her lovely head in firm conviction. "It's heaps different and I'm goin' to know more about such things as clo'es. I ain't plumb *poverty* poor, like lots o' folks, here in th' mountings. I got land down in th' valley I get rent from--fifty dollars, every year! I'm goin' to find out about such things."

He looked at her, almost worried. It would be a pity, he thought instantly, for this charming child of nature to become sophisticated and be fashionably gowned; but, of course, he made no protest.

"You can learn a little something about such things if you stay right here," said he. "I'm going to have visitors, sometime before the summer's over, at my camp. My aunt, Miss Alathea, will be here, and our old friend, Colonel Sandusky Doolittle. He's a great horseman."

Instantly the girl showed vivid interest, not, as he had thought she would, in his aunt, Miss Alathea, but in the Colonel from the Bluegrass, who also was a horseman.

"Horseman, is he?" she exclaimed, her eyes alight.

"Yes; he's famous as a judge of horses."

"At them races that they tell about? Oh, I'd like to see one of them races!"

"Yes, he goes to races, everywhere, although he always means to stop immediately after the next one. It has been the races which have kept him poor and kept him single."

"How've they kept him poor?"

He told her about betting, while she listened, wide-eyed with amazement at the mention of the sums involved.

"How've they kept him single?"

"He's been in love with my Aunt Alathea for a good many years, but she won't marry him until he keeps his promise to avoid the race-tracks."

"What makes your aunt hate hawsses?"

"Oh, she loves good horses, but the Colonel always bets, and, as I have said, it keeps him poor. It's the gambling that she hates, and not the horses. Every year he plans to keep away from all horse-racing for her sake; every year he tries to do it, but quite fails."

She laughed heartily. "An' she thinks he loves th' races more than he does her?" she asked. Then, more soberly: "I don't know's I blame her, none. When's she comin'? I'll be powerful glad to see her."

"I don't know just when she's coming, but she's promised me to have the Colonel bring her up here. I want to have her see the beauty of the mountains."

"I'll like him, sure, whether I like her or not."

He was astonished. "But you said you would be sure to love her!"

"Uh-huh; but I'd be surer to like anyone who is as fond of hawsses as you say he is. Why, when I ride--"

"I didn't know you ever rode a horse. I've only seen you on your ox."

"Poor old Buck! It's true, I have been ridin' him, when I felt lazy, lately, but my pony--ah, that's *fun*!"

"Where is he?"

They had started strolling down the trail and were near the pasture bars, where she had left Joe Lorey on the morning of her bath, after having ridden down to them upon her ox.

She hurried to them, now, and, leaning over them, puckered her red lips and sent a shrill, clear whistle out across the pasture. Immediately from a thicket-tangle at the far end of the half-cleared lot appeared a shaggy pony, limping wofully, but with ears pricked forward as a sign of welcome to his mistress.

"Come on, Little Hawss!" she called. "Come on! It hurts, I know, for you to step, but come on, just th' same. I got a turnip for you."

She turned to Layson with an explanation. "He's lame, poor Little Hawss is. Don't know's he'll ever get all right ag'in."

"Oh!" said Layson. "And I didn't even know you had a horse." Horses are less common in the mountains than are oxen, although nearly every mountain farm has one, for riding. Oxen, though, are the section's draught-animals.

"Didn't think I had a hawss?" she said, and laughed. "I'd *die* without a hawss! Why, they say, here in the mountains, that I'm a good rider. I've raced all the boys and beat 'em on my Little Hawss."

She petted the affectionate, uncouth little beast and fed him slowly, lovingly. "Little Hawss, before he hurt his hoof, was sure-footed as a deer. Didn't have to be afraid to run him anywhere, on any kind of road at any time of day or night," said she. "Never stumbled, never missed the way, and, while he don't *look* much--he never did--he could just carry *me* to suit me! But--well, I don't know as he will ever carry me again!"

Layson, himself a great horse lover, went up to the shaggy little beast and petted him. The pony knew a friend instinctively and rubbed his nose against the rough sleeve of his jacket while he munched the turnip.

Madge stooped and lifted the poor beast's crippled foot.

"Looks bad, don't it?" she said anxiously, asking Frank's opinion as an expert.

He looked the bad foot over carefully and shook his head.

"Madge, I am afraid it does," said he. "But wait until the Colonel comes. He'll tell you what to do. No man knows horses better than the Colonel does.

"I've never told you of my horse, have I?" he asked.

"Why, no; you got one, too?"

He drew a long breath of enthusiasm at the mere thought of his greatest treasure. "Such a mare," said he, "as rarely has been seen, even in Kentucky. She's famous now and going to be more so. She's the very apple of my eye."

The girl looked at him wide-eyed with a fascinated interest. "What color is she?"

"Black as night."

"And gentle?"

"Ah, gentle as a dove with friends; but she's not gentle if she happens to dislike a man or woman! Why, if she hates you, keep away from her. She'll side-step with a cunning that would fool the wisest so's to get a chance for a left-handed kick; she'll bite; she'll strike with her forefeet the way a human fighter would."

"Oh!" said the girl. "Ain't it a pity she's so ugly?"

"I said she's gentle with her friends. She'd no more kick at me than I would kick at her. She knows it. She's intelligent beyond most horseflesh."

"Has she ever won in races?"

"She's won in small events, and great things are expected of her by more folk than I when she gets going on the larger tracks. I'm counting on her for good work this year, after I go home again."

"Ah," sighed the girl, carried quite away by his excited talk about his favorite, "how I'd love to see her run!"

"It's poetry," he granted; "the true poetry of motion."

"And this Cunnel--Cunnel--"

"Colonel Doolittle?"

"Uh-huh. Will he help me, do you s'pose, to get my Little Hawss cured of his lameness?"

"You may count on that."

"Who else is comin' here to see you?" she inquired, as they left Little Hawss wistfully agaze at them across the old log fence.

Layson, for no reason he could think of, felt a bit uncomfortable, as he replied. He temporized before he really told her of what worried him.

"Well," said he, "there'll be old Neb--"

"Who's he?"

"A servant who has been in our family for years. He is a fine old darkey and we love him--everyone of us."

"And will he be all?"

"No; I understand that Mr. Horace Holton, also, will come with the party. Mr. Holton and his daughter."

It is possible that he may have flushed a little, as he spoke about this matter, or there may have been some slight hint of the unusual in his voice. At any rate, the notice of the girl was instantly attracted.

"Daughter?" she inquired.

"Yes," said Frank, "his daughter Barbara."

"How old is she?" Madge's curiosity had been aroused at once.

"About your age."

She was delighted. "And will I surely see her?"

"Yes; of course."

"Do you suppose she'll like me?"

Layson, from what he knew of Barbara Holton, scarcely thought she would. He could not make his fancy paint a picture of the haughty lowlands beauty showing much consideration for this little mountain waif; but he did not say so. He answered hesitatingly, and she noticed it.

"You don't think she'll like me!" she exclaimed.

"I didn't say so. Certainly she'll like you. Who could help it, Madge?" He smiled. It did not seem to him, as his eyes studied her, that anybody of sound sense could.

She sighed. "A woman could." She spoke with an instinctive wisdom which her isolated life among the crags and peaks had not deprived her of. "A woman always can. But, my, I hope she will!"

"She will," said Frank. "She will. And my dear Aunt--oh, you will love her."

"Miss Aluth--Aluth--?" She stopped, questioningly, still bothered by the name.

"Miss Alathea," he prompted. "She'll like you and you'll love her."

The girl smiled happily. "Uh-huh." Her acquiescence was immediate. "Reckon maybe I'll love *her*, all right, and I *hope* the other will come true, too." Suddenly she was stricken with a fear. "But she won't, though--dressed the way I be!"

"What you wear would make no difference to my Aunt Alathea," Frank protested, "any more than it would make to Colonel Doolittle."

She did not speak again for quite a time, walking along the narrow mountain-path with eyes fixed, but unseeing, on the trail. It was plain that in her mind grave problems were being closely studied.

"Maybe," she said, at length, "I won't be so very *awful* as you *think*!"

They had reached the path which led first to the bridge across the mountain-chasm making the rock on which her cabin stood an island, and then, across this draw-bridge, to the cabin itself. She waved a gay and unexpected good-bye to him.

He felt strangely robbed. He had expected another half-hour with her. It astonished him to learn through this tiny disappointment how agreeable the little mountain maid's society had come to be.

He was wakeful that night till a later hour than usual.

Somehow he was not as thoroughly delighted as he felt that he should be by the prospect of his guests' arrival. His journey to the mountains and his sojourn there had been considered rather foolish by his friends, but he had wished to make quite sure that what was said about the wild mountain lands which formed the greater portion of his patrimony--that they were practically valueless--was true, ere he gave up all hope of profiting from them.

The building of the railroad through the valley had imbued him with some hope that they might not prove to be as useless as they had been thought to be, and it had been that which had induced him, at the start, to make the journey.

Once arrived he had found the mountain air delightful, the fishing fine, the shooting all that could be wished, and had enjoyed these to their full, investigating, meanwhile, his rough property; but as he lay there in his shack of logs and puncheons he acknowledged to himself that it was none of these things which now made the mountains so attractive. It was the nymph of the woods pool, the mountain-side Europa on her bull, his little pupil of the alphabet, in plain reality, who now held him to the wilderness.

He wondered just what this could mean. Could it be possible that he was thinking seriously of the little maid *in that way*?

He almost laughed at the idea, there alone in the woods cabin, with the stars in their deep velvet canopy twinkling through the window at him and the glow of his cob pipe for company.

But his laugh was not too genuine. He found himself, to his amazement, comparing Madge, the mountain girl, with Barbara Holton, the elegant daughter of the lowlands, and finding many points in favor of the little rustic maiden. He wondered just how serious his attentions to fair Barbara had been thought to be by her, her father, Horace Holton, and by other people. There were many things about Madge Brierly, which, as he sat there, reflective, he found admirable, besides her vivid, vigorous young beauty. He could not bring himself, as he sat thinking of the two girls, widely separated as they were in the great social plane, unevenly matched as they had been in early training, to admit that the whole advantage was upon the side of Barbara Holton.

And above him, in her lonely little cabin on the towering rock, upon all sides of which the mountain-torrent, making it an isle of safety for her there in the wilderness, roared rythmically, the mountain maiden who so occupied his thoughts was busy with her crude wardrobe.

In complete dissatisfaction she put aside, at length, every garment of her own which she possessed as unsuitable for the great day when she was to meet the blue-grass gentlefolk.

Then, remembering suddenly an old chest which held her mother's wedding finery, she strained her fine young muscles as she dragged it out of storage; and sitting on the floor beside it where the great blaze of pine-knots in the big "mud-and-broke-rock" fireplace lighted it and her with flickering brilliance, she went through it with reverent fingers, searching, searching for such garments and such adornments as it might hold to make her fit to meet the friends of the young lowlander who had captured her imagination with his bravery, resource and courtesy.

There were a few things in the chest which pleased her, and she smiled as she discovered them, smiled as she tried them on, smiled as she saw the image wearing them in the cracked mirror by the side of the big fireplace. She had to make experiments with dripping tallow dips before she got a light which would enable her to get the full effect of an ornate old poke-bonnet which was the chief treasure from the chest, but finally she did so, and exclaimed in pleasure as she managed it.

It was, indeed, a charming picture which she saw there in the glass--a face with rosy cheeks, bright eyes, red lips set off with softly waving auburn hair and framed delightfully in the old arch of shirred red silk--and when she took it off, at last, she was convinced that one, at least, of her big problems had been solved. She had a bonnet, certainly, which was as lovely as the finest thing that any bluegrass belle could wear. There was not the slightest doubt that all its shirring was of real, *real* silk! She had run her fingers over it caressingly, delighted by its sheen and gloss when she had been a little girl; now she fondled it with loving touch, high hopes. Surely no young lady visitor, even from the far off and to her mysterious bluegrass could have anything much finer than that bonnet with its silken facings! She tied the wide strings underneath her chin in a great, flaring bow, and peeped forth from the cavernous depths of the arched "poke" with quite unconscious coquetry, flirting, with the keenest relish and most completely childish pleasure with the charming creature whom she saw reflected on the little mirror's cracked, imperfect surface.

It was while she stood thus, innocently coquetting with her own delightful picture, that a great plan for the plenishment of her otherwise imperfect wardrobe popped into her active, searching mind. Carefully she considered this, first before the glass and then, with feet crossed and clasped hands between her knees, before the roaring fire of resinous pine-knots in the old fireplace.

Having finally decided that it was a good one, she went about the cabin seeing to the fastenings of doors and windows, wholly unafraid despite her solitude. There was but one way of approaching this, her fastness in the rocks, and the bridge, had been drawn up for the night. Safe she was as any Rhenish baron in his moated stronghold.

Conscious that a busy day was looming large before her, she now blew out her candles and crept into her little curtained bed, to dream, there, vividly, of haughty beauties from the bluegrass staring in astonishment as they first glimpsed the beauty of a little mountain girl in such a gorgeous outfit as they had not in all their pampered lives conceived; of lovely aunts who smiled with pleasure when they saw their handsome nephews step up to this splendid maiden and take her hands in theirs; of wondrous youths--ah, these images were never absent from the scenes her fancy painted!--who scorned the haughty bluegrass beauties in favor of the freckled little fists of those same brilliant mountain maidens, and, lo! by taking those same freckled fists in theirs, removed the freckles and the callouses of work as if by magic, making them as white and fine--aye, whiter, finer!--than the haughty bluegrass beauty's. And in her dreams, too, was a gallant horseman, wise in equine ways, who came to her with handsome chargers trailing from fair-leather lead straps to present her with the thoroughbreds because her little, shaggy pony limped.

Queer fancies of the strange life of the lowlands which he had described to her, flashed, also, through her ignorant but active brain in fascinating visions. She thought she saw the houses on the tops of houses which he had described to her, in efforts to assist her to imagine structures more elaborate than the little, single storied cabins which were all that she had ever seen. Strange conceptions of the railroad, with its monstrous engines puffing smoke and fire would have been terrifying had there not been, ever at her side as dreams revealed them, a stalwart youth in corduroys to bear her from their path through rings of burning thickets.

Again she trembled in imagination at the thought of meeting the fine ladies who would be dressed with such elaboration and impressive elegance; but each time, when her dream seemed actually to lead her to them, there he was to help her through the great ordeal with heartening smiles and comforting suggestions.

Her sleep was restless, but delightful. Once she woke and left her bed to peer out of the window, wondering if, by chance, she might not glimpse a light in Layson's camp far down the mountain-side. She was disappointed when she found she could not, but went back to bed to find there further compensating dreams.

There might have been still greater compensation for her had she known that at the very moment when she peered out through the darkness, looking for some vagrant glimmer of a light from Layson's camp, he had, himself, just gone back to his cabin after having stood a long time staring through the darkness toward her own small cabin in its fastness.

He was thinking, thinking, thinking. The little mountain maid had strangely fascinated the highly cultivated youth from the far bluegrass. He did not know quite what to make of the queer way in which her fresh and lovely, girlish face, obtruded itself constantly into his thoughts. And as for the haughty bluegrass belle whom poor Madge dreaded so--he did not think of her, at all, save, possibly, with half acknowledged annoyance at the fact that she was coming to spy out his wilderness and those who dwelt therein. He would have been a little happier if he could have remained there, undisturbed, for a time longer.

Day had not dawned when Madge awoke. The sun, indeed, had just begun to poke the red edge of his disc above Mount Nebo, when, having built her fire and cooked her frugal breakfast, she loosed the rope which held the crude, small draw-bridge up and lowered the rickety old platform until it gave a pathway over the deep chasm and carried her to the mainland, ready for the journey to the distant cross-roads store.

Dew, sparkling like cut diamonds, cool as melting ice, was everywhere in the brilliant freshness of the morning; the birds were busy with their gossip and their foraging, chattering greetings to her as she passed; in her pasture her cow, Sukey, had not risen yet from her comfortable night posture when she reached her. The animal looked up gravely at her, chewing calmly on her cud, plainly not approving, quite, of such a very early call. While the girl sat on the one-legged stool beside her, sending white, rich, fragrant streams into the resounding pail, her shaggy Little Hawss limped up, nosing at her pocket for a turnip, which he found, of course, abstracted cleverly and munched.

Having finished with the cow she set the milk in a fence-corner to wait for her return, and, when she left the lot, the pony followed her, making a difficult, limping way along the inside of the rough stump-fence until he came to a cross barrier. Then, as he saw that she was going on and leaving him behind, he nickered lonesomely, and, although she planned, that day to accomplish many, many things, and, in consequence, was greatly pressed for time, she went back to him and petted him a moment and then found another turnip for him in her pocket.

The journey which began, thus, with calls on her four-footed friends, was solitary, afterward, although in the narrow road-bed, here and there, she saw impressions of preceding footsteps, big and deep. They aroused her curiosity, and with keen instinct of the woods she studied one of them elaborately. Rising from her pondering above it she decided that Joe Lorey had gone on before her, and wondered what could possibly have sent him down the trail so early in the morning. When she noted that his trail turned off at the cross-roads which might lead to Layson's camp (or other places) her heart sank for a moment. She realized how bitterly the mountaineer felt toward the bluegrass youth whom he considered his successful rival and she hoped that trouble would not come of it. She did not love Joe Lorey as he wished to have her love him, but she had a very real affection for him, none the less. And--and--she did--she did--she *did*--this morning she acknowledged it!--love Layson. The matter worried her, somewhat. Trouble between the men was more than possible, she knew; but, on reflection, she decided that Joe had not been bound for Layson's camp, but, by a short cut, to the distant valley. This alone would have explained his very early start. He was not one to seek to take his enemy while sleeping, and she knew and knew he knew that the lowlander slept late. Lorey would not do a thing dishonorable. She put the thought of trouble that day from her, therefore, yielding gladly to the joyous and absorbing magic of the growing, splendid morning.

The rising sun, with its ever changing spectacle, exhilerating, splendid, awe-inspiring, there among the mountains, raised her spirits as she travelled, and drove gloomy thoughts away as it drove off the brooding mists which clung persistently, tearing themselves to tattered ribbons ere they would loose their hold upon the peaks beyond the valley and behind her.

A feeling of elation grew in her--elation born of her abounding health, fine youth, the glory of the scene, the high intoxication of first love.

She beguiled the way with mountain ballads, paused, here and there, to pluck some lovely flower, accumulating, presently, a nosegay so enormous as to be almost unwieldy, whistled to the birds and smiled as they sent back their answers, laughed at the fierce scolding of a squirrel on a limb, heard the doleful wailing of young foxes and crept near enough their burrow to see them huddled in the sand before it, waiting eagerly for their foraging mother and the breakfast she would bring.

When the trail crossed a clear brook she paused upon the crude, low bridge and watched the trout dart to and fro beneath it; where it debouched upon a hill-side of commanding view she stopped there, breathing hard from sheer enjoyment of the glory of the prospect spread before her in the valley.

She was very happy, as she almost always was of summer mornings. The mountain air, circulating in her young and sturdy lungs, was almost as intoxicating as strong wine and made the blood leap through her arteries, thrill through her veins.

The worries of the night before seemed, for a time, to have been groundless. She ceased to fear her meeting with the bluegrass gentlefolk and looked forward to it with real confidence and pleasure. Her confidence in Layson was abounding, and she assured herself till the thought became conviction that he never would permit her to subject herself to anything which properly could be humiliating.

The problem of her garb, too, began to seem far less insoluble than it had seemed the night before. She felt certain, as she travelled with her springing step, that she would find it possible to meet creditably the great emergency with what she had at home and could discover at the little general-store which she was bound for.

When she reached the tiny, mud-chinked structure at the cross-roads, though, and caught her first glimpse of its lightly burdened shelves, her heart sank for an instant. Could it be possible that from its stock she would be able to select material with which she could compete with folk from the far bluegrass in elegance of garb?

But after she had made investigation and had interested in her project the lank mountain-woman who presided at the counter, she lost fear of the result. Together they made careful study of the fashion-papers which the woman had preserved and which the girl had, the night before, remembered with such vividness. Through discussion and reiterated reassurance from her friend, she finally arrived at the decision that with what she had at hand at home and what she could buy here, she could prepare herself to meet the elegant lowlanders with a fairly ample rivalry.

There were few bolts of cloth, of whatever quality or character in the pitiful little general-store's stock which both women did not finger speculatively that morning; there was not a piece of pinchbeck jewelry in the small showcase which they did not study carefully. Especially Madge dwelt on combs, for Layson, once, had mentioned combs as parts of the adornment of the women whom he knew. There in the mountains young girls did not wear them, save of the "circular" variety, designed to hold back "shingled" tresses. But from underneath a box of faded gum-drops and the store's one carton of cigars, came some of imitation tortoise-shell, gilt ornamented, of the sort old ladies sometimes stuck into their hirsute knots for mountain "doings" of great elegance, and the best of these Madge bought. Also she bought lace--great quantities of it, although, even after she had made the purchase, she had some doubt of just what she would do with it; she also had some doubt about its quality, for in the chest at home there had been lace, ripped from her mother's wedding gown, of far different and more convincing texture and design. She realized, however, that what was there must be what must suffice and purchased nearly all the woman had of cheap, machine-made mesh and home-worked, coarse-threaded tatting.

She could not manage gloves. The store had never had gloves in its stock designed for anything but warmth, and, although Layson had explained to her, in answer to her curious pleadings, that the girls he knew down in the bluegrass sometimes wore gloves covering their bare arms to the elbows, she gave up the hope of finding anything of that sort without a visit to the distant valley town, and this was quite impossible, now that her pony had gone lame, so she sighed and gave up gloves entirely.

But she bought ribbons by the bolt, some gay silk-handkerchiefs, a little of the less obtrusive of the jewelry, and needles, thread and such small trifles by the score to be utilized in making alterations in the finery from her dead mother's treasure chest at home there in the mountain cabin. It was with heart not quite so doubtful of her own ability to shine a bit, that, after she had borrowed every fashion-plate the woman owned (many of them ten years old; not one of them of later date than five years previous), she set out upon the long and weary homeward way.

Instinctively as she progressed she searched the soft mud in the shadowed places of the road, the soft sand wherever it appeared, for signs that those great foot-marks which she had thought she could identify as Lorey's in the morning, had returned while she was at the store. Nowhere was there any trace that this had happened, and again she thrilled with apprehension. Almost she made a detour by the road which led to Layson's camp to make quite sure that all was right with the young "foreigner," but this idea she abandoned as much because she felt that such a visit would necessitate an explanation which she would dislike to make, as because her many burdens would have made the way a long and difficult one to tread. How could she tell Layson that Joe Lorey might resent his helping her to study, might resent the other hours which they had spent so pleasantly among the mountain rocks and forest trees together, might, in short, be jealous of him?

Her shy, maiden soul revolted at the thought and perforce she gave investigation up, her thoughts, finally, turning from the really remote chance of a difficulty between the men to the pleasanter task of carrying on her planning for new gowns and small accessories of finery.

The homeward way was longer than the journey down had been, because of her new burdens and the frequently steep mountain slopes which she must climb, but she travelled it without much thought of this.

Never in her life had come excitement equal to that which possessed her as she thought about the visitors, longed to make a good impression and not shame her friend, wondered how the bluegrass ladies would be dressed, would talk, would act, and what they all would think of her. She had decided, in advance, that she would like Miss Alathea, aunt of her woodland instructor; she knew positively that she would like the doughty colonel, lover of god horses, barred from racing by his love for Frank's inexorable aunt.

But the other members of the party he had told about--the Holtons--she was not so sure that she would care for them. Frank, himself, when he had told her of them, had spoken of the father without much enthusiasm, and she felt quite sure that she could never like the daughter. She had noticed, she believed, that when it came to talk of her her friend had hesitated with embarrassment. Could it be possible that this young lady who had had the chances she, herself, had been denied, for education and for everything desirable, would seem to him, when she appeared upon the scene, less lovely, less desirable, than a simple little mountain maid like poor Madge Brierly? The thought seemed quite incredible and the worry of it quite absorbed her for a time and drove away forebodings about the possible hatred of Joe Lorey for Layson and his possible expression of resentment. She even ceased her wonderings about the footsteps which had gone down the road, that morning, and which, so far as she could see, had not come back again.

CHAPTER VI

They were, indeed, the great imprints of Joe Lorey's hob-nailed boots, quite as she suspected. Long before the sun had risen the young mountaineer, distressed by worries which had made his night an almost sleepless one, had risen and wandered from his little cabin, lonelier in its far solitude, even than the girl's. For a time he had crouched upon a stump beneath the morning stars with lowering brows, sunk deep in harsh, resentful thought, forgetful of the falling dew, the chill of the keen mountain air, of everything, in fact, save the gnawing apprehension that the "foreigner," who had invaded this far mountain solitude might, with his better manners, infinitely better education and divers other devilish wiles of the low country, snatch from him the prize which he had grown up longing to possess.

The youthful mountaineer's distress was not without its pathos. He loved the girl, had loved her since they had been toddling children playing in the hills together. Never for an instant had his firm devotion to her wandered to any other of the mountain girls; never for an instant had he had any hope but that of, some day, winning her. That he recognized the real superiority of Layson made his worry the more tragic, for it made it the more hopeless.

A dull resentment thrilled him, not only against this man, but against the whole tribe of his people, who were, in these uncomfortable days, invading the rough country which, to that time, had been the undisputed domain of the mountaineer. He thought with bitterness about the growing valley towns, which he had sometimes visited on court days when some mountain man had been haled there to trial for moonshining or for a feud "killing." He did not understand those lowland people who assumed the right to dictate to him and his kind as to the lives which they should lead in their own country, and he hated them instinctively. Vaguely he felt the greater power which education and a rubbing of their elbows with the progress of the world had given them and definitely resented it. Scotch highlander never felt a greater hatred and distrust of lowland men than does the highlander of the old Cumberlands feel for the people who have claimed the rich and fertile bottom lands, filled the towns which have sprung up there, established the prosperity which has, through them, advanced the state. The mountain men of Tennessee and of Kentucky are almost as primitive, to-day, as were their forefathers, who, early in the great transcontinental migration, dropped from its path and spread among the hills a century ago, rather than continue with the weary march to more fertile, fabled lands beyond.

It had not been, as Madge had feared, his definite hatred of Frank Layson which had started him upon the road so early in the morning, but, rather, an unrest born of the whole problem of the "foreigners'" invasion of the mountains. His restless discontent with Layson's presence had left him ready for excitement over wild tales told in store and cabin of what the young man's fellows were doing in the valley. He had determined to go thither for himself, to see with his own eyes the wonder-workers, although he hated both the wonders and the men who were accomplishing them.

What did the mountain-country want of railroads? What did it want of towns? The railroads would but bring more interlopers and in the towns they would foregather, arrogant in their firm determination to force upon the men who had first claimed the country their artificial rules and regulations. Timid in their fear of those they sought to furtively dislodge and of the rough love these men showed of a liberty including license, they would huddle in their storied buildings, crowd in their trammelled streets, work and worry in their little offices absurdly, harmfully to the rights of proper men. Like other mountaineers Joe had small realization of the advantages of easy interchange of thought and the quick commerce which come with aggregation. He thought the concentration of the townsfolk was a sign of an unmanly dread of those first settlers whom they wished to drive away unjustly, subjugate and ruin.

Throughout the mountains blazed a fierce resentment of the railroad builders' presence and their work; in no heart did it burn more fiercely than in poor Joe Lorey's, for the fear obsessed him that a member of the army of invaders had succeeded in depriving him of the last chance of getting that which, among all things on earth, he longed for most--Madge Brierly's love. He did not stop to think that before the "foreigner" had come the girl had more than once refused to marry him, begging him to remain her good, kind friend. Such episodes, in those days, had not in the least disheartened him. He had always thought that in the end the girl *would* "have him." But now he was convinced his chance was gone, his last hope vanished. The "foreigner" had fascinated Madge, made him look cheap and coarse, uncouth and undesirable.

As he had walked along the roads which, later in the morning, Madge had followed, he had frowned blackly at the sunrise and the waking birds, kicked viciously at little sticks and stones which chanced along his way. Never a smile had he for chattering squirrel or scampering chipmunk; fierce, repellant was the brown brow of the mountaineer, despite the glory of the morning, and black the heart within him with sheer hatred of Frank Layson and the class he represented.

His journey was much longer than the girl's, for it did not end till he had reached the rude construction camp of the advancing railroad builders in the valley far below the little mountain-store. There he gazed at what was going on with a child's wonder, which, at first, almost made him lose his memory of what he thought his wrongs, but, later, aggravated it by emphasizing in his mind his own great ignorance.

Through a tiny temporary town of corrugated iron shanties, crude log-and-brush and rough-plank sheds, white canvas tents, ran the raw, heaped earth of the embankment. About it swarmed a thousand swarthy laborers, chattering in a tongue less easy to his ears than the harsh scoldings of the squirrels he had seen while on his way. Back behind them stretched two lines of shining rails, which, even as he watched, advanced, advanced on the embankment, being firmly spiked upon their cross-ties so as to form a highway for the cars which brought more dirt, more dirt, more dirt to send the raw embankment on ahead of them.

At first the puffing, steam-spitting, fire-spouting locomotive with its deafening exhaust and strident whistle, clanging bell and glowing fire-box actually frightened him. As he stood close by the track and it came on threateningly, he backed away, his rifle held in his crooked arm, ready for some great emergency, he knew not what. A laborer laughed at him, and his hands instinctively took firmer grip upon the rifle. The laborer stopped laughing.

Some lessons of the temper of the mountaineers already had been learned along the line of that new railroad, and, driven from his wrath by the appearance of new marvels, Joe, at greater distance, sat upon a stump and watched, wide-eyed, and undisturbed, unridiculed.

For a long time his resentment wholly drowned itself in wonder at the puzzle of the engines, the mechanism of the dump-cars, the wondrous working of the small steam crane which lifted rails from flat-cars, and, as a strong man guided them, dropped them with precision at the time and place decided on beforehand. He noted how the men worked in great gangs, subject to the orders of one "boss," a phenomenon of organization he had never seen before, with unwilling admiration.

But presently, from a point well in advance of that where rails already had been laid and upon which his attention had been concentrated because of the machinery there, there came a mighty boom of dynamite. It startled him so greatly that he sprang up, bewildered, ready for whatever might be coming, but wholly at a loss as to just what the threatening danger might be. His fright gave rise to jeering laughter from the men who had been watching with a covert eye the rough, determined looking mountaineer, squatting on the stump with rifle on his arm. He turned on them so fiercely that they shrank back, terrified by the look they saw in his grey eyes.

Then, noting that the noise had not appalled them in the least and assuming that what was surely safe for them was safe enough for him, he sauntered down the line, attempting to seem careless in his walk, until he reached the gang which was busy at destruction of a high, obstructive cropping of grey granite.

For hours he sat there watching them with curiosity. He saw them pierce the rocks with hammered drills; he saw them then put in a small, round, harmless looking paper cylinder which, of course, he knew held something like gunpowder; he saw them tamp it down with infinite care, leaving only a protruding fuse; he saw them light the fuse and scamper off to a safe distance while he watched the sputtering sparks run down the fuse, pause at the tamping, then, having pierced it, disappear. The great explosions which succeeded were, at first, a little hard upon his nerves, but he saw that those who compassed them did not flinch when they came, and, after he had dodged ridiculously at the first, received the second with a greater calm, keyed himself to almost motionless reception of the third, and managed to sit listening to the fourth with self-possession quite as great as theirs, his face impassive and his frame immovable.

He noted with amazement the great force of the infernal power the burning fuses loosed, and knew, instinctively, that the explosive was a stronger one than that with which he had been thoroughly familiar since his earliest childhood--gunpowder. He wondered mightily what it could be, and, finally, summoned courage to inquire of one of the swart laborers.

These were the first words he had spoken that day, and, although the man was courteous enough in answering, "Dynamite," he thought he saw a smile upon his face of veiled derision, and resented it so fiercely that instead of thanking him he gave him a black look and sauntered off. But he had learned what the explosive was; before he went away he had seen it used in half-a-dozen ways and had a visual demonstration of the necessity for caution in its handling. One of the young and cocky engineers, whom he so hated, dropped by dread mischance a heavy hammer on a stick of it, and the resulting turmoil left him lying torn and mangled on the rocks.

Lorey felt small sympathy for the man's suffering, although he never had seen any human being mutilated thus before. Many a man he had seen lying with a clean hole through his forehead, the neat work of a definitely aimed bullet; assassination and the spectacles it carried with it could not worry him: his childhood and young manhood had been passed where "killings" were too frequent; the man, like all the others there at work, was his enemy, and he sorrowed for him not at all; but this tearing, mangling laceration of human flesh and bone was horrifying to him.

Later, though, a certain comfort came to him from it. The whole scene had impressed him and depressed him. He remembered what Madge Brierly had said about the engineers with their blue paper plans and their ability to read from them and work by them. He saw them at their work, and the spectacle made him feel inferior, which had never happened in his free, untrammeled life of mountain independence before. There were a dozen men about the work of the same type as Layson's, and their calm cocksureness as they directed all these mysteries amazed him, overwhelmed him, made him feel a sense of littleness and unimportance which was maddening. Why should they know all these things when he, Joe Lorey, who had lived a decent life according to his lights, had labored with his muscles as theirs could not labor if they tried to force them to, had lived upon rough fare and in rough places while they had had such "fancinesses" as he saw spread before them at their mess-tent dinner (and crude fare enough it seemed to them, no doubt) knew none of them? He could see no justice in such matters and resented them with bitter heart. If their own infernal powder had killed one of them he would not mourn. He tried to look back at the accident with satisfaction.

Had he gone down to that crude construction camp without the jealousy of Layson in his heart, he might, possibly, have merely gazed in wonder at the cleverness of all this work, despite his mountaineer's resentment of the coming of the interlopers; but, with that resentment in his heart to nag and worry him, he achieved, before the day was over, a real hatred of the class and of each individual in it. Layson had come up there to his country to rob him of the girl he loved; now these men were coming with their railroad to change the aspect of the land he had been born to and grown up in, making it a strange place, unfamiliar, unwelcoming and crowded. He hated every one of them, he hated the new railroad they were building, he hated their new-fangled and mysterious machinery which puzzled him with intricate devices and appalled him with its power of fire and steam.

By the time the afternoon was two hours old he was in a state of sullen fury, silent, morose, miserable on the stump which he had chosen as his vantage point for observation. More than once an engineer looked at him with plain admiration of his mammoth stature in his eyes; many a town-girl, seeing him, like a statue of The Pioneer upon a fitting pedestal, made furtive eyes at him, for he was handsome and attractive in his rough ensemble; but he paid no heed to any of them. He was giving his mind over to consideration of his grievance against these men who came, with steam and pick and shovel, dynamite and railroad iron, invading his domain.

He thought about his secret still, hidden in its mountain fastness, and realized that this new stage of settlement's inexorable march meant danger to it; he thought about the game which roamed the hills and realized that with the coming of the crowd it would soon scatter, never to return; he thought about the girl up there, his companion in adversity, his fellow sufferer from mutual wrong, the one thing which he had had to love, the shining prize which it had been his sole ambition to possess for life; he thought of her and then about the man, who (product of the same advantages which made these men before him clever with their blue-prints and their puffling monsters) had come there searching profit from the land which he had never loved or lived on, and, seeing Madge, had, Joe thoroughly believed, exerted every wile of a superior experience to win her from him by fair means or foul. He thought of them and hated all of them!

He was a most unhappy mountaineer who sat there on the stump, impassive and morose as the sun progressed upon its journey toward the western horizon. All the organized activity in the scene about him filled him with resentment and despair. In the hills he ever felt his strength: they had presented in his whole lifetime few problems which he could not cope with, conquer; but here in that construction camp he felt weak, incompetent, saw full many a puzzling matter which he could not understand. He watched the scene with bitter but with almost hopeless eyes. These new forces working here at railroad building, working in the hills to rob him of the girl he loved, seemed pitilessly strong and terribly mysterious. He never had felt helpless in all his life, before. It made him grind his teeth with rage.

But, though it angered him, the tense activity of the construction camp was fascinating, too. Especially was his attention held spellbound by the ruthless work of the advancing blasting gangs. What power lay hidden in those tiny sticks of dynamite! How lightly one of them had tossed that poor unfortunate in air and left him lying mangled, broken, helpless on the ground when it had spent its fury! ***What a weapon one of them would make, upon occasion***!

This thought grew rapidly in his depressed and agitated mind. What a weapon, what a weapon! Presently the blasting gangs and what they did absorbed his whole attention. He no longer paid the slightest heed to the puffing locomotives, busy with their dump-cars, to the mysterious steam-shovel, to the hand cars with their pumping, flying passengers. The dynamite was greater than the greatest of them. One stick of it, if properly applied, would blow a locomotive into junk, would tear a dump-car, with its massive iron-work and grinding wheels, apart and leave mere splinters!

His thoughts roamed back to his home mountains and pondered on the probable effect of this incursion on his personal affairs. Not satisfied with tearing up the placid valley, these foreigners would, presently, invade the very mountains in their turn. He saw the doom of that small, hidden still which had been his father's secret, years ago, was now his secret from the prying eyes of law and progress. That the "revenuers," soon or late, would get it, now that their allies were building steel highways to swarm on, was inevitable. His heart beat fast with a new anger, anticipatory of their coming to his fastness.

Lying not six feet from him as he sat there thinking bitterly of all these things, the foreman of the blasting gang had gingerly deposited a dozen sticks of dynamite upon a soft cushion of grey blankets. Joe looked at them as they lay there, innocent and unimpressive. If he had some of them in the hills and the revenuers came to raid his still--

The thought sprang into being in his mind with lightning quickness and grew there with mushroom growth. Never in his life had Lorey stolen anything, although the government would have classed him as a criminal because he owned that hidden still. His standards, in some things, were different from yours and mine, but he had never stolen anything and scorned as low beyond the power of words to tell a man who would. But now temptation came to him. He wanted some of that explosive. Should he buy it, its purchase by a mountaineer would certainly attract attention and might thus precipitate the very thing he wished to ward away--a watch of him, and, through that espionage, discovery of his secret place among the hills. And were not the railroad and the men who owned it robbing him by their progression into his own country? They were robbing him of peace and quiet, of the possibility of living on the life he had been born to and had learned to love! One of the class which fostered him was robbing him, he feared with a great fear, of the sweet girl whom he loved better than he loved his life. Surely it would be no sin, no act of real dishonesty for him to slip down from his stump when none was looking and secure a stick or two of the explosive!

Speciously he argued this out in his mind and reached the wrong conclusion which he wished to reach.

If he could but get one of those sticks of dynamite! When progress came, as, now, he felt convinced it would, to drive him from his mountains and the still which made life possible to him, he could meet it, at the start, with one of its own weapons. That, even though he had a hundred such, he could fight the fight successfully, could, in the end, find triumph, he did not for an instant think. The might of the encroaching army had impressed him, and he knew that, soon or late, he would be forced to yield to it; but he coveted those sticks of dynamite. One of them would give him some slight power, at least. He acknowledged to himself that he would steal one if he got the chance, despite his innate hatred of all pilferers. Such theft would merely be the taking of an unimportant tribute from the power which would, eventually, claim much, indeed, from him.

From the distance came the screaming whistle of a locomotive pulling in along the newly built roadway to eastward. It was followed by a flurry of excitement among all the men at work around about him.

"There comes the mail," he heard one handsome young chap shout.

He wore a suit like that which Joe had learned to hate because Frank Layson wore it.

This youth started running down the track, bright-eyed, expectant, and a dozen others ran to follow him, leaving blue-prints, their surveyors' instruments and other tokens of their mysterious might of education, lying unheeded on the ground behind them. There was much excitement. Even the rough laborers stopped delving at their tasks for a few minutes, to straighten from their work and stand, with curious eyes agaze down-track.

In the distance Joe saw smoke arise above the tops of the invaded forest-trees. Then he heard the growing clangor of a locomotive's bell, then other whistling and the approaching rumble of steel wheels upon steel rails, the groan of brake shoes gripping, the rattle of contracted couplings, the impact of car-bumpers.

The excitement grew among the working gangs. Even the laborers left their tasks and started down the rough surface of the new embankment toward the place, a quarter-of-a-mile away, where the train would stop at the end of the crude ballasting.

Lorey sat there on his stump, apparently impassive, watching all this flurry with resentful, discontented eyes. He himself was infinitely curious about the coming train; but he could not bring himself to go to see it. He had never seen a railway train, but it somehow seemed to him that if he hurried with the rest to meet this one it would mean a certain sacrifice of dignity in the face of the invading conqueror. He sat there, grimly wondering what it might be like, what the people whom it brought were like, until, suddenly, he discovered that he was alone. The last workman yielding to temptation, free from supervision for the moment, had run down the bank to meet the train, get mail, see who had come. Lying not a dozen feet away from Joe on their grey blanket were the sticks of dynamite.

Lithe, quick and silent as one of the mountain wild-cats he had so often trailed through his domain, he slipped down from his stump, caught up a stick of the explosive, tucked it carefully into his game-bag, took his place again upon the stump, impassive, calm, apparently quite unexcited.

When the men came trooping back, opening letters, tearing wrappers from their newspapers, gossiping, he still sat on the stump as they had left him. Not one of them suspected that he once had left it.

"Bright and lively as a cigar-store Indian," he heard one care-free youth exclaim as he went by him.

He did not know what the man meant; he had never seen a cigar-store Indian; but he knew a jibe was meant. It did not anger him, as it would have done, a few moments earlier. Now he had exacted his small tribute. They could stare at him and jibe, if they were so inclined. Hidden carefully there in his game-bag was one of their own weapons for their fight against the wilderness, which, in course of time, might be a weapon of the wilderness in fighting against some of them.

Presently he climbed down from the stump and strolled back along the raw embankment toward the little group still standing near the train which had arrived.

CHAPTER VII

The young moonshiner stiffened instantly as he neared the group of newly arrived travellers, for the first word he heard from them was the name of him whom, among all foreigners, he hated with most bitterness. An old darky, plainly the servant of the party, and such a darky as the mountain country had never seen before, was inquiring of a bystander where he could find "Marse" Frank Layson.

The man of whom he asked the question had not the least idea, nor had anyone about the railroad working. Most of the men had never heard of Layson, and the few who had become acquainted with him through chance meetings since he had been stopping in his cabin in the mountains, knew most indefinitely where the place was located. Lorey could have quickly given the information, but had no thought of doing so. He stood, instead, staring at the party with wondering but not good-natured eyes, and said no word. He certainly was not the one to do a favor to his rival or his rival's friends.

The group of strangers were thrown into confusion by the difficulty of getting news of him they sought, and, while they discussed the matter, Lorey had a chance to study them. He stood upon the rough plank platform, leaning on his rifle, with the game-bag and its burden of purloined explosive hanging slouchily beneath one arm, his coon-skin cap down well upon his eyes, those eyes, half closed, gazing at the newcomers with all the curiosity which they would have shown at sight of savages from some far foreign shore.

He was not the only one about the temporary railroad station who eyed the group with curiosity and interest. Two of the travellers were ladies from the bluegrass and scarcely one of all the natives lingering about the workings had ever seen a lady from the bluegrass, while, to the young surveyors and the group of civil engineers who had, for months, been exiled by their work among the mountains from all association with such lovely creatures, it was a joy to stand apart and covertly gaze at them. Many a young fellow, months away from home, who had grasped the newspapers and letters which had come in with the other mail with eager fingers, anxious to devour their contents, had, after the two ladies had descended from the train, almost forgotten his anxiety to get the news from home, and stood there, now, with opened letters in his hands, unread.

The ladies were very worthy of attention, too. Miss Alathea Layson, the elder of the two, was slight, beautifully groomed despite the long and dirty trip on rough cars over the crude road-bed of a newly graded railway. A woman whose thirtieth birthday had been left behind some years before, she still had all the brightness and vivacity of the twenties in her carriage and her manner. Her voice, as it drifted to the young moonshiner, was a new experience to him--soft, well modulated, culti-vated, it was of a sort which he had never heard before, and, while it seemed to him affected, nevertheless thrilled him with an unacknowledged admiration.

It was she who showed the greatest disappointment about the general igno-rance concerning Layson's whereabouts, and that voice made instantaneous and irresistible appeal to the older men among the party of engineers and surveyors, who, finding an excuse in her discomfiture, flocked about her, hats off, backs bent in humble bows, proffering assistance, three deep in the circle.

The other lady traveller, whom Miss Alathea called Miss Barbara, more espe-cially attracted the attention of the younger men, and, as they stood aloof to gaze at her, held such mountain dwellers as were near, paralyzed with wonder and admira-tion. Nothing so brilliantly beautiful as she in form, carriage, face, coloring or dress had ever been seen there in the little valley.

She was a florid girl of twenty, or, perhaps, of twenty-one or two. Her eyes were the obtrusive feature of her face, and she used them with a freedom which held callow youth spellbound. Her gown was more pretentious than that of her more elderly companion. This, of course, was justified by the difference between their ages; but there seemed to be, beyond this, a flaunting gayety about it and her manner which were not, in the eyes of the older and wiser men among the group who watched, justified by anything. It would have been a hard thing for the most critical of them to have definitely mentioned just what forced this strong impression on their minds, but it was forced upon them very quickly. One of them, a cute and keen observer as he was, of many years experience, decided the moot point, though, and whispered his decision to a grizzled man (the engineer in charge of the whole enterprise upon that section of construction) who stood next him.

"The elder one is of the old-time Southern aristocracy," he said. "The younger one is one of the newcomers--her father has made money and she is breaking in by means of it."

His companion nodded, realizing that the guess was shrewd and justified, even if it might, conceivably, be inaccurate.

"She certainly is very striking," he said, nodding, "but the elder one is the aristocrat."

The other member of the party was a big man, nearing fifty, with a broad face on which geniality was written in its every line, wearing the wide-brimmed Southern hat, typical long frock-coat with flaring skirts, black trousers, somewhat pegged, and boots of an immaculate brilliance.

His voice was loud, hearty and attractive, as he made inquiries, here and there, about the young man whom they had hoped to find in waiting for them at the station, although they had arrived, owing to the exigencies of travel by a new road, not yet officially opened to traffic, a day before they had expected to.

"I suh," said this gentleman, "am Cunnel Doolittle--Cunnel Sandusky Doolittle, and am looking for this lady's nephew, Mr. Layson, suh. If you can tell me where the youngster is likely to be runnin', now, you will put me under obligations, suh."

None, however, knew just how Layson could be reached. Most of them knew him or had heard of him, but they were not certain just where his camp in the mountains was located.

"I regret, Miss 'Lethe," said the Colonel, turning to the disappointed lady at his side, after having completed his inquiries, "that there is no good hotel heah. If there were a good hotel heah, I would take you to it, ma'am, and make you comfortable. Then, ma'am, I would search this country and I'd find him in short order. He probably did not receive my letter saying that we would arrive to-day and not to-morrow."

One of the engineers proffered to the ladies the use of his own canvas quarters till some course of action should have been decided on, an offer which was gratefully accepted.

Soon afterward inquiries by the Colonel brought out definite information as to the exact location of Frank's camp. A railway teamster, also, it appeared, was starting in that direction after ties and offered to transport a messenger as far as he was going, directing him, then, so that he could not lose his way. Old Neb, the darky, thereupon, was started on the search.

He was a different sort of negro from any which the mountain folk had ever seen, and wore more airs than his "white folks." Dressed in a black frock-coat as ornate as the Colonel's, although its bagging shoulders showed that it had been a gift and not made for him, his hat was a silk tile, a bit too large, and in one hand was a gold-headed cane on which he leaned as his old legs limped under him. Among the mountaineers about he was an object of the keenest curiosity, although down in the bluegrass, where old family negroes frequently were let to grow into a childish dignity of manner after years of faithful service and were not disturbed in their ideas of their own importance, he would have been regarded as merely an amusing infant of great age, reaping a reward for by-gone merits in the careful consideration and indulgence now extended to him. His inordinate vanity of his personal appearance and his dignity might have given rise to smiles, down there; here there were those upon the platform who laughed loudly as he walked away, boasting vaingloriously, although he evidently feared the trip with the rough teamster, that he would find "young Marse Frank" in a jiffy and have him there in no time.

It was while the aged negro was climbing somewhat difficultly to the side of the good-natured railroad teamster who had promised to give him a lift upon his way and then supply directions for his further progress, that Joe Lorey, who had been an interested spectator of the affair, contemptuous, amused by the old darky, saw, coming through the crowd behind him and well beyond the range of the newly arrived strangers, the roughly dressed, mysterious old man whom he had seen, once or twice, up in the mountains, whom Madge had seen, tapping with his little hammer at the rocks. Lorey looked toward him with a face which scowled instinctively. He disliked the man, as he disliked all foreigners who dared invasion of his wilderness; he would have feared him, too, had he known that it had really been him and not young Layson and Madge Brierly who had made the noise there in the thicket which had disturbed him, that day, when, armed to meet a raid of revenuers, he had rushed out from his still to find the girl and the young bluegrass gentleman in a close company which worried him almost as much as the appearance of the officers, in fact, could have done.

He was a "foreigner," this old man with the manner of the mountains, and, sometimes, their speech, for he wore bluegrass clothes; therefore he was one to be classed with the others in his bitter hatred. He was standing almost in his path, and, by stepping to one side, could have saved him a small detour round a pile of boxed supplies; but he did not move an inch, stiffening, instead, delighted at obstructing him.

The old man, as he went around, looked sharply at him, and then smiled, almost as if he recognized him and could read his thoughts; almost as if he realized the man's instinctive hate; almost as if he felt a certainty, deep in his soul, that so great was the disaster hovering above the mountaineer that it would be scarcely worth his own while, now, even to think resentfully of this small insult.

A moment later, though, and the expression of his face had changed completely. The first glimpse of the new come party standing, now, deep in discussion of the railway work, before the engineer's white, hospitable tent, made him start back in amazement.

For an instant he stood wavering, as if he were considering the plan of trying to depart without approaching them or being seen by them, but then he shrugged his shoulders and advanced, trying to show upon his face surprised good-nature.

"Wall, Colonel Doolittle!" he cried. "And you, Miss Layson, and--why, there's Barbara!"

"*Father!*" said the girl, in absolute amazement, hurrying toward him.

"Ah, Mr. Holton!" said Miss 'Lethe, bowing to him as the Colonel, plainly not too greatly pleased by the necessity for doing so, advanced toward him with extended hand.

"What brings you all up here?" asked Holton, after the greetings had been said.

"We came up to see Frank and the beauties of his long-forgotten land," Miss 'Lethe answered, in her softly charming voice. "He has property up here, you know, which has been for years a family possession, but which has been considered valueless, or almost so. When he learned that this new railway was to pass quite close to it, he decided to investigate it carefully and see just what it really amounted to."

Holton smiled a little wryly as she completed her explanation. "He's stayed here, studyin' it, a long time, ain't he?"

"Yes," Miss Alathea answered. "When he once reached here he seemed to find new beauties in the country every day. He wrote us the most glowing letters of it, and these letters and--and--other things, decided me to come and see him and the property he is so fond of. The Colonel was polite enough to volunteer as escort, your daughter to come as a companion."

Holton winked mysteriously at Colonel Doolittle. "You come at the right time," said he. "I'll have some things to tell you of this country and just what the railroad's going to do for it if you should care to listen."

The Colonel's eyes, plainly those of one who read the tale of character upon the faces of the people whom he met, looked at him with no great favor, but he smiled. "We've already learned some things which have astonished us," he said. Then, though, despite the fact that his remark had greatly aroused Holton's curiosity, evidently, he changed the subject somewhat abruptly, and turned grandiosely to Miss 'Lethe.

"May I offuh you my ahm, ma'am, for a little stroll about heah?" he inquired. "The greatest disadvantage which I see about this country is the lack of level places big enough to put a race-track in, ma'am. So far as I can see from lookin' round me, casual like, you couldn't run a quahtuh, heah, without eitheh goin' up a hill or comin' down one."

"*Isn't* it rough!" said Barbara, with a gesture of aversion which seemed a bit affected.

Holton looked at her with what was plainly admiration. It was clear enough that, in a way, he was fond of his showy daughter. He ran his eye with satisfaction over her costume, from head to foot, and nodded.

"You ain't never seen much of rough life, now have you, Barbara?" He turned, then, to Miss Alathea. "These young folks, raised the way we raise 'em, nowadays, get thinkin' that the whole world has been smoothed out for their treadin'--an' they ain't far wrong. We *do* smooth out the world for 'em. Now, there's your nephew, Frank; he--"

"Oh, he *likes* it, here, as I have said," she answered.

"But it is so-- ***uncouth*** " said Barbara, plainly for the benefit of one or two admiring youths from the surveying party, who were standing near. "And some of the people look so absolutely vicious--some of the natives, I mean, of course, you know. Now look at that young fellow, over there!"

The girl had nodded toward Joe Lorey, who was standing not far off, observing them with an unwavering and disapproving, almost definitely hostile stare.

"He looks," the girl went on, "as if he hated us and would be glad to do us harm. So violent!"

"He's from up the mountains," one of the young engineers said, glancing toward him. "It's funny how those mountain people ***all*** hate us. You see, they say, the hills around about here are all full of moonshiners and they believe the coming of the railroad will bring with it law and order and that when that comes, of course, their living will be gone."

"Moonshiners?" said Barbara. "Pray, what are moonshiners?"

Her father grimly smiled again. He knew that she knew quite as well what moonshiners were as any person in the group, but her affected ignorance of rough things and rough men amused him.

"Distillers of corn whisky who refuse to pay their taxes to the government," the youth replied. "The revenue officials have had dreadful times with them, here in the Cumberland, for years. Sometimes they have really bloody battles with them, when they try to make a raid."

"How terrible!" said Barbara, and shuddered carefully. She looked again at Lorey, who, conscious that he was the subject of their conversation and resentful of it, stared back boldly and defiantly. "And do you think that he--that very young man there--can possibly have ever actually ***killed*** a man?"

The engineer laughed heartily. "That he may ***possibly*** have killed a man," said he, "there is no doubt. I don't know that he has, however, and it is most improbable. I don't even know that he's a moonshiner."

Among the others who had left the train, which, now, had been switched off to a crude side-track, the cars left there and the locomotive started at the handling of dirt-dump-cars, were two tall, sunburned strangers, whom Miss Alathea, who had noted them as she did everyone, had classed as engineers or surveyors, but who had not, when they had arrived, mingled with the other men employed on the construction of the railroad. While the young man and Barbara were talking about moonshiners, one of them had drifted near and he gave them a keen glance at the first mention of the word. Now he turned, but turned most casually, to follow with his own, their glances at Joe Lorey. Then he sauntered off, and, as he passed Holton, seemed to exchange meaning glances with him.

Soon afterward Lorey turned away. The day was getting on toward noon. The long tramp back to his lonely cabin in the mountains would consume some hours. The sight of all these strangers, all this work on the new railroad worried him, made him unhappy, added to and multiplied the apprehension which for weeks had filled his heart about Madge Brierly and young Layson. He battled with a mixture of emotions. There was no ounce of cowardice, in Joe. Never had he met a situation in his life before which he had feared or which had proved too strong for him. All his battles, so far, and they had been many and been various, as was inevitable from the nature of his secret calling, had resulted in full victories for his mighty strength of body or his quick foot, certain hand, keen knowledge of the mountains and the woods resource and wit that went with these; but now things seemed to baffle him. His soul was struggling against acknowledgment of it, while his mind continually told him it was true. Everything seemed, now, to be against him.

He knew, but would not admit, even to himself, that the march of progress must inevitably drive out of existence the still hidden in his cave and make the marketing of its illicit product doubly hazardous, nay, quite impossible. He knew that he must give it up; he realized that real good sense would send him home, that day, to bury the last trace of it in some spot where it never could be found again. But his stubborn soul revolted at the thought of being beaten, finally, by this civilization which he hated; he would not admit, even in his mind, that it had bested him, or could ever best him. He ground his teeth and pressed his elbow down against the stock of his long rifle with a force which ground the gun into his side until it hurt him. He would never give up, never! Let them try to get him if they could, these lowlanders! He would not be afraid of them. His father had not been--and he would never be.

And there was a voice within him which kept whispering as did the one which counselled the abandonment of his illegal calling, the abandonment of that other effort, infinitely dearer to him, to win Madge Brierly's love and hand in marriage.

His common-sense assured him that she was not made for such as he, that, while she had been born there in the mountains there were delicacies, refinements in her which would make her mating with his rude and uncouth strength impossible, would make it cruelly unhappy for her, even should it come about. But this voice he steadfastly declined to listen to, even more emphatically than he did to that which counselled caution in his calling. Again he ground his teeth. His heels, when they came down upon the rocky mountain trails up which he soon was climbing, fell on the slopes so heavily that, constantly, his progress was followed by the rattle of small stones down the inclined path behind him, constant little landslides. And, at ordinary times, Joe Lorey, awkward as he looked to be, could scale a sloping sand-bank without sending down a sliding spoonful to betray the fact that he was moving on it to the wild things it might startle.

Heavily he resolved within his soul, against his own best judgment, to keep up both fights and win.

The dynamite which he had stolen and which nestled in his game-sack comforted him, although he did not know how he would use it. Many times, as he worked through the narrow trails, jumped from stepping-stone to stepping-stone in crossing mountain-streams, pulled himself up steep and rocky slopes by clutching swaying branches, or rough-angled boulders, he let his left hand slip down to the side of the old game-sack, where, through the soft leather, he could plainly feel the smooth, terrific cylinder.

He swore a mighty mountain oath that none of the advancing forces ever should win victory of him. If the revenuers ever tried to get him, let God help them, for they would need help; if Frank Layson stole his girl from him, then let God help him, also, for even more than would the revenuers the young bluegrass gentleman would need assistance from some mighty power.

But a fate was closing on Joe Lorey which all his uncouth strength could not avert. As he had left the railway those two men whom simple-minded Miss Alathea had supposed were engineers, but who had not mingled with the throng of railway builders had looked at Horace Holton for confirmation of their guess. In a quick glance, so keen that they could not mistake its meaning so instantaneous that none else could suspect that the three men were even casual acquaintances, he had told them they had guessed aright.

They sauntered off and disappeared in the direction whence the mountaineer had gone, and, though his feet were well accustomed to the trails and were as expert in their climbing as any mountaineer's for miles, these men proved more expert; though his ear was as acute as a wild animal's, so silently they moved that never once a hint that they were following, ever following behind him, reached it; their endurance was as great as his, their woods-craft was as sly as his.

A fate was closing on Joe Lorey. The march of civilization was, indeed, advancing toward his mountain fastnesses at last. And nothing stays the march of civilization.

CHAPTER VIII

The afternoon was waning as Joe climbed a sudden rise and saw before him Layson's camp.

Through a cleft in the guardian range the sun's rays penetrated red and fiery. Already the quick chill of the coming evening had begun to permeate the air. A hawk, sailing from a day of foraging among the hen-yards of the distant valley, flew heavily across the sky, burdened with plunder for its little ones, nested at the top of a black stub on the mountain-side. Squirrels were home-going after a busy day among the trees. The mournful barking of young foxes, anxious for their dinners, thrilled the air with sounds of woe. Among the smaller birds the early nesters were already twittering in minor among the trees and thickets; a mountain-eagle cleft the air in the hawk's trail, so high that only a keen eye could have caught sight of him. Daylight insects were beginning to abate their clamor, while their fellows of the night were tuning for the evening concert. Mournfully, and very faintly, came a locomotive's wail from the far valley.

Joe Lorey paused grimly in his progress to stare at the rough shack which housed the man he hated. He was no coward, and he would not take advantage of the loneliness and isolation of the spot to do him harm surreptitiously, but vividly the thought thrilled through him that someday he would assail him. Smoke was curling from the mud-and-stick chimney of the little structure, and he smiled contemptuously as he thought of how the bluegrass youth was doubtless pottering, within, getting ready to go down into the valley to greet his fine friends and be greeted. He had no doubt that long ere this the aged negro had reached him with the news of their arrival. He wondered, with a fierce leap of hope, if, possibly, their coming might not be the signal for the man's departure from the country where he was not wanted.

This hope keenly thrilled him, for a moment, but, an instant later, when, through the small window, he saw the youth seat himself, alone, before a blazing fire of logs, stretch out his legs and lounge in the comfort of the blaze, it left him. He wondered if Layson did not intend to go down at all to meet his friends.

Just then his quick ear caught the sound of stumbling, hurried footsteps, plainly not a mountaineer's, down in the rough woodland, below. Instantly his muscles tautened, instantly he brought his rifle to position; but he soon let it fall again and smiled, perhaps, for the first time that day.

"Lawsy! Lawsy!" he could hear a scared voice muttering. "Lawsy, I is los', fo' suah!"

His smile broadened to a wide, malicious grin of satisfaction. The black messenger who had been started with the news, evidently had not fared well upon the way, and was, but now, arriving. "It's that nigger wanderin' around up hyar," he mused. And then: "I'm goin' to have some fun with him."

Silently he slipped down the path by which he had so recently ascended, and, at a good distance from the cabin, but still well in advance of the unhappy negro, hid behind a rock, awaiting his approach.

Old Neb, advancing, scared tremendously, was talking to himself in a loud, excited voice.

"Oh, golly!" he exclaimed. "Dis am a pretty fix for a bluegrass cullud gemman! Dis am a pretty fix--los', los' up heah, in de midst of wolves an' painters!"

Joe, from behind his rock, wailed mournfully in startling imitation of a panther's call.

The darkey almost fell prone in his fright. "Name o' goodness!" he exclaimed. "Wha' dat? Oh--oh--dere's a painter, now!"

Joe called again, more mournfully, more ominously than before.

Neb's fright became a trembling panic. "Hit's a-comin' closer!" he exclaimed. "I feel as if de debbil's gwine ter git me!" He stooped and started on a crouching run directly toward the rock behind which Joe was hiding.

As the old man would have passed, Joe jumped out from his ambush, and, bringing his right hand down heavily upon the darky's shoulder, emitted a wild scream, absolutely terrifying in its savage ferocity. With a howl Neb dropped upon his knees, praying in an ecstasy of fear.

"Oh, good Mister Painter, good Mister Debbil--" he began.

Inasmuch as he was not devoured upon the instant, he finally ventured to look up and Joe laughed loudly.

So great was the relief of the old negro that he did not think of anger. A sickly smile spread slowly on his face. "De Lawd be praised!" he said. "Why, hit's a man!"

"Reckon I am," said Joe. "Generally pass for one." Then, although he knew quite well just why the man had come, from whom, for whom, he asked sternly to confuse him: "What *you* doin' in these mountings?"

"I's lookin' fo' my massa, young Marse Frank Layson, suh," Neb answered timidly.

"You needn't to go fur to find him," Lorey answered bitterly. "You needn't to go fur to find him."

The old negro looked at him, puzzled and frightened by his grim tone and manner.

"Why--why--" he began. "Is it hereabouts he hunts fo' deer? He wrote home he was findin' good spo't in the mountains, huntin' deer."

Joe's mouth twitched ominously, involuntarily. The mere presence of Old Neb, there, was another evidence of the great advantage, which, he began to feel with hopeless rage, the man who had stolen that thing from him which he prized most highly, had over him. The negro was his servant. Servants meant prosperity, prosperity meant power. Backwoodsman as he was, Joe Lorey knew that perfectly. His face gloomed in the twilight.

"Yes," he answered bitterly, "it's here he has been huntin'--huntin' deer--the pootiest deer these mountings ever see." Of course the old negro did not understand the man's allusion. He was puzzled by the speech; but Joe went on without an explanation: "But thar is danger in sech huntin'. Your young master, maybe, better keep a lookout for his-self!"

His voice trembled with intensity.

In the meantime Layson was still seated thoughtfully before his fire of crackling "down-wood," busy with a thousand speculations. Just what Madge Brierly, the little mountain girl, meant to him, really, he could not quite determine. He knew that he had been most powerfully attracted to her, but he did not fail to recognize the incongruity of such a situation. He had never been a youth of many love-affairs.

Perhaps his regard for horses and the "sport of kings" had kept him from much travelling along the sentimental paths of dalliance with the fair sex. Barbara Holton, back in the bluegrass country, had been almost the only girl whom he had ever thought, seriously, of marrying, and he had not, actually, spoken, yet, to her about it. When he had left the lowlands for the mountains he had meant to, though, when he returned. There were those, he thought, who believed them an affianced couple. Now he wondered if they ever would be, really, and if, without actually speaking, he had not led her to believe that he would speak. He was astonished at the thrill of actual fear he felt as he considered the mere possibility of this.

The news which had been brought to him by mail that upon the morrow he would see the girl again, in company with his Aunt and Colonel Doolittle, had focussed matters in his mind. Did he really love the haughty, bluegrass beauty? He was far from sure of it, as he sat there in the little mountain-cabin, although he had been certain that he did when he had left the lowlands.

It seemed almost absurd, even to his young and sentimental mind, that one in his position should have lost his heart to an uneducated girl like Madge, but he definitely decided that, at any rate, he had never loved the other girl. If it was not really love he felt for the small maiden of the forest-fire and spelling-book, it surely was not love he felt for the brilliant, showy, bluegrass girl.

He was reflecting discontentedly that he did not know exactly what he felt or what he wanted, when he heard Joe Lorey's startling imitation of the panther's cry, outside, and, rising, presently, when careful listening revealed the fact that the less obtrusive sound of human voices followed what had seemed to be the weird, uncanny call of the wild-beast, he went to the door and opened it, so that he could better listen.

Joe and the negro had not been in actual view of Layson's cabin, up to that time. A rocky corner, rising at the trail's side, had concealed it. Now they stepped around this and the lighted door and windows of the little structure stood out, despite increasing darkness, plainly in their view.

Almost instantly old Neb recognized the silhouette of Layson's figure there against the fire-light from within.

"Marse *Frank*!" he cried. "Marse *Frank!*"

Layson, startled by the unexpected sound of the familiar voice there in the wilderness, rushed from the door, took Neb's trembling hand and led him to the cabin.

"Neb, old Neb!" he cried. "By all that's wonderful! How did you get here alone? I thought you all were to come up to-morrow. Where is Aunt 'Lethe, and the Colonel, and--and--"

Neb, his troubles all forgotten as quickly as a child's, stood wringing his young master's hand with extravagant delight. Joe Lorey disappeared like a flitting shadow of the coming night.

"Dey're all down at de railroad, suh," said Neb. "Dey're all down at de railroad. Got heah a day befo' dey t'ought dey would, suh, an' sent me on ahead to let you know. I been wanderin' aroun' fo' a long time a-tryin' fo' to fin' yo'. Dat teamster what gib me a lif', he tol' me dat de trail war cleah from whar he dropped me to yo' cabin, but I couldn't fin' it, suh, an' I got los'.'"

"And the others all are waiting at the railroad for me? I was going down to meet them to-morrow."

"Dey don't expect you till to-morrow, now, suh. Ev'rybody tol' 'em that you couldn't git dar till to-morrow. I reckon dey'll be com'fable. Fo'ty men was tryin' fo' to make 'em so when *I* lef'." The old darky laughed. "Looked like dat dem chaps wat's layin' out dat railroad, dar, ain't seen a woman's face fo' yeahs an' yeahs, de way dey flocked aroun'. Ev'y tent in de destruction camp war at deir suhvice in five minutes."

Frank was busy at the fire with frying-pan and bacon. The old negro was worn out. The young man disregarded his uneasy protests and made him sit in comfort while he cooked a supper for him.

"So you got lost! Who finally set you straight? I heard you talking, there, with someone."

"A young pusson, suh," said Neb, with dignity. Lorey had befriended him, he knew, at last; but he had scared him into panic to begin with. "A young pusson, suh," he said, "what made me think he was a paintuh, suh, to staht with. Made me think he was a paintuh, suh, or else de debbil, wid his howlin'.'"

Layson laughed long and heartily. "Must have been Joe Lorey," he surmised. "I heard that cry and thought, myself, it was a panther. He's the only one on earth, I guess, who can imitate the beasts so well. Where is he, now?'

"Lawd knows! I see him dar, close by me, den I seed you in de doah, an' when I looked aroun' ag'in, he had plumb faded clean away!"

"They're wonderful, these mountaineers, with their woods-craft."

"Debbil craf, mo' like," said Neb, a bit resentful, still.

Frank smiled at the thought of his dear Aunt, precise and elegant, compelled to spend the night in a construction camp beneath white-canvas.

"What did Aunt 'Lethe think about a night in tents?" he asked.

"Lawd," said Neb, plainly trying to gather bravery for something which he wished to say, "I didn't ax huh. Too busy with my worryin'."

"Worrying at what, Neb?"

"Oveh dat Miss Holton an' her father."

"Mr. Holton didn't come, too, did he?"

"No; he didn't come wid us, suh; but he met us dar down by de railroad. Wasn't lookin' for him, an' I guess he wasn't lookin', jus' exactly, to see us. But he was dar an' now he's jus' a membuh of ouah pahty, suh, as good as Cunnel Doolittle. Hit don't seem right to me, suh; no suh, hit don't seem right to me."

"Why, Neb!"

"An' dat Miss Barbara! She was dead sot to see you, an' Miss 'Lethe was compelled to ax her fo' to come along. She didn't mean to, fust off; no suh. But she had to, in de end. Den I war plumb beat when I saw Mister Holton stalkin' up dat platfohm like he owned it an' de railroad an' de hills, and de hull yearth. But he's bettuh heah dan down at home, Marse Frank. He don't ***belong*** down in de bluegrass."

"I'm afraid you are impertinent, Neb. Don't meddle. You always have been prejudiced against Barbara and her father."

The old negro answered quickly, bitterly. "I ain't likely to fuhgit," said he, "dat de only blow dat evuh fell upon my back was from his han'! I guess you rickollick as well as I do. He cotch me coon-huntin' on his place an' strung me up. He'd jes' skinned me dar alive if you-all hadn't heered my holler in' an' run in."

Layson was uneasy at the turn the talk had taken. "That was years ago, Neb," he expostulated.

"Don't seem yeahs ago to me, suh. Huh! De only blow dat evuh fell upon my back! But yo' snatched dat whip out of his ban' an' den yo' laid it, with ev'y ounce of stren'th war in yo', right acrost his face!"

Layson, unwilling to be harsh with the old man and forbid him to say more, ostentatiously busied himself, now, about the table with the frying-pan and other dishes, hoping, thus, to discourage further talk of this sort.

"No, suh," Neb went on with shaking head, "I jus' nachelly don' like him. Don't like *either* of 'em. An' he, Marse Frank, he nevuh *will* fuhgit dat blow, an' don't you think he will!"

"That's all over, long ago," said Frank, as he put the finishing touches on the old man's supper. "And what had Barbara to do with it? She can't help what her father does."

Neb drew up to the table with a continuously shaking head. For months he had desired to speak his mind to his young master, but had never dared to take so great a liberty. Now the unusual circumstances they were placed in, the fact that he had been lost in the mountains in his service and half scared to death, imbued him with new boldness.

"She kain't he'p what he does, suh, no," said he. "But listen, now, Marse Frank, to po' ol' Neb. De pizen vine hit don't b'ar peaches, an' nightshade berries--dey ain't hulsome, eben ef dey're pooty."

"Neb, stop that!" Layson commanded sharply.

The old negro half slipped from the chair in which he had been sitting wearily. Once he had started on the speech which he had made his mind up, months ago, that, some day, he would screw his courage up to, he would not be stopped.

"Oh, honey," he exclaimed, holding out his tremulous old hands in a gesture of appeal, while the fire-light flickered on a face on which affection and real sincerity were plain, "I's watched ovuh you evuh since yo' wuh a baby, an' when I see dat han'some face o' hers was drawin' of yo' on, it jus' nigh broke my ol' brack heaht, it did. It did, Marse Frank, fo' suah."

The young man could not reprimand the aged negro. He knew that all he said came from the heart, a heart as utterly unselfish and devoted in its love as human heart could be.

"Oh, pshaw, Neb!" he said soothingly. "Don't worry. Perhaps I did go just a bit too far with Barbara--young folks, you know!--but that's all over, now." Again he wondered most uncomfortably if this were really true, again his mind made its comparisons between the bluegrass girl and sweet Madge Brierly. "There's no danger that Woodlawn will have any other mistress than my dear Aunt 'Lethe for many a long year," he concluded rather lamely.

The emotion of the ancient darky worried him. It was proof that evidence of a love affair with Barbara Holton had been plain to every eye, he thought.

Neb now slid wholly from the chair and dropped upon his knees close by the youth he loved, grasping his hand and pressing it against his faithful heart.

"Oh, praise de Lawd, Marse Frank; oh, praise de Lawd!" he cried.

Old Neb slept with an easier heart, that night, than had throbbed in his old black bosom since the probability that Barbara Holton would be a member of the party which was to visit his young master in the mountains, had first begun to worry him. But long after he had found unconsciousness on the boughs-and-blanket bed which he had fashioned for himself under Frank's direction, Layson, himself, was wandering beneath the stars, thinking of the problem that beset him.

He was sorry Barbara was coming to the mountains. Why had his Aunt 'Lethe brought her? What would that dear lady think about Madge Brierly, wood-nymph, rustic phenomenon? What had Horace Holton been doing in the mountains, secretly, to have been surprised, discomfited as Neb had said he was, at sight of the Colonel, Miss 'Lethe and his daughter?

But before he had finished the pipe which he had carried into the crisp air of the sharp mountain night for company, his thought had left the Holtons and were seeking (as they almost always were, these days and nights), his little pupil of the spelling-book, his little burden of the brush-fire flight. He looked across the mountain-side toward where her lonely cabin hid in its secluded fastness. There was a late light to-night ashine from its small window.

"She'll like her," he murmured softly in the night. "She'll *love* her. Aunt 'Lethe'll understand!"

And then he wondered just exactly what it was that he felt so very certain his Aunt 'Lethe would be sure to understand. He did not understand, himself, precisely what had happened to him, his life-plans, heart-longings.

Strolling there beneath the stars he gave no thought to poor Joe Lorey, until, like a night-shadow, the moonshiner stalked along the trail and passed him. Layson called to him good-naturedly, but the mountaineer gave him no heed. Frank stood, gazing after him in the soft darkness, in amazement. Then a quick, suspicious thrill shot through him. The man was bound up the steep trail toward Madge's cabin. Presently he heard him calling. He went slowly up the trail, himself.

The girl came quickly from her cabin in answer to the shouting of the mountaineer.

"What is it, Joe?" she asked.

"I want a word with you. I've come a purpose," Lorey answered sullenly.

The girl was almost frightened by his manner. She had never seen him in this mood; he had never come to her, alone, at night, before. "Well, Joe, you'll have to wait," said she. "I've got some things to do, to-night." Her sewing was not yet half finished.

Standing on her little bridge, she held with one hand to the worn old rope by means of which she presently would pull it up. She did not take Joe very seriously; in the darkness she could not see the grim expression of his brow, the firm set of his jaw, the clenched hands, one of which was pressed against the game sack with his powerful plunder hidden in it. She laughed and tried to joke, for, even though she did not guess how serious he was, her heart had told her that some day, ere long, there must of stern necessity be a full understanding between her and the mountaineer, and that he would go from her, after it, with a sore heart. In the past she had not wished to marry him, but she had never definitely said, even to herself, that such a thing was quite impossible for all time to come. Now she knew that this was so, although she would not acknowledge, even to herself, the actual reason for this certainty. No; she could never marry Joe. She hoped that, he would never again beg her to.

"Come back some other time, when I ain't quite so busy," she said trying to speak jokingly. "Tomorrow, or nex' week, or Crismuss."

He stood gazing at her sourly. "I'll come sooner," he said slowly. "Sooner. An' hark ye, Madge, if that thar foreigner comes in atween us, I'm goin' to spile his han'some face forever!"

"What nonsense you do talk!" the girl exclaimed, but her heart sank with apprehension as the man stalked down the path. She did not pull the draw-bridge up, at once, but stood there, gazing after him, disturbed.

Again he met Layson, still strolling slowly on the trail, busy with confusing thoughts, puffing at his pipe. The mountaineer did not call out a greeting, but stepped out of the trail, for Frank to pass, without a word.

"Why, Joe," said Layson, "I didn't see you. How are you?" He held out his hand.

The mountaineer said nothing for an instant, then he straightened to his lank full height and held his own hand close against his side. "No," he said, "I can't, I can't."

Layson was astonished. He peered at him. "Why, Joe!" said he; and then: "See here--what have I ever done to you?"

Joe turned on him quickly. "Done?" he cried. "Maybe nothin', maybe every-thin'." He paused dramatically, unconscious of the fierce intentness of his gaze, the lithe aggressiveness of his posture. "But I warns you, now--you ain't our kind! Th' mountings ain't no place for you. The sooner you gits out of 'em, the better it'll be fer you."

Layson stood dumbfounded for a moment. Then he would have said some fur-ther word, but the mountaineer, his arm pressed tight against that old game-sack, stalked down the trail. Suddenly Layson understood.

"Jealous, by Jove!" he said. "Jealous of little Madge!" Slowly he turned about, puffing fiercely at his pipe, his thoughts a compound of hot anger and compassion.

Madge, filled with dread of what her disgruntled mountain suitor might be led to do by his black mood, had not yet re-crossed her draw-bridge, but was standing by it, listening intently, when she heard Layson's footsteps nearing. Her heart gave a great throb of real relief. She had not exactly feared that trouble really would come between the men, but--Lorey came of violent stock and his face had been dark and threatening.

She saw Layson long before he knew that she was there.

"Oh," she cried, relieved, "that you?"

He hurried to her. "I thought you mountain people all went early to your beds," said he, and laughed, "but I met Joe Lorey on the trail and here you are, standing by your bridge, star-gazing."

Of course she would not tell him of her worries. She took the loophole offered by his words and looked gravely up at the far, spangled sky. "Yes," said she, "they're mighty pretty, ain't they?"

Layson was in abnormal mood. The prospect of his Aunt's arrival, the certainty that something more than he had thought had come out of his mountain sojourn, the fact that he was sure that he regretted Barbara Holton's coming, old Neb's arrival, and his raking up of ancient scores against the lowland maiden's father, his meeting with Joe Lorey and the latter's treatment of him, had wrought him to a pitch of mild excitement. The girl looked most alluring as she stood there in the moonlight.

"My friends are in the valley and are coming up to-morrow," he said to her. "Do you know that this may be the last time I shall ever see you all alone?"

She gasped. He had not hinted at a thing like that before. "You ain't going back with them, are you?" she asked, her voice a little tremulous from the shock of the surprise. "You ain't going back with them--never to come hyar no more, are you?"

He stepped nearer to her. "Why, little one," he asked, "would you care?"

"Care?" she said with thrilling voice, and then, gaining better self-control, tried to appear indifferent. "Why should I?" she said lightly. "I ain't nothin' to you and you ain't nothin' to me."

His heart denied her words. "Don't say that!" he cried. "You don't know how dear you've grown to me." He stepped toward her with his arms outstretched. He almost reached her and he knew, and she knew, instinctively, that if he had he would have kissed her.

She shrank back like a startled fawn, when his foot was almost on the bridge that spanned the chasm between them and her cabin.

"Don't you dare to touch me!" she said fiercely.

She sped back upon the little bridge, and, when he would have followed, held her hand up with a gesture of such native dignity, offended womanhood, that he stopped where he was, abashed.

"No--no, sir; you can't cross this bridge," said she. "No man ever can, unless--unless--"

Almost sobbing, now, she left the sentence incomplete; and then: "Oh, you wouldn't dared act so to a bluegrass girl! But I know what's right as well as them. It don't take no book-learnin' to tell me as how a kiss like that you planned for me would be a sign that really you care for me no more than for the critters that you hunt an' kill for pastime up hyar among the mountings."

He would have given much if he had never done the foolish thing. He stood there with lowered eyes, bent head, abashed, discomfited.

"An' I 'lowed you were my friend!" said she.

Now he looked up at her and spoke out impulsively: "And so I am, Madge, really! I was ... wrong. Forgive me!"

She dropped her hands with a weary change of manner. "Well, I reckon I will," said she. "You've been too kind and good for me to bear a grudge ag'in you; but ... but ... Well, maybe I had better say good-night."

She walked slowly back across the bridge without another word, pulled on its rope and raised it, made the rope fast and slowly disappeared within her little cabin.

"Poor child!" said he, and turned away. "I was a brute to wound her."

As he went down the trail, darkening, now, as the moon slid behind the towering mountain back of him, his heart was in a tumult. "After all," he reflected, "education isn't everything. All the culture in the world wouldn't make her more sincere and true. She has taught *me* a lesson I shan't soon forget."

His thoughts turned, then, to the girl who would come up with the party on the following day.

"I--wonder! Was there ever, really, a time when I loved Barbara?... If so, that time has gone, now, never to return."

CHAPTER IX

His visitors took Layson by surprise, next morning. They had started from the valley long before he had supposed they would.

Holton saw him first and nudged his daughter, who was with him. They were well ahead of Miss Alathea and the Colonel, who had been unable to keep up with them upon the final sharp ascent of the foot-journey from the wagon-road. The old man grinned unpleasantly. He had rather vulgar manners, often annoying to his daughter, who had had all the advantages which, in his rough, mysterious youth, he had been denied.

"Thar he is, Barb; thar he is," he said, not loudly. Miss Alathea and the Colonel, following close behind, were a restraint on him.

The girl's face was full of eagerness as she saw the man they sought. He was busy polishing a gun, but that his thoughts were occupied with something less mechanical and not wholly pleasant the slight frown upon his face made evident. "Mr. Layson! Frank!" she cried.

The young man turned, on hearing her, and hurried toward her and her father with his hands outstretched in welcome. He was not overjoyed to have the old man visit him, just then; he was even doubtful of the welcome which his heart had for the daughter; but he was a southerner and in the gentle-born southerner real hospitality is quite instinctive.

"Mr. Holton--Barbara," said he. "I am delighted. Welcome to the mountains." He grasped their hands in hearty greeting. "But where are Aunt Alathea and the Colonel?"

Holton tried to be as cordial as his host. That he was very anxious to appear agreeable was evident. "Oh, them slow-pokes?" he said, laughing. "We didn't wait for them. We pushed on ahead. We reckoned as you would be glad to see us."

"And so I am."

"One in particular, maybe," Holton answered, with a crude attempt at badinage. He glanced archly from the young man to his daughter.

"Father!" she exclaimed, a bit annoyed, and yet not too unwilling that the fact that she and Layson were acknowledged sweethearts should be at once established.

"Oh, I ain't been blind," said Holton, gaily, going much farther than she wished him to. "I've cut *my* eye-teeth!"

Then he turned to Layson with an awkward lightness. "Barbara told me what passed between you two young folks afore you come up to the mountings," he explained. And then, with further elephantine airyness: "I say, jest excuse me--reckon I'm in the way." He made a move as if to hurry off.

Layson was not pleased. The old man was annoying, always, and now, after the long revery of the night before about Madge Brierly, this attitude was doubly disconcerting. "Not at all, Mr. Holton," he said, somewhat hastily. "I'm sure we'd rather you'd remain. Are you sure the others are all right?"

"Close behind us."

"I'll go and make sure that they do not lose their way."

Holton looked at his daughter in a blank dismay after the youth had started down the hill. "I say, gal," said he, "there's somethin' wrong here!"

She was inclined to blame him for the deep discomforture she felt. "Why couldn't you let us alone?" she answered angrily. "You've spoiled everything!"

The old man looked at her, with worry on his face. "Didn't you tell me 't was as good as settled? You said you were dead sure he meant to make you his wife."

She was still petulant, blaming him for Layson's unexpected lack of warmth. "Yes, but you needn't have interfered!"

Holton was intensely puzzled, worried, almost frightened. He was as anxious to have this young man for a son-in-law as his daughter was to have him for a husband. Her marriage into such a celebrated bluegrass family as the Laysons were, would firmly fix her social status, no matter how precarious it might be now, and the match would be of great advantage to him in a business way, as well. He stood there, thinking deeply, very much displeased.

"There's somethin' more nor me has come between you," he said finally, his face flushing with a deep resentment. "I tell you, gal, what I believed at first, deep in my heart, air true. He was only triflin' with you. Them aristocrats down in the bluegrass don't hold us no better than the dust beneath their feet, even if we have got money. It's *family* that counts with them. Didn't he lay his whip acrost my face, once, as if I was a nigger?" His wrath was rising. "And now he shows that he was only triflin' with you with no real intentions of doin' as we thought he would!" The man was tremulous with wrath. "Oh, I'll be even with him!"

Barbara was greatly worried by the situation. All her life, despite the fact that she was beautiful, despite the fact that her father was a rich man--richer, by a dozen times, than many of the people for whose friendship she longed vainly--she had vaguely felt that there was an invisible gulf between her and the girls with whom she came in contact at the exclusive schools to which she had been sent, between her and the gentlefolk with whom, in some measure, she had mixed since she had left school-walls. "Father," she asked anxiously, "why do people look down on us so?"

He faced her with a worried look, as if he feared that she might guess at something which he wished should remain hidden. "They say I made my money tradin' in niggers," he replied, at length. "Well, what of it? Didn't I have the right?"

"Are you sure there's nothing else?"

He seemed definitely startled. "Girl, what makes you ask?"

"Because sometimes memories come to me."

"Memories of what?"

"Of--my childhood," she said slowly, "of passes among mountains--mountains much like these."

He regarded her uneasily. "Oh, sho, gal!" he exclaimed, trying to make light of it. "Reckon you've been dreamin'. You were never hyar before."

But she looked about her, unconvinced, and, when she spoke, spoke slowly, evidently trying to recall with definite clarity certain things which flitted through her mind as vague impressions only. "Why does everything seem so familiar, here, then, as if I had just wakened in my true surroundings after a long sleep in which I had had dreams?" There was, suddenly, a definite accusation in her eyes. "Father, you are trying to deceive me! I was once a child, here in these very mountains!" She stared about intently.

The speech had an amazing effect on the old man. He stepped close to her. "Hush!" said he, imperatively. "Don't you dare speak such a word ag'in!"

She peered into his eyes. "There *is* a secret, then! We lived here, long ago!"

"Stop, I tell you!" he commanded. "Don't hint at such things, for your life." He dropped his voice to hoarse whisper. "Suppose I did live hyar, once. I was a smooth-faced youngster, then; my own mother wouldn't know me, now."

The sound of voices coming up the mountain-trail interrupted the dramatic scene.

"Sh!" said he. "They're comin'!"

Frank was piloting his Aunt and Colonel Doolittle. "This way, Aunt 'Lethe," they could hear him say.

An instant later he appeared, leading the way up the steep trail. His Aunt, Neb and the Colonel followed him.

"Now, Aunt 'Lethe," he said gaily, "you can rest at last. Colonel, I can welcome you in earnest. This is, indeed, a pleasure."

The Colonel was puffing fiercely from the hard work of the climb, but his broad face glowed with pleasure. He took a long, full breath of the exhilerating mountain air. "Pleasure? It's a derby-day, sir, metaphorically speaking." As he rested he eyed the youngster with approval. "Frank," said he, "you've grown to be the very image of my old friend, Judge Layson. Ah, five years have made their changes in us all--except Miss 'Lethe." He bowed gallantly in her direction, and she gaily answered the salute.

Barbara advanced, enthusiastically, looking at the Colonel with arch envy in her eyes. "Five years you've been in Europe, surrounded by the nobility. Oh, Colonel, what happiness!"

He shook his head. "Happiness away from old Kentucky, surrounded by a lot of numb-skulls who couldn't mix a fancy drink to save their lives, who know nothing of that prismatic, rainbow-hued fountain of youth, a mint-julep? Ah!"

"But, Colonel," said the girl, "the masterpieces of art!"

"Give me," said he, "the masterpieces of Mother Nature--the bright-eyed, rose-cheeked, cherry-lipped girls of old Kentucky!"

There was a general laugh. The Colonel's gallantry was ever-blooming. Frank applauded and the ladies bowed.

"By the way, Frank," said the Colonel, after they had been made comfortable in a merry group before the cabin-door, "where is that particular masterpiece of Nature which you've written us so much about? Where is the--Diana?"

Miss Alathea smiled at her somewhat worried nephew. "The 'phenomenon,'" said she.

"According to Neb, who told us of her as we worked up that steep trail," said Barbara, "the 'deer.'" She laughed, not too good naturedly Neb, who was standing waiting orders near, grinned broadly.

"Neb, you rascal!" exclaimed Frank.

"Come, where is she, Frank; where is she?" asked the Colonel.

The youth was not too much embarrassed, but he gave a quick, side-glance at Barbara. "She is probably getting ready to receive you," he replied. "I told her I expected you and she's been very much excited over it."

"Adding to nature's charms the mysteries of art," the Colonel said, approvingly. "We shall expect to be overwhelmed. And, meantime, while we're waiting, we might as well explain to you the business which has brought us up here."

His face showed him to be the bearer of good news. He rose, excitedly, and went to Frank, to put his hand upon his shoulder. "Now, my boy, keep cool, keep cool! I tell you, Frank, it's the biggest thing out. It'll make a millionaire of you as sure as Fate before the next five years have passed!"

Layson was taken wholly by surprise. No one had in the least prepared him for anything of this sort. He had supposed the party had come up to see him merely for the pleasure of the trip. "I don't understand," said he.

"Keep cool, keep cool!" the Colonel urged. "It is colossal, metaphorically. You see, I was over there in Europe, promoting a South American mine, when I happened to see in a Kentucky paper that the Georgetown Midland was to be put through these mountains near the land your father bought. That land, my boy, is rich in coal and iron!"

The young man's face shone with delight. "He always said so!" he exclaimed. "I meant, sometime, to investigate."

"I've saved you the trouble. I came back on the next steamer, organized a syndicate in New York City, sent an expert out to carefully look into things, and, on his report, a company is willing to put in a $200,000 plant to develop your land. All you've got to do is to take $25,000 worth of stock and let your coal-land stand for as much more."

The youth's face fell. "Twenty-five thousand dollars!" he exclaimed. "Why, Colonel, I have not one fifth of it!"

"Ah," said the Colonel, smiling, "but here, like a good angel, comes in your dear Aunt 'Lethe!" He smiled at her. "Isn't it so, Miss 'Lethe?"

Frank spoke up quickly. "Surely," he exclaimed to her as she advanced toward him, with smiles, "you know I'd never take your money!"

"You must, Frank," she insisted. "The Colonel says it is the chance of a lifetime."

"Why, Auntie, it's your whole fortune. I wouldn't risk it."

"But you could pay it all back in a month."

"How?" he asked, not understanding in the least.

"By selling Queen Bess."

He flinched. The thought had not occurred to him. "Sell Queen Bess!" said he. "The prettiest, the fastest mare in all Kentucky! Never!"

"My boy," said the Colonel, "the odds are far too heavy--a million against the mare. You can't stand 'em."

"Oh, Frank," said his Aunt, impulsively, "if you'll only take the money and give up racing!"

He laughed. Miss Alathea's strong prejudice against the race-tracks was proverbial. "So that's what you're after!" he exclaimed. "You dear old schemer!"

"With your impulsive, generous nature, racing is sure to ruin you."

The Colonel looked first at Frank with ardent sympathy aglow in his eyes; then, after a hasty glance at Miss Alathea, he quickly changed the meaning of his look and spoke admonishingly. "The voice of wisdom!" he exclaimed. "Ah, Frank, from what I hear I judge you're too much of a plunger--like a young fellow I once knew who thought he could win a fortune on the race-track." He began, now, to speak very seriously. "He was in love with the prettiest and sweetest girl in old Kentucky, but he wished to wait till he could get that fortune, and he chased it here and there, looking for it mostly on the race-tracks, until he had more grey hairs than he had ever hoped to have dollars; he chased it till his dream of happiness had slipped by, perhaps forever. My boy, the race-track is a delusion and a snare."

Miss Alathea looked at him with pleased surprise. "Colonel, your sentiments astonish and delight me."

"How can you refuse," the Colonel said, "when such a woman asks? For one who loves you, you should give those pleasures up without a pang."

In the pause that followed he reflected on the history of the youth to whom he had referred, for that young man was himself. He had loved Miss Alathea twenty years, but the Goddess Chance had kept him, all that time, too poor to ask her hand in marriage. His heart beat with elation as he realized that, possibly, the scheme which he had come there to the mountains to propose to Frank, might remedy the evils of the situation.

Frank had been thinking deeply. "But what certainty is there," he inquired, "that I can sell Queen Bess at such a price?"

Now the Colonel spoke with animation. "Absolute. I've a written offer from the Dyer brothers to take her for twenty-five thousand dollars, if she is delivered, safe and sound, on the morning she's to run in the Ashland Oaks. It's a dead sure thing, my boy. You can't refuse."

The young man hesitated, still. "I'll investigate, and--well, I'll see." He walked away, deep in thought.

The Colonel turned from him to Miss Alathea. "Miss 'Lethe, congratulate yourself. The victory is won."

Frank turned upon his heel and spoke to Holton. "What do you think of this investment?" he inquired.

"Wal," said Holton, "I think it's a blamed good thing. I'd only like the chance to go into it, myself." He went closer to the youth and spoke in an instinctively low tone. "By the way, this gal, hyar, Madge Brierly, owns fifty acres o' land down there in the valley, that's bound to be wuth money. Like enough, with your help, I could buy it for a song. I'll make it all right with you. What do you say? Is it a bargain, Layson?" He held out his hand, evidently with no thought but that the questionable offer would be snapped up at once.

Layson drew back angrily. "No," he replied.

Holton, seeing that he had made a serious mistake, tried to correct it. "Oh, shucks, now! I didn't mean no harm. That's only business."

Layson was intensely angered. "I won't waste words on you," he said, "but think twice before you make me such a proposition again."

Holton's wrath rose vividly. "Damn him!" he muttered as he walked away. "I'll pay him back for that! I'll get that gal's land in spite of him, and I won't stop at that. I'll pay him back for ... everythin'! I'll teach him what it air to stir the hate o' hell in a man's heart!"

Barbara, distressed anew by this unpleasant episode, had started to go after him, when the weird cry of an owl, a long drawn, tremulous: "Hoo-oo-oo!" came from somewhere in the forest, close at hand. It startled her. "Heavens!" said she. "What's that?"

Neb, who also had been startled at the first penetrating, weird call, bethought himself, now, and answered her: "It's de deah."

"The phenomenon!" exclaimed Miss Alathea.

"The Diana!" said the Colonel, looking at Frank slyly.

"Yes; she's coming," Frank said gaily, and then, looking down the path, started violently. "Heavens, she's coming!"

The Colonel, who also had looked down the path, hurriedly approached him, feigning worry. "Frank, I haven't got 'em again, have I?"

Madge approached them slowly in the quaint, old-fashioned costume she had resurrected from the chests of her dead mother's finery and re-made, very crudely, in accordance with the fashion-plates which she had found down at the cross-roads store. The result of her contriving was a startling mixture of fashions widely separated as to periods. Her untutored taste had mixed colors clashingly. Her unskilled fingers had sewed very bunchy seams.

The girl was much embarrassed: it required the last ounce of her bravery to advance. Before she actually reached the little group, she half hid, indeed, behind a tree. It was from this shelter that she called her greeting: "Howdy, folks, howdy!"

Frank went toward her with an outstretched hand. "Come, Madge," said he, encouragingly.

"Reckon I'll have to," she assented, with a bashful smile and took a step or two reluctantly. But she had never seen folk dressed at all as were these visitors from the famed bluegrass, and her courage again faltered. Instantly she realized how wholly her own efforts to be elegant had failed. She hung back awkwardly, pathetically.

"Don't be nervous, Madge; just be yourself," Frank urged her.

"Free and easy? Well, I'll try; but I'm skeered enough to make me wild and reckless."

Frank led her forward, while she made a mighty effort to accept the situation coolly. "These are my friends, Madge. Let me introduce you."

She got some grip upon herself and smiled. "Ain't no need. Know 'em all by your prescription." With a mighty effort she approached the Colonel. "Colonel Sandusky Doolittle, howdy!"

The Colonel was delighted. Her knowledge of his name was flattering. He had forgotten her strange costume the moment his glance had caught her wonderful, deep eyes. "Howdy, howdy!" he said heartily, shaking her hand vigorously. "Why, this is real Kentucky style!" It won't take *us* long to get acquainted."

"Know all about you now," she said. "Great hossman. Colonel, I'll have a race with you, sometime."

"What, you ride?" said the delighted Colonel.

"Ride! Dellaw!" said she, with, now, unembarrassed animation. The subject was that one, of all, which made her most quickly forget everything beside. "Why, me and my pony takes to racin' like a pig to carrots. Before he lamed himself, whenever th' boys heard us clatterin' down th' mounting, they laid to race us back. Away we went, then, clickity-clip, up th' hills and around th' curves--an' I allus won."

The Colonel realized with a great joy that he had found a kindred spirit. "Shake again!" he said to her, after further most congenial talk, and then turned to Frank. "My boy, you're right. She *is* a phenomenon--a thoroughbred, even if she hasn't any pedigree."

Up to this time the ladies had remained somewhat in the background, watching the young mountain girl as the Colonel drew her out.

Madge now turned to Frank, but looked at Barbara. "Is that the young lady from the bluegrass?" The girl was hurt and really offended by the stranger's aloof manner. "Looks like she can't see common folks."

"That is Miss Barbara." He led the mountain girl toward her. "Barbara, this is my friend--er--Madge." He was, himself, a little disconcerted.

The maiden from the lowlands bowed, but said no word. For an instant Madge shrank back, but then she advanced with an unusual boldness. Her spirit was aroused.

"Howdy, Miss Barbarous, howdy!" she exclaimed and held her hand out to the handsomely dressed girl.

But Miss Barbara was annoyed by the whole happening. She felt that this uncultivated country girl was getting far too much attention. The child's unconscious pun upon her name infuriated her. She did not answer her, but raised a lorgnette and stared at her.

Madge was ready with an instant sympathy. "Oh, that's why you couldn't see, poor thing! Spectacles at your age!" Whether she really thought this was the case, not even Frank could tell by looking at her.

Miss Holton was incensed. The haughty treatment she had planned to, give the mountain girl had not had the results she had expected. "There's nothing whatever the matter with my eyes!" she exclaimed hastily.

"Wouldn't think you'd need a machine to help you star-gaze at folks, then," said the mountain girl. "But maybe it's the fashion in the bluegrass."

Frank hurried up with Holton, planning a diversion. "This is Mr. Holton, Madge."

"Howdy, sir," said she, and then started in astonishment. "Ain't I seen your face before, sir?"

"Wal, I reckon not," said Holton most uneasily. "I was never hyar in these hyar mountings afore."

She stepped closer to him, gazing straight at his grey eyes. They seemed strangely to recall the very distant past, she knew not how. There were other things about him which seemed much more immediately familiar, although his more elaborate garb prevented her, for the moment, from recognizing him as the stranger with the hammer, who had, that day of the forest-fire, been tap-tapping on the rocks upon her pasture-land. "Your eyes seem to bring something back." She plainly paled. She knew that their suggestion was a dreadful one, but could not make it definite.

Miss Alathea noted her agitation instantly, and hurried to her side. "Poor child, what is the matter?"

Madge had regained control of her features, which, for an instant, had shown plain horror. "Tain't nothin', ma'am. It couldn't be. It's all over now." She smiled gratefully at Miss Alathea. "An' you're his aunt, ain't you? I'd know you for his kin, anywhere. Why, somehow, you remind me of my lost mother."

"Thank you, my dear. You must be very lonely, up here all alone."

"I am, sometimes," said the girl, "but I have lots of fun, too. The woods are full of friends. Th' birds an' squirrels ain't afraid o' me. They seem to think I'm a wild thing, like 'em."

"It's true," said Frank, with an admiring, cheering look at the little country girl. "Their confidence in her is wonderful."

The bluegrass girl's annoyance was increasing. She had come up to the mountains thinking that, among such crude surroundings, her gowns and the undoubted beauty they adorned, would hold the center of the stage, and by contrast, hold Layson quite enthralled; but here, instead, was a brown-faced country maid in grotesque, homemade costume, attracting most of his attention. She was conscious that by showing her discomfiture she was not strengthening her own position, but she could not hide it, could not curb her tongue.

"A rider of races," said she; "a tamer of animals! What accomplishments! Do you actually live here, all alone?"

"Come," said Madge, determined to be pleasant, "and I'll show you." She led the bluegrass girl to a convenient point from which her cabin was in sight.

"In that little hut!" said Barbara, not impressed as Madge had innocently thought she would be. "Shocking!"

The girl was angered, now. "So sorry I didn't have your opinion afore! But, maybe, you wouldn't think it were so awful, if you knowed how 'twere I come to live there."

Frank had written something of the poor girl's tragic story to his aunt. She was all interest. "Won't you tell us, please?" she asked.

Holton seemed to show a strange disinclination to listen to the narrative. "Ain't got no time for stories," he objected. "Gettin' late."

"We'll take time, then," said Frank.

"Go on, little one," urged Colonel Doolittle. "We're listening."

Impressed and touched by the sympathy in the horseman's tone and the interest in Miss Alathea's eyes, Madge told with even greater force and more effect than when she had related it to Layson the story of the tragedy which had robbed her at a blow of father and of mother, the black, dreadful tale of merciless assassination which had left her orphaned in the mountains. Her audience attended, spellbound, even the disgruntled and unsympathetic Barbara listening with unwilling fascination. Only Holton turned away, with a gesture of impatience. He plainly did not wish to waste time on the girl. Or was it that? He seemed to be uneasy as he walked to and fro upon the rock-ledge near them, whence, had he cared for it, he could have had a gorgeous view of mountain scenery. But, although he said, as plainly as he could without actual rudeness, that the girl and her sad tale of tragedy were not worth attention, he was not successful in his efforts wholly to refuse to listen to her.

"Infamous!" said Miss Alathea, when the child had finished.

"And that scoundrel has gone free!" exclaimed the Colonel, in disgust.

" *That's* how I come to live alone, here," Madge went on, addressing Barbara, particularly. The girl had made her feel it necessary to offer some defense. "After my mammy died I didn't have no place to go, an' so I just stayed on here, an' th' bridge my daddy built for his protection I have kept for mine. Maybe he has told you of it." She indicated Frank. They nodded.

"And nothing has been heard of the infernal traitor, all these years?" the Colonel asked.

"He left the mountings when he found how folks was feelin'--they'd have shot him, like a dog, on sight. But it don't make no differ where he goes; it don't make a bit of differ where he goes."

"What do you mean by that?" the Colonel asked, and as he spoke, Holton, suddenly intent, paused in his pacing of the ledge to listen.

"I mean, no matter where he goes he'll have to pay for it, come soon, come late. Th' day air sure to come when Joe, Ben Lorey's son, 'll meet him face to face an' make him answer for his crime!"

"God-speed to him!" exclaimed the Colonel, fervently.

Madge, in a gesture full of drama, although quite unconscious, raised her head, looking off into the vastness of the mountains, her hands thrust straight down at her sides and clenched, her shoulders squared, her chest heaving with a mighty intake. The little mountain-girl, as she stood there, thrilling with her longing for revenge, with prayers that some day the sinner might be punished for his dreadful crime, made an impressive figure.

"Come soon or late!" she sighed. "Come soon or late!"

The party watched her, fascinated, till Holton took his daughter's arm and urged her, uneasily, out of the little group.

Later Madge asked the Colonel to go with her to the pasture lot and take a look at Little Hawss. Gladly he went with her, tenderly this expert in Kentucky racers, the finest horses in the world, examined the shaggy little pony's hoof. He told Madge what to do for him and promised to send up a lotion with which to bathe the injured foot, although he gently warned her that she must not hope that Little Hawss would ever do much racing up and down the mountain trails again. She choked, when he said this, and the horseman's heart went out to her.

"Little one," said the Colonel, as the party was preparing to go down the mountain, "you're a thoroughbred, and Colonel Sandusky Doolittle is your friend from the word 'go.'" He took her hand in his and smiled down into her eyes.

Then, turning to Miss 'Lethe: "Do you know, Miss 'Lethe, there's something about this little girl that puts me in mind of you, when I first met you? You remember?"

"Ah, Colonel, that was twenty years ago--the day I was eighteen."

"And I was twenty-five. Now I'm forty-five and you--"

"Colonel!"

"Are still eighteen.' He bowed, impressively, with that charming, gallant smile which was peculiar to him.

"Aren't you going down with us, Frank?" asked Barbara, looking at the youth with plain surprise when she noted that he lingered when she and her father were ready for the start.

"I wish to speak to Madge, a moment. I'll overtake you."

The bluegrass beauty looked at him, wrath blazing in her eyes, then turned away with tossing head.

"Good-bye," said Madge, and held her hand out to her.

Barbara paid no attention to the small, brown hand, but, instead, opened her parasol almost in the face of the astonished mountain-girl, who jumped back, startled. "Oh, very well," said Barbara to Frank.

Madge turned to him, the softness of the mood engendered by her talk with the Colonel and Miss 'Lethe all gone, now. Her face was flushed with anger. "Dellaw!" said she. "Thought she was goin' to shoot!"

Now Barbara spoke haughtily. "Good afternoon, Miss Madge. You have entertained us wonderfully, wonderfully."

CHAPTER X

It was late on an afternoon several days after the party from the bluegrass had gone down from the mountains when Layson, with a letter of great import in his pocket sought Madge Brierly.

He was very happy, as, a short time before he reached her isolated cabin, he stepped out to the edge of that same ledge where Horace Holton had found the view too full of memories for comfort, to look off across the lovely valley spread before, below him. There were no memories of struggle and bloodshed to arise between him and that view and for a time he gloried in it with that bounding, pulsating appreciation which can come to us in youth alone, as his eyes swept the fair prospect of wooded slope and rugged headland, stream-ribbon, mountain-meadow, billowy forest. Then, with a deep breath of the wondrous air of the old Cumberlands, which added a physical exhileration almost intoxicating to the pleasure of the thoughts which filled his mind, he went slowly up the rugged twisting path to Madge's cabin. There, standing by the bridge he called, and, presently, the girl appeared.

He smiled at her. He did not wish to tell her, too quickly, of the news the letter held.

The girl was still full of the visit and the visitors. They had seemed to her, reared as she had been in the rough seclusion of the mountains, like denizens of another, wondrously fine world, come to glimpse her in her crude one, for a few hours, and then gone back to their own glorious abiding place.

She did not admit it to herself, but they had left behind them discontent with the life she knew, her lack of education, almost everything with which, in days gone by, she had been so satisfied.

Layson, watching her as she approached, was tempted to enjoy her as she was, for a few minutes, before telling her the news which, young and inexperienced as he was, he yet knew, instinctively, would change her for all time.

"Well," he said, "how did you like them, Madge?"

The girl sat upon a stump and looked off across the valley. Her hands were clasped upon one knee, as she reflected, the fading sunlight touched her hair with sheening brilliance, her eyes, at first, were dreamy, happy.

"Oh, I loved your aunt!" said she. "She made me think of my own mammy.... She made me think of my own mammy."

"And she was quite as much in love with you."

"Was she?... And Cunnel Doolittle! Ain't he *splendid*? And how he do know hosses! Wouldn't I *love* to see some of them races that he told about? Wouldn't I love to have a chance to learn how to become a lady like your aunt? She's just the sweetest thing that ever lived."

"And ... and ... Miss Barbara?" said Layson, with a little mischief in his wrinkling eyelids.

The girl shrugged herself together haughtily upon her stump. He had seen lowlands girls use almost the same gesture when, in drawing-rooms, some topic had come up which they did not wish to talk about.

"Huh! Her!" said Madge and would have changed the subject had he let her.

"Really?" he asked, wickedly. "Didn't you like her?"

"I ain't sayin' much," said Madge, "because she's different from me, has had more chance, is better dressed, knows more from books an' so on, an' it might seem like I was plumb jealous of her. Maybe I am, too. But, dellaw! Her with her pollysol! When she opened it that way at me I thought it war a gun an' she war goin' to fire! Maybe I ain't had no learnin' in politeness, but it seems to me I would a been a little more so, just the same, if I'd been in her place. She don't like me, she don't, an' I-- why, I just *hates* her! Her with her ombril up, an' not a cloud in sight!"

Layson looked at her and laughed. The letter in his pocket made it seem probable that she would not need, in future, to submit to such humiliations as the blue-grass girl had put upon her, so his merriment could not be counted cruel.

"Jealous of her?" he inquired, quizzically.

She sat in deep thought for a moment and then frankly said: "I reckon so; a leetle, teeny mite. Maybe it has made me mean in thinkin' of her, ever since."

"You're honest, anyway," said he, "and I shall tell you something that will comfort you. She was as jealous of you as you were of her."

"*She* was!" the girl exclaimed, incredulous, surprised. "Of *me*?" You're crazy, ain't you?"

"Not a bit."

"What have *I* got to make *her* jealous?"

"A lot of things. You've beauty such as hers will never be--"

"Dellaw!" said Madge, incredulously. She had no knowledge of her own attractiveness. "Don't you start in makin' fun o' me."

"I'm not making fun of you. You're very beautiful--my aunt said so, the Colonel said so, and *I've* known it, all along."

No one had ever said a thing like this to her, before. She looked keenly at him, weighing his sincerity. When she finally decided that he really meant what he had said, she breathed a long sigh of delight.

"They said that I--was *beautiful*!"

"They did, and, little girl, you are; and you have more than beauty. You have health and strength such as a bluegrass girl has never had in all the history of women."

"Oh, yes," said she, "I'm strong an' well--but--but--"

"But what?"

"But what?" she quoted bitterly. "But I ain't got no eddication. What does strength and what does what you tell me is my beauty count, when I ain't got no eddication? Why--why--I looked plumb *foolish* by the side of her! You think I don't know that my talk sounds rough as rocks alongside hers, ripplin' from her lips as smooth as water? You think I don't know that I looked like a scare-crow in all them clo'es I had fixed up so careful, when she come on with her gowns made up for her by *dressmakers*? Why--why--I never *see* a dressmaker in all my life! I never even see one!"

"Well," said he, and looked at her with a slow smile, "there probably will be no reason why you may not see as many as you like, in years to come,"

She was amazed. "This some sort o' joke?"

"No, Madge. How would you like to be rich?"

"Me?... Rich? Oh ... oh, I'd like it. *Then* I could go down in th' bluegrass, study, l'arn, an'--I could do a heap o' good aroun' hyar, too" She sighed. "But thar never was nobody rich in these hyar mountings an' I reckon thar never will be."

"Perhaps you may be," said the youth, and there was a serious quality in his voice which made her start and then lean forward on her stump to gaze at him with searching, eager eyes.

"Your land down in the valley," he went on, "may contain coal and iron enough to give you a fortune. Now there are bad men in this world, and I want you to promise me to sell it to nobody without first coming to me for advice."

"Promise?" said the girl, the wonder all ashine in her big eyes. "In course I'll promise that. But is there r'ally a chance of it?"

"There really is."

"Oh, if I only knowed, for shore! Seems like I couldn't wait!"

"You shall know, to-night, or, maybe, sooner. I have the engineers report, but I must study it out carefully and make sure what boundaries he means. I'm almost certain they include your land. As soon as I find out I'll come back here and call to you and let you know."

"I reckon you won't have to call! I'll be watchin' for you every minute."

"Well, I'm off. But remember what I said about letting anyone buy any of your land from you. Don't sell an inch, don't give an option at whatever price, to anyone without consulting me."

When he had left, the girl still sat there, dreaming on her stump after she had watched him out of sight.

The news that she might become rich had stirred her deeply for a moment, but, soon she wondered if riches, really, would mean everything, and decided that they would not.

"Somehow," she mused, "somehow I don't care much about it, not unless--unless--oh, I can't think of nothin' in th' world but him! An' he says he's goin' to go away, never to return no more!... Other folks has gone away, afore, but it didn't seem to hurt my heart like this. I wonder what is ailin' me."

Her thought turned back to that half-bitter, half-delightful moment when he had tried to kiss her at the bridge. "Why, even then," she mused, "thar were somethin' seemed to draw me to him in spite o' myself. Never felt anythin' like it afore. It war--just as if I war asleep, all over, an' never wanted to wake up! I wonder if I wish he warn't comin' back, to-night--not half so much, I reckon, as I wish he warn't never goin' away!"

She left her resting place upon the stump, and, torn by varying emotions, found a place upon the trail where she could look off to his camp. She was standing there, leaning listlessly against a tree, when the sound of someone coming made her turn her head. She saw Joe Lorey.

"Madge," said he, approaching, "I wants a word with you,"

She did not wish to talk with him. Her mind was far too busy with its thoughts of Layson, its dismay at the prospect of his departure. "No time, Joe; it's too late," said she. She started to go by him toward her little bridge.

But he was not inclined to be put off. The mountaineer's slow mind had been at work with his great problem and he had quite determined that he would take some action, definite and unmistakable, without delay. He had leaned his ever-present rifle up against a stump, had laid the old game-sack, still burdened with the stolen dynamite, upon the ground, close to it, and was prepared to talk the matter out, to one end or the other. He loved her with the fierce love of the primitive man; his rising wrath against the circumstances amidst which he seemed to be so powerless had made him sullen and suspicious; mountain life, continual defiance of the law, unceasing watchfulness for "revenuers," does not teach a man to be smooth-mannered, half-way in his methods. He made a move as if to catch her arm; she darted by him, running straight toward the old game-sack.

That burden in the game-sack had been a constant horror to him ever since he had first stolen it down at the railroad workings. The mighty evidence of the power of the explosive which had been shown to him when it had torn and mangled its poor victim there, had filled him with a terror of it, although it had also filled him with determination to make use of that great power if necessary. But now, as he saw her running, light-footed, lovely, toward the bag which held it, running in exactly the right way to stumble on it if a mis-step chanced, his heart sprang to his throat. What if the dire explosive he had planned to use upon his enemies should prove to be the death of the one being whom he loved? He sprang toward her with the mighty impulse of desperate muscles spurred by a panic-stricken mind and caught her, roughly, just before her foot would have touched and spurned the game-sack.

"Stop!" he cried, in desperation.

She was amazed that he should take so great a liberty. She stopped, perforce, but, after she had stopped, she stood there trembling with hot anger. "Joe Lorey," she exclaimed, "you dare!"

Now he was all humility as he let his hand fall from her arm. "It was for your sake, Madge," said he. "A stumble on that sack--it mout have sent us both to Kingdom Come!"

She looked at him incredulously, then down at the sack. "That old game-sack? Why, Joe, you're plumb distracted!"

"I'm in my senses, yet, I tell you," he persisted. "T'other day I went down where they're blastin' for th' railroad. I see 'em usin' dynamighty, down thar, an' I watched my chance an', when it come, I slipped one o' th' bombs into that game-sack. Ef you'd chanced to kick it--"

She was impressed. "Dynamighty bombs? Dellaw! What's dynamighty bombs?"

"It's a giant powder, a million times stronger nor mine." He reached into the sack and, with cautious fingers, took out the cartridge and the fuse, exhibiting them to her. "See here. I seed 'em take a bomb no bigger nor this one, an' light a fuse like this, an' when it caught it ennymost shook down a mounting! I seed a poor chap what war careless with one, an' when they picked him up, why--"

"Don't, Joe!" said the girl, looking at the cartridge with the light of horror shining in her eyes. "What you doin' with such devil's stuff?"

"I got it for th' revenuers," he said frankly. The mountaineers of the old Cumberland, to this day, make no secret of their deadly hatred for the agents of the government excise. "They're snoopin' 'round th' mountings, an' if they find my still I plan to blow it into nothin', an' them with it."

She recoiled from him. "No, no, Joe; you'd better gin th' still up, nor do such work as that!"

"I'll never gin it up!" said he, with a set face. "It's mine; it war my father's long before me. There's only one thing could ever make me gin it up."

"What's that?" The girl was still spellbound by the fascination of the dynamite which she had come so near to treading on. Her eyes were fixed upon the cartridge in his hand with horror, wonder.

He stepped closer to her. "I mout gin it up for you!"

"For me?"

"You know I've loved ye sence ye were that high," said he, and measured with his hand a very little way up the side of the old stump. "Many a time I've listened hyar to your evenin' hymn, an' thought I'd rather hear you singin' in my home than hear th' angels singin' in th' courts o' Heaven. Say th' word, Madge--say you'll be my little wife!"

The girl was woe fully affected. Her eyes filled and her bosom heaved with feeling. It cut her to the soul to have to hurt this playmate of her babyhood, defender of her youth, companion of her budding womanhood; their lives had been linked, too, by the great tragedy which, years ago, had orphaned both of them. But, of late, she had felt sure that she could never marry him. She would not admit, even to herself, just why this was; but it was so. "No, no, Joe; it can never be," she said.

He knew! "And why?" said he, his face blackening with bitter feeling, his brows contracting fiercely. "Because that furriner from the blue grass has come atween us!"

Madge, surprised that he should guess the secret which she had scarcely admitted, even to herself, was, for a second, frightened by his keenness. Had she shown her feelings with such freedom? But she quickly regained self-control and answered with a clever counterfeit of lightness. "Him? Oh, sho! He'd never think o' me that way!"

"Mebbe so," said Joe, "but I know you think more o' th' books he teaches you from than o' my company. From th' thickets borderin' th' clearin' where you've studied, I've watched you settin' thar with him, wen I'd give th' world to be thar in his place. Why, I'd ennymost gin up my life for one kiss, Madge!" He looked at her with pitiful love and longing in his eyes; but this soon changed to a sort of mad determination. "I'll have it, too!" he cried, advancing toward her.

She was amazed, not in the least dismayed. Indeed the episode took from the moment some of its emotional strain. That he should try to do this utterly unwarrantable thing took a portion of the weight of guilty feeling from her heart. It had been pressing heavily there. "You shan't!" she cried. "Careful, Joe Lorey!"

She eluded him with ease and ran across her little bridge. He paused, a second, in astonishment, and, as he paused, she grasped the rope and pulled the little draw up after her.

"Look out, Joe; it air a hundred feet, straight down!" she cried, as she saw that the baffled mountaineer was trembling on the chasm's edge, as if preparing for a spring. "Good night, Joe. Take my advice--gin up th' still, an' all thought of makin' a wife of a girl as ain't willin'."

Half laughing and half crying she ran up the path which wound about among the thickets on the rocky little island where her rough cabin stood, secure, secluded.

The mountaineer stood, baffled, on the brink of the ravine. Much loneliness among the mountains, where there was no voice but his own to listen to, had given him the habit of talking to himself in moments of excitement.

"Gone! Gone!" he said. "Gone laughin' at me!" He clenched his fists. "And it is him as has come atween us!" He turned slowly from the place, picked up his rifle, slung the game-sack, saggin with the weight of the dynamite, across his shoulder by its strap, and started from the place.

He had gone but a short distance, though, before he stopped, considering. Murder was in Joe Lorey's heart.

"She said he war comin' back," he sullenly reflected. "I'll ... lay for him, right hyar."

He looked cautiously about. His quick ear caught the sound of footsteps coming up the trail.

"Somebody's stirrin', now," he said. "Oh, if it's only him!"

He slipped behind a rock to wait in ambush.

But it was not his enemy who came, now, along the trail. Horace Holton, held to the mountains by his mysterious business, had left the others of the party to go home alone, as they had come, and returned to the neighborhood which housed the girl who owned the land he coveted.

Joe, suspicious of him, as the mountaineer who makes his living as a moonshiner, is, of course, of every stranger who appears within his mountains, stepped forward, suddenly, his rifle in his hand and ready to be used. He had no idea that the man had been a member of the party from the bluegrass.

"Halt, you!" he cried.

CHAPTER XI

Holton, full of scheming, was returning up the trail after having said good-bye to Barbara, Miss Alathea and the Colonel at the railway in the valley, climbing steadily and skillfully, without much thought of his surroundings. The locality, familiar to him years before (although he had at great pains indicated to everyone but Barbara that it was wholly strange to him) showed but superficial change to his searching, reminiscent eyes. His feet had quickly fallen into the almost automatic climbing-stride of the born mountaineer, and his thoughts had gradually absorbed themselves in memories of the past. Joe Lorey's sudden command to halt was somewhat startling, therefore, even to his iron nerves. Instinctively and instantly he heeded the gruff order.

Dusk was falling and he could not very clearly see the moonshiner, at first, as he stepped from behind the shelter of his rock. He moved slowly on, a step or two, hands half raised to show that they did not hold weapons, recovering quickly from the little shock of the surprise, planning an explanation to whatever mountaineer had thought his coming up the trail at that hour a suspicious circumstance. That he was one of Layson's friends from the low-country would, he thought, be proof enough that he was not an enemy of mountain-folk. Layson, he knew, was generally regarded with good will by the shy dwellers in this wilderness.

But when he clearly saw Joe Lorey's face a thrill shot through him far more lasting than the little tremor born, at first, of the command to halt.

He had not seen the youth before. Joe, half jealous, half contemptuous, of Layson's fine friends from the bluegrass, had kept out of their sight, although he had watched them furtively from covert almost constantly; and, it chanced, had not been so much as mentioned by either Frank or Madge while the party from the bluegrass lingered at the camp, save when Madge told the tragic story of her childhood while Holton stood aloof, for reasons of his own, hearing but imperfectly.

Now the unexpected sight of the young man, for some reasons, made the old one gasp in horror. There was that about the face, the attitude, the very way the lithe moonshiner held his gun, which made him seem, to the astonished man whom he had halted, like a grim vision from the past. "My God!" he thought. "Can the dead have come to life?"

For an instant he went weak. His blood chilled and the quick beating of his heart changed the deep breathing of his recent swinging stride into short, sharp gasps.

It was only for an instant, though. His life had not been one to teach him to falter long in the face of an emergency. Quickly he regained poise and reasoned calmly.

"No," he thought, "it's Joe, Ben Lorey's son. Th' father's layin' where he has been, all these years. I'm skeery as a girl."

Joe advanced upon him truculently. "Say," he demanded, "what's yer name an' what ye want here?" His ever ready rifle nested in the crook of his left arm, his brow was threatening, his mouth was firmly set an instant after he had spoken.

Holton, recovering himself quickly, spoke calmly, propitiatingly. "My name's Holton. I want to see th' gal as lives up yander. Want to buy her land of her."

Lorey, satisfied by this explanation that the stranger was not a government agent, as he had, at first suspected, relaxed his tense rigidity of muscles. From fear of revenuers his disturbed mind returned quickly to the bitterness of his resentment of what he thought Madge Brierly's infatuation for the young lowlander.

"It's too late," he said. "Thar's only one man as she'd let down that bridge for, now--th' man I thought ye might be--Frank Layson."

Holton, quick to see the possibility of gaining an advantage, realizing from the young man's tone that he was certainly no friend of Layson's, guessing, with quick cunning, at what the situation was, decided that the thing for him to do was to reveal the fact that, in his heart, he, also, hated Layson.

"So ye took me for a revenuer or Frank Layson, eh?" said he. "I know what th' mountings think o' revenuers, an' I reckon, from yer handlin' o' that rifle, that you're no friend o' Layson's."

Joe, full of the fierce bitterness of his resentment, was ready to confide in anyone his hatred of the "furriner" who had come up and won the girl he loved. He let the barrel of his rifle slip between his fingers till its stock was resting on the ground.

"I hates him as I hates but one man in th' world!" he said, with bitter emphasis.

"Who's that?" said Holton, thoughtlessly, although, an instant afterward, he was sorry that he had pursued the subject.

"Lem Lindsay," Lorey answered; "him as killed my father. Frank Layson's come between me an' Madge Brierly, an' he's got to cl'ar my tracks!" His voice thrilled with the intensity of his emotion, and, suddenly, he caught his rifle up, again, into his crooked elbow, where it rested ready for quick usage. "If you plans to warn him--" he began.

"Warn him!" said the older man, with a bitterness, real or counterfeited, whichever it might be, as fierce as that which rang in the young moonshiner's own voice, "I hate him as much as you. I'd rather warn you."

"Warn me o' what?" Lorey had begun to lose suspicion of the stranger. If, really, he hated Layson, he might make of him a useful ally.

"Your name's Lorey," Holton answered, with his keen eyes fixed intently on those of the man who stood there, tensely listening to him, "an' yo' keep a still."

Now Lorey again caught his rifle quickly in both hands; his face showed new apprehension, and a terrible determination, desperate and dreadful. If this stranger knew about the still, was it not certain that he was a government spy and therefore worthy of quick death?

"Keerful!" he said menacingly. "Hyar in th' mountings that word's worth your life!" The youth, with frowning brow and glittering, wolfish eyes, stood facing Holton like an animal at bay, with what amounted to a threat of murder on his lips.

"I'm speakin' it for your own good," the old man answered, throwing into his voice as much of frankness as he could command. "I tell you that th' revemooers have got word about your still."

"Then somebody's spied an' told 'em."

Here was Holton's chance. The vicious scheme came to him in a flash. Layson he hated fiercely; this youth he hated fiercely. What plan could be better than to set the one to hunt the other? If Lorey should kill Layson it would remove Layson from his path and make his way clear to the purchase of Madge Brierly's coal-lands at a small fraction of their value. And, having killed him, Lorey would, of course, be forced to flee the country, for the hue and cry would be far-reaching. Such a killing never would be passed over as an ordinary mountain murder generally is by the authorities. Thus, at once, he might be rid of the young bluegrass gentleman he hated and the young mountaineer he feared.

"You're right," said he. "Somebody's spied an' told 'em. Somebody as stumbled on yore still while he was huntin'."

Lorey looked at him, wide-eyed, infuriated. Instantly he quite believed what Holton said. It dove-tailed with his own grim hate of Layson that Layson should hate him and try to work his ruin by giving information to the revenuers. "Somebody huntin'!" he exclaimed. "Frank Layson! Say it, say it!"

"Promise you'll never speak my name?" said Holton. He had no wish to be mixed up in the tragic matter, and he knew, instinctively, that if Joe Lorey gave his word, moonshiner and lawbreaker as he was, it would be kept to the grim end.

"I promise it, if it air th' truth you're tellin' me," said Lorey.

"It's true, then," Holton answered. "You can see for your own self that I'm a stranger hyar. I couldn't a' knowed o' th' still exceptin' through Frank Layson."

The simple, specious argument to Lorey was convincing. "It air true," he admitted slowly. "Nobody else would a' gin ye th' word." The angry youth paused in black, murderous thought. "He air a-comin' hyar, to-night," he went on presently. "I heered him tell Madge Brierly that he war comin' back, this evenin'. You better--maybe you had better git along." He had no wish for witnesses to what he planned, now, to accomplish, when Layson should come back to Madge, as he had promised, with the engineer's report upon her coal lands.

Holton nodded, grimly satisfied that he had planted a suspicion which might flower into his own revenge. That blow which Layson had delivered on his face, in the old days, had left a scar upon his soul, and now that the young man seemed likely to add to this unforgotten injury the new one of retiring from the field as suitor for his daughter, and, further, interfering with his plans to rob Madge Brierly of her coal lands, his hatred of him had become intense, insatiable. What better fortune could he wish than to pit this mountain youth, whom, also, for a reason carried over from dark days in his past life, he hated, against the young man from the bluegrass whom he hated no less bitterly?

"Go by *that* path, thar," said Lorey, suddenly, and pointing, as Holton started to return by the direct route he had followed as he came. "It air round-about, but it'll lead you to th' valley. I'll run no risk o' your warnin' him."

"Don't you be skeered," said Holton. "I'll keep mum, no matter what happens."

With a grim smile he started down the path which the mountaineer had pointed out.

"Laid his whip across my face!" he muttered as he went. "Trifled with my gal! Him an' Ben Lorey's son--let 'em fight it out! I'm so much th' better off."

And Lorey, slipping back into the shadow of a rock, after he had made quite certain that the stranger was following his directions, was reflecting, bitterly: "He's come atween me an' th' gal I love! He's put th' revenoo hounds upon my track! Oh, if he had a dozen lives, I'd have 'em all!"

For ten alert and watchful minutes, which seemed to stretch to hours, he crouched there, waiting, waiting, waiting, for the coming of the man he hated. During five of these he listened to the sounds of Holton's downward progress, brought to his keen ear on the soft breezes of the young night. There came the crackling of a twig, the thud, thud, thud of a dislodged stone bounding down the slope, the rustle of leaves as the old man shuffled through a pocket of them gathered in the lea of some protruding rock by vagrant winds. Then all was still. He did not guess that Holton had been anxious that these sounds should reach him; that he had stumbled down the trail with awkward feet with no thought in his mind but to be certain that the sounds should reach him. Such was the case, however, and, after he felt sure that the crouching mountaineer above must be convinced that he had gone on to the valley, the old man turned, catlike, re-ascended with a skill as great as Lorey's own, and, with not a sound to warn the mountaineer that he had retraced any of his steps, took cautious place behind a rock upon the very edge of the open space where, when Layson came, he felt quite sure a tragedy would be enacted.

Then Layson came blithely up the trail. He had gone through the engineer's report with care. The coal prospects included the girl's land. He was full of rare elation at thought of the good luck which had descended on the little mountain-maid, full of pleasant plans for a bright future from none of which she was omitted.

His dreams were rudely interrupted as Joe Lorey stepped ominously from behind the rock where he had waited for him.

"Hold up your hands!" the mountaineer commanded, with his rifle levelled at the advancing youth.

"Joe Lorey!" exclaimed Layson.

"You know what air between us. Your time air come. If you want to pray, do it quick, for my finger air itchin' to pull th' trigger."

Layson's blood and breeding told, in this emergency. He did not flinch a whit. "I'm ready," he said calmly. "I'm not afraid to die, though it's hard to meet death at the hands of a coward."

"Coward!" said the mountaineer, amazed. "You call me that?"

"The man who shoots another in cold blood, giving him no chance for his life, deserves no better name."

This appealed to Lorey. So had his father died--at the hands of one who killed him in cold blood, giving him no chance for his life. "You shan't die callin' me that!" he cried. He leaned his rifle against a nearby rock, threw his knife upon the ground beside it, pulled off his coat, and thus, unarmed, advanced upon his enemy. "We're ekal now," he said with grim intensity, and pointed to the chasm through which ran the stream which made Madge Brierly's refuge an island. "That gully air a hundred feet straight down," he said, "an' its bottom air kivered with rocks. When we're through, your body or mine'll lay there. Air you ready?"

Holton, tense with excitement, was watching every move of the two men from his hidden vantage point. Upon his face was the expression of an animal of prey.

"Ready!" said Frank, quietly.

It was a terrific struggle which ensued. The trained muscles of the lowland athlete were matched against the lithe thews of the mountaineer so evenly that, for a time, there was doubt of what the outcome might be. Holton, watching, watching, thrilled with every second of it. Little he cared which man won; the best thing which possibly could happen, for his own good, he reflected, would be that both should crash down to the bottom of the gully locked in one of their bear-hugs, to fall together on the jagged rocks below. The fierce breathing of the contestants, the shuffle of their struggling feet upon the ground, the occasional involuntary groan from one man or the other as his adversary crushed him in embrace so painful that an exclamation could not be suppressed, were all music to the ears of the old man behind the rock. Both youths were perils to him. Let them kill each other. He would be the gainer, whatever the outcome of the battle.

Suddenly Frank's foot slipped on a rolling pebble. Instantly Lorey had taken advantage of the mishap, and, with a quick wrench, thrown him crashing to the earth. He lay there, scarcely breathing, utterly unconscious.

The mountaineer bent over him, ready to meet the first sign of revival with renewed attack, his bloodshot eyes strained on the face of the young man upon the ground. Then, anxious to be satisfied that his prostrate enemy was not feigning, he knelt by him and peered into his face, placed his hand upon his chest above his heart, felt his pulse with awkward fingers. He wondered, now, if he had not killed him, outright, for Frank's head had struck the ground with a terrific impact. But Layson's nostrils soon began to dilate and contract with a spasmodic breathing. He still lived.

Rendered careless by the excitement of the moment, Joe again yielded to the habit engendered by much solitude and spoke his thoughts aloud.

"It'll be long afore he'll stir," he muttered. "I'll throw him down into th' gully."

He rose, and, going to the side of the ravine, peered over with a fearful curiosity at the brawling torrent, cut into foam-ribbons by a horde of knife-edged rocks. Then he went to Layson and stretched out his hand to grasp his shoulder.

Occurred a psychological phenomenon. He found his courage fail at thought of laying hands upon the man as he was stretched there helpless.

"I--I can't touch him!" he exclaimed. "It'd be--why, it'd be like handlin' th' dead!"

He drew back, nonplussed, ashamed of his own timidity, yet unable to overcome it. He had felled the man and meant to kill him, yet, now, he could not bring himself to lay a hand upon him.

The thought then flashed into his mind of the dreadful contents of his old game-sack.

"Th' bomb," he said. "Th' dynamighty bomb that I was savin' for th' revenuers! Let that finish out th' man as set 'em onto me!"

He took the bomb from the old sack with trembling fingers, laid it by Frank's side and, with a match which flickered because the hands which held it were unsteady as a palsied man's, set fire to the fuse. Then he drew off to one side.

"Now, burn!" he said, with set teeth and lowering brow. "Burn! Burn!"

For a second he stood there, watching the sparking sputter of the powder as it slowly ate its way along the little paper tube. Then, suddenly, a dreadful thought occurred to him. The girl! What if Madge Brierly should come to meet the lowlander before the bomb exploded, should see him lying there, should hurry to him, frightened, and get there just in time to--

He shuddered. He must protect the girl he loved! She could reach the side of the endangered man only by means of the small bridge. But one rope held it in position above the deep, precipitous-sided gully.

He raised his rifle to his shoulder. It was a hard shot, one which most men would have deemed impossible, but there was a star in line. He fired. The bridge crashed down, a ruin, the severed rope now dangling limply, freed of the burden it had held for many years.

"She's safe!" said he.

For another instant he stood studying the spluttering fuse. From what he had seen at the railroad workings he knew it was destined to burn long enough so that many workmen could get out of danger before the spark reached the strong explosive in the cartridge. He need not hurry.

"In three minutes it'll all be ended," he reflected. "He's as helpless as a baby; he can't strike back, now; it's no more nor he deserves. I'm goin'."

He straightened up and would have hurried off, had not, at just that moment, the sweet voice of the girl he loved rung through the brooding, fragrant evening air, in song.

It brought him to himself, it filled him with a horrified realization of the foulness of the deed which he was contemplating.

"No--no!" said he. "Why, I'd be the coward that he called me!"

He hurried to the fuse and, with trembling eagerness, stamped out the spark which, now, was creeping close indeed to that point where it would have blossomed into the terrifying flower of death.

"I'll fight him ag'in," he said; and then, addressing the now extinguished fuse, the harmless cartridge of explosive: "You lie thar and prove ter him I ain't no coward!"

He hurried down the trail.

Holton, vastly disappointed, crept out from his hiding place. "The fool!" he muttered. "Oh, the fool! That thar little spark would a' put me even an' made me safe fer life! An' it war lighted--it war lighted!"

His regret was keen. He raged there like a madman robbed of his intended prey. Then, suddenly:

"But--who'll believe him when he says he put it out? I'll--do it!"

He hastily took out a match, struck it, relighted the dead fuse.

"It'll be his work, not mine!" he thought, exultantly, as he paused to see that the fuse would surely burn.

As he turned to hasten from the spot he caught a glimpse of something white across the gully at the thresh-hold of the girl's cabin. For a second this was terrifying, but he quickly regained poise. The bridge was gone. She could not reach the side of the endangered man to save him, she could not reach the mainland to pursue him and discover his identity. He fled.

The girl was worried by the long delay in Layson's coming. For fully half an hour she had been listening for his cheery hail--that hail which had, of late, come to mean so much to her--as she worked about her household tasks. The last words he had said to her had hinted at such unimagined possibilities of riches, of education, of delirious delights to come, that her impatience was but natural; and, besides this, Joe's words had worried her. She did not think the mountaineer would ever really let his jealousy lead him to a foul attack upon his rival, but his words had worried her. She stood upon her doorstep, hand above her eyes, and peered across the gorge toward where the trail debouched into the little clearing.

Nothing was in sight there, and her gaze wandered along the little rocky field, in aimless scrutiny. Finally it chanced upon the prostrate form of the young man.

"What's that lyin' thar?" she thought, intensely startled. And then, after another moment's peering: "Why, it's Mr. Frank!"

She was amazed and frightened. Then her eye caught the little sputtering of sparks along the fuse. It further startled her.

"It's Mr. Frank and somethin's burnin' close beside him!"

Suspicion flashed into her mind like lightning, followed, almost instantly, by firm conviction.

"It's a fuse," she cried, "an' thar by him is th' bomb! It's Joe Lorey's work! Oh, oh--"

She sprang down the rough path toward the place where, ever since she could remember, the little bridge had swung. Now, though, it was gone.

"The bridge!" she cried. "The bridge! It's gone! I can't cross! I've got to see him die!"

Her frantic eyes caught sight of the frayed rope, dangling from the firm supports which had so long held up the bridge by means of it. Instantly her quick mind saw the only chance there was to save the man whom, now, she knew she loved. She sprang for the rope and caught it, gave herself a mighty push with both her agile feet, and, hanging above certain death if hold should fail or rope break, swung across the chasm and found foothold on the mainland.

In another second she was at the side of the unconscious man. Another and she had the cartridge, sputtering fuse and all, in her right hand, another and the deadly thing was hurtling to the bottom of the deep ravine, whence an almost immediately ensuing crashing boom told her that she had not arrived a moment sooner than had been essential to the salvation of the man she loved.

She knelt by Frank, pulled his head up to her knee, chafed at his insensate hands, and called to him wildly, fearing that he was dead.

CHAPTER XII

Joe Lorey was unhappy in his mountains. After the visiting party had gone down from Layson's camp, and, in course of time, Layson himself had followed them because of the approach of the great race which was to make or mar his fortunes, the man breathed easier, although their coming and the subsequent events had made, he knew, impressions on his life which never could be wiped away. He hated Layson none the less because he had departed. He argued that he had not gone until he viciously had stolen that thing which he, Lorey, valued most: the love of beautiful Madge Brierly. He brooded constantly upon this, neglecting his small mountain farm, spending almost all his time at his illegal trade of brewing untaxed whisky in his hidden still, despite the girl's continual urgings to give up the perilous occupation before it was too late. He had told her that he would, if she would marry him; now that she would not, he told her surlily that he would continue to defy the law even if he knew that every "revenuer" in the state was on his trail. He was conscious that there was real danger; he believed that Layson knew about the still and that the bitter enmity resulting from the fight which had so nearly proved his death might prompt him to betrayal of the secret; but with the stubbornness of the mountaineer he clung doggedly to his illegal apparatus in the mountain-cave, kept doggedly at the illegal work he did with it. It was characteristic of the man, his forbears and his breed in general, that, now, when he knew that deadly danger well might threaten, he sent more moonshine whisky from the still than ever had gone from it in like length of time, either in his father's day or his.

That his actual and only dangerous enemy was Holton, he did not, for an instant, guess. He knew of not the slightest reason why this stranger should include him in the hatred he had sworn he felt for Layson--that hatred which, he had assured him, was as bitter as his own. He would have been as much astonished as dismayed had he known that Holton's almost instant action, upon arriving at the county-seat, had been to make a visit to the local chief of the Revenue-Service-- cautiously, at night, for to be known as an informer might have cost his life at other hands than Lorey's, would have made the mountain for far miles blaze vividly with wrath against him.

So, defiant of the man he thought to be his foe, unconscious of the hatred of the man who really was, Lorey was working in his still when a small boy, sent up from a cabin far below, dashed, breathless, to him with the news that revenue-men were actually upon their way in his direction. He had scarcely time to put his fire out, hide the lighter portions of his apparatus and flee to a safe hiding-place, near-by, before, clambering with lithe skill and caution almost equal to his own along the rocky pathways of the mountain-side, armed like soldiers scouting in a hostile country, cool-eyed as Indians, hard-faced as executioners, they actually appeared.

For a time, as Lorey watched their progress from his covert, he held his rifle levelled, held his finger on its trigger, determined to kill them in their tracks; and it was no thrill of mercy for the men or fear of consequences to himself which saved their lives. It was rather that he did not wish further to risk his liberty until he had had opportunity to glance along the gleaming barrel of his rifle as it was pointed at Frank Layson's heart.

After the men had gone he went back to his still to view the ruins they had left behind them. His wrath was terrible. Madge, who had, of course, learned what had happened almost instantly, for the still was scarcely out of hearing of her cabin, tried vainly to console, to calm him. He turned on her with a rage of which, in all her life among hot-tempered mountaineers, she had never seen the equal, and chokingly swore vengeance on the man who had given the information which had resulted in the raid.

"They come straight to th' still," he told her, "never falterin', never wonderin' if, maybe, they was on th' right path. Ev'ry inch o' th' hull way had been mapped out for 'em, an' they didn't make a mis-step from th' valley to th' very entrance o' th' cave. I'll git th' chap that planned their course out for 'em thataway! I'll git 'im, Madge! I'll git 'im, sure!"

Her heart sank in her breast like lead. She knew perfectly whom Lorey meant. She knew as perfectly that Layson never had informed upon the moonshiner, but she also knew that Heaven itself could not, then, convince the man of that.

"Who do you mean you'll git, Joe?" she faltered, hoping against hope that she was wrong in her suspicions.

"You know well enough," he answered. "Who would I mean but that damn' furriner, Frank Layson? He warn't satisfied with comin' here an' stealin' you away from me! He had to put th' revenuers on th' track o' th' old still that was my dad's afore me, an' has been th' one thing, siden you, I've ever keered fer in my life."

"You're wrong, Joe," she insisted. "You're shore wrong. Frank Layson'd never do a coward's trick like that!"

"He done it!" Lorey answered doggedly. "He done it, an' as there is a God in Heaven he air goin' to pay th' price fer doin' it!"

With that he stalked off down the trail, his rifle held as ever in the crook of his elbow, his brows as black as human brows could be.

For a time she sat there on a rock, gazing after him, half-stupefied, with eyes wide, terror-stricken. What could a mere girl do to avert the dreadful tragedy impending? Tireless as he was, she knew that he could keep upon the trail for twenty-four hours without a pause, and that such travelling, with the lifts which he would get from mountain teamsters, would take him to the home of the man whose life he had determined to snuff out at any hazard. Beside herself with fright for Frank, she sped back to her cabin, took what food was ready-cooked and could be bundled up to carry on the journey, put on her heaviest shoes and started for the door. But, suddenly, the thought flashed through her mind that, even as Joe Lorey was bound down the trails to meet his rival, so would she be bound down them to meet her own. She could not bear the thought of facing Barbara Holton, clad, as she was now, in rough, half-shapeless, mountain-homespun. She made another bundle, larger than the one which held her food, by many times, and, when she finally set off, this bundle held the finery which she had so laboriously prepared in the mad hope of rivaling the work of the bluegrass belle's accomplished city dressmakers.

Down in the bluegrass home of the ancient Layson family all was excitement in anticipation of the race which was to mean so much to the fortunes of the young master of the fine old mansion which, with pillared porticos and mighty chimneys, dominated the whole section. Layson's heart was filled with confidence whenever he went to the stables to view the really startling beauty of the lovely animal on which his hope was pinned; it sunk into despair, when, seated in his study in the house, away from her, he counted up the cost of all which he would lose if she did not run first in the great race.

None but the Colonel, Miss Alathea and himself had an idea of the real magnitude of the stakes dependant on Queen Bess. Upon the glossy shoulders of the lovely mare rested, indeed, a great burden of responsibility. If she won she would not only secure the large purse for the owner, but be salable for a price which would enable him to take advantage, fully, of the offer which the syndicate had made to develop his coal lands. If she failed--well, the fortunes of the house of Layson would be seriously shattered.

No wonder, then, that Uncle Neb, in whom his master's confidence was absolute, had strict injunctions closely to guard the mare. The faithful negro watched her with a vigilance which was scarcely less unremitting in the daytime than it was at night when he slept upon the very straw which bedded her.

Miss Alathea, intensely prejudiced against horse-racing and the gambling which invariably goes with it, by the Colonel's wasted life and her own ensuing loneliness, nevertheless prayed night and day that Queen Bess would be victorious, for Frank had finally refused, point-blank, to let her risk her fortune in the scheme for the development of his coal-lands, and so, if the mare lost and the eastern firm refused to purchase her at the large price which would enable him to join the syndicate, his great chance would be gone. Perhaps not once in the world's history had any maiden-lady, constitutionally opposed to betting and the race-track, given as much thought to an impending contest between horses on which great sums were certain to be won and lost, as Miss Alathea did, these days.

And if Miss Alathea was excited, what should be said about the gallant Colonel? Every day he visited the Layson place; every day he scrutinized the mare with wise and anxious eyes; every day he from his soul assured her owner and her owner's aunt that it was quite impossible that she should lose; every day he cautioned Neb, her guardian, to let no human being, whom he did not know and whom he and his master had not every cause to trust implicitly, approach the splendid beast. Wise in the ways of race-tracks and the unscrupulous men who have, unfortunately, thrown the sport of kings into sad disrepute, he feared some treachery continually.

Neb scarcely left the stable-yard, by day, unless the mare went with him, by night he slept so that he could, by reaching out a wrinkled, ebon hand, actually touch her glossy hide. He fed her himself with oats and hay which he examined with the utmost care before they found her manger or her rack; he watered her himself with water from a well within the stable and guarded by locked doors, drawn in a pail which, invariably, he rinsed with boiling water before he filled it up for her. No drugs should reach that mare if *he* could help it! None but himself or his "Marse Frank" was under any circumstances permitted to get on her back. If watchfulness could possibly preserve the mare unharmed and in fine shape until the day of the great race, Neb plainly meant to see that this was done. Even the amateur brass-band and glee-club into which he had organized the stable-boys and other negro lads about the place, and of which he acted as drum-major--the proudest moment of his life were when he donned the moth-eaten old shako which was his towering badge of leadership--must practice nowhere save within the stable-yard, where he could train them and, at the same time, keep watchful eyes upon Queen Bess' quarters.

The negroes, young and old, about the place, indeed, were wild with their enthusiasm for the mare. The day before the race a delegation of them, full of eagerness, met Neb as he came out of the stable.

"Say, Unc Neb," said one of them, "we-all's made a pool."

"Pool on de races?"

"Uh-huh! An' we-all wants to know jes' what we ought to put ouah money on."

They well knew what he would say.

"Queen Bess, fo' suah," he answered, to their vast delight. "Queen Bess ebery time. She's fit to run fo' huh life."

The boys accepted the suggestion with a shout, and he was about to enter into one of the long dissertations on the strong points of his equine darling, when he was informed that some stranger was approaching. He peered down the road with his old eyes, but could not recognize the visitor.

"Who is it?" he asked one of the black lads.

"Marse Holton."

"Marse Holton!" he repeated dryly. "Run along, now, honiest. Unc' Neb gwine be busy. I won't hab dat ar Marse Holton pryin' round dat mare. Hoodoo her fo' suah." He sidled to the stable door, and, careful to see that his bent body hid the operation from the coming visitor, turned the key in the big lock. The key he then slipped into his capacious trousers pocket.

"Hello, Neb," said Holton, affably, as he came up.

"Ebenin', suh." Neb added nothing to this greeting and went nonchalantly to a distant bench to sit down on it carelessly.

"I say, Neb," said Holton, "I expect to do a little betting, so I thought I'd jest drop over and take a look at Layson's mare."

Neb sat immovable upon his bench. At first, indeed, he did not even speak, but, finally, he looked at Holton calmly, took the key out of his pocket, tossed it in the air, caught it as it came down, put it back into his pocket and dryly said: "T'ink not, suh."

Holton, paying no attention to him, had gone on to the stable-door and tried it. Finding it to be fast locked, he turned back toward the darkey. "The door's locked, Neb," he said.

"Knowed dat afore, suh," Neb replied.

Holton was nettled by his nonchalance. "Open that door!" he ordered.

"Not widout Marse Holton's ohduhs, suh," Neb answered calmly.

"What do you mean?" demanded Holton, angrily.

"Jus' what I say, suh."

Holton made a slightly threatening movement toward him, but Neb did not even wink.

"Don't git riled, suh--bad fo' de livuh, suh."

Holton, now, was very angry. "Look here," he said, advancing on the aged negro angrily. "Do you dare insult a friend and neighbor of Mr. Layson?"

Neb slowly rose and answered with some dignity: "I dares obey Marse Frank's plain ohduhs, suh. Dat mare represents full twenty-fi' thousan' dolluhs to him" (Neb rolled the handsome figures lovingly upon his tongue), "an' dere's thousan's more'll be bet on huh to-morruh." He looked at Holton with but thinly veiled contempt. "Plenty men 'u'd risk deir wuthless lives to drug huh."

"Oh, shucks!" said Holton, trying to control his temper because of his great eagerness to get in to the mare. "She would be safe with me; you know it."

"I knows Marse Frank hab barred ebery window an' sealed ebery doah but dis one, an' gib me ohduhs to let no one in 'cept he is by. I stan's by dem ohduhs while dere's bref in my ol' body."

Holton was infuriated. "It's lucky for you I'm not your master!"

"Dat's what I t'ink, suh."

"If you **was** my nigger, I'd teach you perliteness with a black-snake whip! I'll see what Layson'll say to such sass as you've gin me. Jest you wait till you hear from him."

Neb was not impressed by the man's wrath. "Huhd from him afoah, suh. Oh, I'll wait, I'll wait."

He went up to the stable-door, unlocked it and stood in the open portal. Holton would have followed him, but Neb began to close the door.

"You'll wait, too, suh," said the negro, grinning, "on de outside, suh."

He closed and locked the door on the inside.

Holton was beside himself with wrath. "Damn him! Damn him!" he exclaimed. "Damn him and damn his proud young puppy of a master! I'll ruin him! I'll set my foot on him and smash him, yet!"

Baffled, he walked down the drive.

"There's a way," he told himself. "It's bold and risky, but nobody'll suspicion me. I've kept straight here in the bluegrass. The mountains and all as ever knowed me thar are far away!"

But all who had known him in the mountains were not as far away as he supposed. Even as he spoke a dusty, weary figure in worn homespun, carrying a mammoth bundle, limping sadly upon bruised and blistered feet, came through the shrubbery, approaching the great stables from the far side of the big house-lot. Holton looked at this wayfarer with amazement.

"Madge Brierly!" he cried. "Gal, what are you a-doin' here?"

"Don't know's I've got any call to tell you," Madge replied, almost as much astonished at the sight of him as he had been at sight of her. Then she smiled roguishly at him. "Maybe you'll find out, though."

"I tell you this ain't no place for you," he admonished her. "Lordy! They takes up folks that looks like you, for vagrants. Take my advice, turn back to the mountings."

She looked at him with that same smile, still unimpressed.

For no reason which he could have well explained the man was almost panic-stricken in his keen anxiety to get the girl away from the old Layson homestead and the possibility of meeting those who dwelt therein.

"Here, if you'll go," he added, and thrust his hand into his pocket, "I'll give you money--money to help you on your way."

Still she smiled at him with that aggravating, meaning smile; that smile which he could by no means fathom and of which she scarcely knew the meaning. "No," she said, "I don't want your money. You couldn't hire me to leave the bluegrass till I've seen Frank Layson."

Seeing that she was determined, unable to conjecture what she had come down for, realizing, upon second thought, that it was most improbable that she had any tale to tell of him, he reluctantly gave way. "As you will, then," he said slowly. "But let me warn you that you won't be welcome hyar. You'll learn the difference between the mounting and the bluegrass folks. You'd better think it over and turn back."

"I'll not," said she.

As he walked disgustedly away she watched him curiously. "I wonder why he is so sot on makin' me go back?" she mused. "Maybe he air right in sayin' that I won't be welcome; but I'll do my duty, just th' same!"

Neb came out from the stable. The girl saw him with delight. "Dellaw!" she said. "How tired I be! Howdy, Uncle Neb; howdy!"

"Sakes alive!" he cried. "It's de frenomenom, come down frum de mountains! Howdy, honey, howdy!" He hurried toward her and saw that she was near to tears from weariness and the strain of what she had gone through and what she had to tell. "Why, chil', what's de mattuh?"

"Pebble in my shoe," she answered, and busied herself as if removing one. "All right in a minute. This air a long way from th' mountings."

"Honey, you don't mean you **walked**!"

"Had to. Wings ain't growed, yet. Say; I've come to bring a word to Mr. Frank. Is he to home?" She motioned toward the stable, which was the finest building she had ever seen.

"Yes; but he don't lib dar, honey."

"Don't he? Who does, then?"

"Queen Bess."

"Queen Bess!" The girl was thunderstruck; her worry choked her. She knew Frank owned a blooded mare, but did not know her name, and she had but vaguely heard of queens. "Well--air she to home?"

"Yes; an' Marse Frank, an' Miss 'Lethe, an' Miss Barbara's comin', purty soon, to see huh."

"Miss Barbarous!" said Madge, aroused by the mere mention of the girl who, from the start, she had recognized, instinctively, as her real enemy. It had been thought of her, alone, which had made her bear the weary burden of the bundle on the long journey from the mountains. "I'd like to fix a little, 'fore she comes. I got some idees o' fashion from her, when she was up thar, an' I been workin' ev'ry minute I could spare, since then, on a new dress. Ain't thar some place I can go to fashion up before they come?"

The old negro was acutely sympathetic. He disliked Miss Barbara and liked the mountain girl. His old black head, thick as it was, sometimes, had quickly recognized the fact that Barbara regarded Madge as one to be despised, humiliated, while his master treated her with much consideration and thought highly of her. He did not like the daughter of Horace Holton any better than he liked the man himself. If he could help the mountain girl he would. The only place where she could possibly find privacy, without going to the house, was in the stable with the race-horse. He would have trusted no one else on earth with her; to distrust Madge, however, did not once occur to him.

"Missy," he said slowly, "I reckon you can go right in dar wid Queen Bess."

She was a bit appalled. "Maybe she wouldn't like it," she objected.

"She won't keer if you don't go too close."

"I'm kinder 'feared."

"Don't gib her no chance to kick. You's all right, den."

"Kick!" said the girl, amazed. Kicking did not seem to her to fit the character of queens.

Neb unlocked the stable door. "Or bite," he added.

"Bite! Dellaw!" the girl exclaimed, still more amazed. How little she had learned of royalty up in the mountains!

The aged negro threw the door wide open. "Go in, honey, now; go in," he said.

"I'm skeered!" she said, and tiptoed to the stable door. She peered in cautiously. Then she turned and faced him with much-puzzled eyes. "I don't see nothin' but a hoss," she said.

"Uh-huh; dat's Queen Bess." Old Neb stood chuckling, looking at her.

"Queen Bess is Mister Frank's race-hoss!" she cried, delighted by the revelation. "Well, now, I feel to home." She went into the stable with her bundle, half-closed the door and then peeped out at Neb. "You won't let any one come in?"

He held the key up reassuringly. "Don't you see I's got de key, honey?"

"I'd feel safer if I had that key myself," said she, and snatched it from him. An instant later and the door was closed and locked on the inside.

Neb was alarmed. He had disobeyed plain orders in letting her go in at all. For him to let that key out of his possession was a further violation which he feared to be responsible for. He pounded on the door. "Open de doah, honey," he implored. "I mus' hab dat key!"

"All right," said she, "soon's I am dressed."

He fell back from the door dismayed. "De Lawd help me!" he groaned. "What's I gwine ter do? An' I war so mighty firm 'bout dat key wid Marse Holton!" He paced the space before the stable door in agitation. "But I reckon she'll be t'rough befo' Marse Frank comes," he comforted himself.

She was not, though. While Neb still paced the stable yard in acute worry, Frank, Miss Alathea, Barbara and Holton came toward him in a laughing group. He almost fainted.

"Here we are, Neb," his master cried, "ready for a look at Queen Bess."

"Yessah, yessah, pwesently!" Neb stammered, and would have paled had nature made provision for such exhibition of his feelings. "I jus' nachelly hab got to speak to dem ar stable boys a minute, fust. Jus' 'scuse me fo' a minute, suh." He vanished hurriedly, hoping that by this diversion he could gain a little time for Madge and for himself.

Layson gazed after him with some astonishment, then went and tried the stable door. "Of course the door's locked," he explained, annoyed, "but he'll be back here in a minute."

Miss Alathea smiled. The attitude of the young master toward the aged negro often was amusing to her. She liked to watch the constant evidence of that rare affection which formed an inseparable bond between them.

Suddenly she heard the crunching of a man's heavy footsteps on the gravel, back of them. Turning, she saw that the newcomer was the Colonel, and the Colonel in great haste. This was most impressive, for the Colonel did not often hurry.

"Here comes the Colonel, Frank," she said, "and see how he is hurrying!"

"Something's up," her nephew answered, "when the Colonel hurries." Then, as the horseman came up to them: "Why, Colonel, what's the matter?"

"A shock! A regular shock! As I came from Lexington, just now, I saw you standing here, so I sent the boy on with the buggy and cut across to meet you. Just as I passed the thicket by the spring I caught a glimpse of a man, who then vanished like a ghost, but I swear that man was that lank mountaineer, Joe Lorey, and that he tried to keep out of my sight."

"Joe Lorey!" Frank exclaimed. "What can he want down here?"

"Who knows? Maybe to finish the work he began in the mountains."

"More than likely," Holton ventured. "A rifleshot in the back, or a match touched to a building."

"*I* don't believe it," Frank said stoutly. "The man who laid down his weapons to give me a fair, square fight, wouldn't stoop to things like that."

"'Pears to me the man who fired that bomb 'u'd do most anythin'," said Holton.

"That was in a fit of anger. Lorey swore to Madge that he thought better of his impulse to do murder, stamped upon the burning fuse, and believed that he had put it out, and I believe him."

He saw, now, that his aunt was badly frightened, and cautioned the other men. "Not another word about him, now, at any rate, or Aunt 'Lethe won't once close her eyes to-night."

"Well," said the Colonel, quite agreeing with him and hastening to change the subject, "here's something much more interesting, anyway. A letter from the Company. Looks official and important."

Frank took the letter, opened it and gazed at it in some dismay. "I should think so," he exclaimed. "An assessment of $15,000 on my stock."

"Fifteen thousand devils!"

"No; fifteen thousand dollars."

The Colonel took the letter from his hand and looked at it with worried eyes. "And you've got to meet it, Frank, or lose what you've put in."

Miss Alathea went to her nephew anxiously. "You'll sell Queen Bess, now, won't you?" she implored. "You could pay it then. Best sell her."

The young man stood there, deep in worried thought. "If I were quite convinced of the Company's good faith in everything, I'd risk it all, even the loss of Woodlawn, my old home," he answered.

Neb now appeared from around a corner of the stable, evidently having decided that the girl had had enough time for her toilet, or afraid to wait another minute. His appearance created a diversion.

"Here, Neb," said Frank, "we've had enough nonsense. Let's see Queen Bess, now."

Neb looked anxiously for signs that Madge was ready to see visitors, he listened at the door. He saw no sign, he heard no signal. He was scared, but he was faithful to his promise to the girl. He planted his old back against the door. "Now de trouble am commencin'!" he assured himself.

Holton looked at him with a sour smile. "I hope," he said to Frank, "that you'll have better luck nor me. Neb wouldn't open that door for me."

"Dem was yo' ohduhs, suh," said Neb, appealing to his master.

"An' he was powerful sassy in the bargain," Holton went on, full of malice, hoping to make Neb suffer for defying him.

Layson, however, much as he was now annoyed by the old darky's hesitation about opening the stable door for him, himself, did not propose to chide him for having kept his trust and held it closed to others. "You mustn't mind Neb," he said to Holton. "He's a privileged character around here. I had told him to admit no one, and, as usual, he obeyed my orders blindly."

"Yes, suh," Neb declared, delighted, "went it blind, suh."

"His obedience," his master went on boastingly, "is really phenomenal. He wouldn't open that door for anybody. He'd guard the key with his own life." He turned to Neb. "Wouldn't you, now, Neb?"

Neb was disconcerted. It was true enough that from most people he certainly would have guarded that key with his life. But at that moment there was one within the stable from whom he had *not* guarded it. "Yes--yessah!" he said hesitantly. And as he said it he would have given anything he had if he could have laid his hands upon that self-same key.

Frank smiled at him. "But I suppose you'll let *me* have a look at her."

"Yes--yessuh--in a--in a minute, suh."

Layson was annoyed. "Why not at once?" He was beginning to be frightened. Could something Neb was trying to hide have happened to the mare?

"Bekase--bekase--" Ned stammered, "well, to tell de trufe, suh, bekase I is afeared she ain't quite dressed."

"Not dressed! The mare not dressed! Have you lost your senses? Open that door--quick!"

"Marse Frank, I cain't. I nachully jus' cain't."

Holton was enjoying this. "You see," he said, "he won't open it for nobody. Not even for th' man as owns it an' th' mare behind it."

"Give me the key!" said Frank.

"De key--de key--" Neb stammered.

"I said the key!"

The old negro advanced pitifully. "Fo' de lawd, Marse Frank, I hasn't got it!"

"He'd guard it with his life!" said Holton, with deep sarcasm.

"Where is it?" Frank demanded.

"In dar," said Neb, and pointed to the stable.

Layson, astonished and annoyed beyond the power of words by the old negro's strange performance, fearful of the safety of his mare, entirely puzzled, sprang toward the stable window and was about to pull himself up by the ledge so that he might look in.

Neb seized him and pulled him from the aperture with a desperate agility which strained his aged limbs. "Fo' de Lawd's sake, now, Marse Frank," he cried, "don't yo' dare look t'rough dat stable winder!"

Frank, now, was badly frightened. "Is there some one in there with Queen Bess?" he asked.

"A young pusson to see you, suh," Neb admitted.

"And you let that person have the key?"

"No, suh; it were taken from me."

Layson was in panic. "Heaven knows," he exclaimed, "what can have happened here!" He rushed to the stable door and pounded on it with his fists. "Open at once, or I'll break in the door," he cried.

Neb, now, had gone up to the window and looked through it with desperate glance. What he saw was reassuring. He turned back toward his master smiling. "Hol' on, Marse Frank, de young pusson am a-comin' out," he said.

"Well," said Layson, threateningly, "I'm ready for him." He braced himself to spring upon some malefactor.

The door opened and Madge appeared before their astonished eyes, garbed in a gown which she had fashioned after that which Barbara had worn up in the hills.

"Madge!" cried Frank, amazed.

The Colonel, laughing, approached the girl with outstretched hand; Neb, relieved, dived through the stable door; Miss Alathea, who had been under a great strain while the dramatic little scene had been in progress, dropped limply on Neb's bench.

Madge, with a retentive memory of the way Miss "Barbarous" had greeted her back in the mountains, stepped toward that much-astonished maiden, opened her red parasol straight in her face, and courtesied to the rest.

"Howdy, folks; howdy!" she said, happily.

CHAPTER XIII

The party stood, nonplussed. Frank was first to show signs of recovery, and, after a moment of completely dazed astonishment, advanced to Madge with hand outstretched. Her appearance, astonishing as it had been, had been as great a relief as he had ever known in all his life. Neb's worry and insubordination had filled him with the keenest apprehension. But he had no doubts of Madge. If she had been there with the mare, the mare was certainly all right, no matter how puzzling the affair might seem to be upon its surface.

"Why, little one, this is, indeed, a great surprise and pleasure!" he exclaimed, with sincere gallantry.

Madge looked at him with doubtful eyes, from which the doubt, however, was fast clearing. "Oh, say; are you-uns r'ally glad to see me?"

"No one could be more welcome," he assured her, and the honest pleasure in his eyes convinced her that he did not speak for mere politeness' sake.

And now Miss Alathea, recovering from the shock of all that had preceded the girl's unexpected appearance, went to her cordially. "We are more than glad, my child," she told her.

"Glad's no name for it," the gallant Colonel said, advancing in his turn.

There could be no doubt of the sincerity of any one who, thus far, had expressed a welcome for her; but the voice which now came coldly from Miss Barbara was less convincing. She did not approach the mountain girl, but sat somewhat superciliously upon a bench and spoke frigidly. "It is an unexpected pleasure."

Madge, not trained to hide her feelings under softened words, turned on her angrily. "Humph! I wasn't askin' you," she said. Then, to the others: "I didn't know but what my droppin' in, permiskus like--"

"A Kentuckian's friends," said Frank, "are always welcome."

"Friends from the word go, remember," said the Colonel.

"Thankee, Colonel," said the girl. "We'll have that race, some day; but I won't ride agin you if you ride Queen Bess. Oh, wouldn't I like to see her go!"

"So you shall," said Frank. "Neb, is she ready?"

"Yessuh; all saddled, sur, an' bridled."

"Oh, let me bring her out," cried Madge. "I'd love to."

"Lawsy, honey," said the negro, "you couldn't bring her out. She's dat fretful an' dat nervous dat she'd kill yo', suah."

"Get out, Neb!" Madge cried, scornfully. "I ain't afeard of her. Wild things allays has made friends with me. I've never seen a horse so skeery that I couldn't manage him--couldn't make him foller me."

She pushed the hesitating Neb out of her path and went into the stable.

Layson, who was for the moment, at a distance, had not heard all her talk with Neb, but saw her as she went into the stall where none but he, himself, and Neb, dared go, and it was stable talk that, soon or late, Queen Bess would prove to be a man killer!

"Neb, stop her! She'll be killed!" he cried.

Neb ran, as fast as his old legs would carry him, into the stable; Frank hurried to the stable door.

"Madge! Madge!" he cried, and then: "Why--look! The mare is following her as might a kitten!"

He stepped aside and Madge came from the stable with Queen Bess behind her, ears pricked forward eagerly as she kept her eyes on Madge's pursed up, cooing lips, head dropped, neck stretched in graceful fashion, lifting her dainty feet as proudly as ever did the queen whom she was named for.

"Come on, you beauty!" the girl cried. "Oh, it would be like heaven to ride you; and I could do it, too!"

"Take her to the track, Neb," Layson ordered. "I'll follow and give her her exercise."

Madge, unable to resist the impulse which was thrilling her with longing, motioned Neb away as he approached to take the mare. "Go 'way! Go 'way!" she said. Then, to the mare: "Come on, you dear, come on." She went on slowly, while the mare, in calm docility, trailed after her. The spectators, who knew the beast, gazed spellbound.

Constantly the girl's pleased eyes were on the beautiful creature following. Never had she seen so perfect an animal; never had she known one giving such plain signs of high intelligence. The mare's big eyes, broad forehead, delicate muzzle, arching neck, strong withers, mighty flanks, and slender ankles marked her, to the veriest novice, a thoroughbred of thoroughbreds; her docile and obedient march showed what seemed like an almost magic power in the delighted mountain maid. Every drop of blood in the girl's body tingled with excitement, all her muscles thrilled with mad desire to mount the wondrous beast and be away as on the wind's wings. She could imagine what the mare's long strides would be, she could imagine how exhilerating she would find the steady, perfect motion of the mighty back.

"Oh, I can't stand it!" she exclaimed, at length. "I've got to do it!"

She paused, and eagerly the mare stepped up to her, nuzzleing her caressing hand. Then, with a bound, the girl was on the graceful creature's back, landing in her place as lightly as a wind-blown thistle-down, as gracefully as a fairy horse-woman.

"Heavens!" cried Barbara. "She's on Queen Bess!"

"She'll be killed!" Miss Alathea screamed, in terror.

The Colonel, only, recognized her instantly as a born horsewoman. His expert eye observed with rare delight the ease with which she mounted, the perfect poise with which she found her seat, the absolute adjustment of her lithe young motions to the movements of the mare beneath her from the very moment she had reached her back.

"No danger; she rides like a centaur."

With the others he had stopped, with eyes for nothing but the girl before them and the splendid animal she rode. "Ah, what a jockey she would make!"

Barbara liked this exhibition of the mountain girl's abilities no better than she had liked anything which Madge had done. Her lip curled somewhat scornfully. "What a pity that her sex should bar her from that vocation!" she said coldly.

She turned to Frank, who was watching Madge with startled eyes, worried as to the result of this mad prank on both the girl and mare.

"Frank," said Barbara, "what a figure she will make to-night at your lawn-party! How your friends will laugh at her!"

Layson cast a quick, sharp glance at her. She was not advancing her own cause by trying, thus, to ridicule the mountain maiden. "I'll run the risk," he said. "She is my guest, you know, and, as such, will surely be given every consideration and courtesy by all."

"Oh, certainly," said Barbara, seeing that she had gone, perhaps, too far. "If you wish it. I should be glad to please you, once again."

"Nothing could please me more than to have you show her what kindnesses you can. I know she will feel strange and worried."

Madge, sitting Queen Bess with an ease and grace which that intelligent mare had never found in any other rider, and, now, far from them at the other end of the great training-field, absorbed the youth's delighted glances.

"Can't you forget her for an instant?" exclaimed Barbara. "You haven't been at all the same since you came back from the mountains! Once we were always together. Now I never see you unless I come over here; and no matter what I do, you don't seem to care."

Layson was uneasy. He had been aware, for a long time, that, sooner or later, a complete understanding of his changed feelings toward this girl, must, in some way, be accomplished. Now seemed a good time for it, yet he hesitated at the thought of it. But the thing had to be gone through with. "I know I used to play the tyrant, Barbara; but it wasn't a pleasant role, and I was always half-ashamed of it."

The girl flared into a passion. "What do you mean?"

"Barbara, I have had no right to go so far, no right to ask so much of you. From the bottom of my heart I beg forgiveness. Let us forget it all and just be friends again." And, even as he spoke, his eyes were wandering toward the girl whom Queen Bess had so utterly surrendered to. The mare, known since she had first been saddled, as a terror to all riders, was carrying her as gently as the veriest country hack had ever borne an old lady from the farm to market.

Barbara saw where his attention was, and resentment thrilled her. "Friends? Never! Frank Layson, I believe I hate you!"

"Oh, very well," said he, plainly not too much impressed, "if you want to be unreasonable, why, of course--"

The girl was frightened at the length to which she had permitted her ill-temper to carry her. "Oh, no, Frank," she hastily corrected, "I didn't mean that. Of course

I am your friend."

"Thank you, Barbara," said he, with a calmness which was maddening to her. "I am sure we understand each other, now." And then, still further maddening her: "I must go now, and look after Madge and dear Queen Bess. I never should forgive myself if anything should happen to the girl. But nothing will. See how splendidly she rides!"

The girl upon the horse, as if conscious of his anxiety about her, now turned her mount back toward the field-end where the onlookers were loosely grouped and came toward them at a slow and gentle canter--a gait which none had ever seen Queen Bess take before, when a stranger was upon her back. She leaped from the mare by Layson's side, and Neb, ever anxious for the welfare of his equine darling, began work without delay at rubbing Queen Bess down.

"Reckon you'll never forgive me," Madge apologized to Layson, "but I just couldn't help it. Never even saw a mare like her, afore. My pony's no-whar along-side of her. I felt like an angel sittin' on a cloud an' sailin' straight to heaven!" She turned and petted the black beauty. "Oh, you darling!"

"Got to take her in, now," Neb said, preparing to lead the mare away. He spoke apologetically as if the girl had rights which, now, should be consulted. He had never made a like concession in the past to anyone except his master.

"Go 'way, go 'way," said Madge, taking the reins from his black hand. "Ain't no use o' leadin' her--you jest watch her foller me!"

She looped the reins about the mare's arched neck, started off, and, without so much as flicking her long tail, Queen Bess fell in behind, obedient to her cooing, murmurous calls.

Frank laughed. "If," he said to the whole party, "you wish to have a look at the mare's quarters, I think Neb will now admit us."

All but the Colonel started toward the stable, but he hesitated, looking toward Miss Alathea. While the others had been spellbound by the girl and horse, he, the most enthusiastic horseman of them all, had been divided in attention between them and the lady whose notice he attracted, now, by means of sundry hems and haws.

"Miss 'Lethe, just a moment," he said softly. She paused and then went up to him. He held out a newspaper, suddenly at a loss for words, now that there was a prospect of a moment with her wholly uninterrupted. "Here," said he, a little panicky, "is a full account of the revival, sermon and all. Make your hair stand on end to read it."

She took the paper, undeceived by his small subterfuge to gain attention, but interested, as she always was in such things, in the account of the revival. "This really is interesting." She sat down on the bench, as they reached the stable-yard again, and pored above the newspaper.

In the meantime the Colonel tried to screw his courage to the sticking point. "Colonel Sandusky Doolittle," he adjured himself, "if you don't say it now, then you forever hold your peace, that's all!" He went to his buggy, which had been brought to the stable yard, and from underneath its seat took a box containing a bouquet of sweet, old-fashioned flowers. Miss Alathea, absorbed in the account of the revival, did not notice him at all. "This will do the business," he reflected. "Now, Sandusky Doolittle, keep cool, keep cool!" Nervously, as he gazed at her, his fingers worked among the flowers, dismembering them unconsciously. "A Kentucky Colonel," he was saying to himself in scorn, "afraid of a woman!" His fingers tore the flowers with new activity as his nervousness increased, making sad work with the magnificent bouquet. "Of course she is an angel," he reflected, and then, with a grim humor, "or will be before I ask her, if I wait another twenty years! But I shall ask her, I shall ask her!" He stepped toward her boldly, but paused before her in a wordless panic when he had approached within a yard. "Heavens!" he thought. "My heart is going at a one-forty gait and the jockey's lost the reins. I'll be over the fence in another minute if I don't hold tight! But I have got to do it, this time." He dropped the stems of the flowers, still bound together by their lengths of wide white ribbon, into the elaborate box from which, so lately, he had taken them in their uninjured beauty, not noting the sad wreck which his too nervous fingers had produced, put on the cover and approached still nearer. With the box held toward her bashfully, he managed, then, another step or two. "Miss 'Lethe," he said stammering, "lawn party to-night--bouquet for you--brought it from Lexington--for you--for you, you know."

The Colonel never was embarrassed save when he was endeavoring to propose marriage to Miss Alathea and he always was embarrassed then. She recognized the situation from the mere tone of his voice and looked up hopefully.

"Oh, Colonel, how kind!" said she, as she held delighted hands out for the box. "I know it is beautiful."

"It was quite the best I could do, Miss 'Lethe," said the Colonel.

"You have such splendid taste! I'm sure it's lovely." She opened the box and looked, expectantly, within. "Why, Colonel," she cried, disappointed, "where are--where are the flowers?"

"Why--why--why," he stammered, and then saw the mutilated blossoms on the ground around him. "Why, I don't know--don't know," said he. "'Don't ask me."

She was rummaging among the stems, nonplussed. "Why, here's a note!" she said.

"Thank heaven!" the Colonel thought, "the note's there yet!" Then, growing bold: "Miss 'Lethe, if you've a kindly feeling for me in your heart, read that note; but don't you get excited; keep cool, keep cool!"

"Why, certainly," said she. "I see no cause for excitement." She unfolded the note and read, aloud, and very slowly, for the Colonel's hand was not too easy to decipher. "'My dear, dear Miss 'Lethe: Woman without her man is a savage.'" She looked up, naturally astonished by this unusual statement. "Why, Colonel," she exclaimed, "what can you mean by saying woman is a savage without her man?"

He stood appalled for just a second and then realized the error into which his ardor had misled him. "Great Scott!" he cried. "I forgot to put in the commas! It ought to read this way: 'Woman, without her, man is a savage.' Go on, Miss 'Lethe, please go on."

She read again: "'I feel that it is time for me to become civilized--in other words, to come in out of the wet. To me you have been, for twenty years, the embodiment of woman's truth, purity and goodness. But constitutional timidity and chronic financial depression, due to the race-track, have hitherto kept me silent.'" Miss 'Lethe looked up at him with a strange expression on her face. "Colonel," she exclaimed, "what does this mean?"

"Go on, Miss 'Lethe," was the answer, "please go on, go on." He made a mighty effort to secure control of his unruly nerves, and, almost unconsciously, while her head was bent above the note, took a small flask from his pocket and imbibed from it. It steadied him.

She read again: "'I am convinced that my interest in the company will yield me a competence; accordingly, behold me at your feet!'"

Miss 'Lethe looked down somewhat mischievously. She did not see the Colonel where his note declared he would be. She glanced again at the paper in her hands and saw a word which, at first, had quite escaped attention. "'Metaphorically,'" she read, and then the signature: "'Colonel Sandusky Doolittle.'"

"Colonel!" she exclaimed.

"Miss 'Lethe," he replied, and, discovering that the flask was still in plain view in his hand, slipped it into his sidepocket upside down.

"Colonel, put that bottle right side up and listen to me," she said calmly. "Do you really love me?"

"Do I love you? With a fervor--er--a--passion--er--will you excuse me if I smoke?" He took a black cigar from his vest pocket, in another effort to control his nerves, and lighted it as might an automatic smoker.

"I am going to put you to the proof," said she. "Could you, for my sake, come down from ten cigars a day to five?"

The Colonel was dismayed. "To five cigars a day! Impossible!" He caught himself. That scarcely was the way to answer the request of the woman he adored so fervently. "I mean," he hastily corrected, "is--is that all?" He made a motion as if to throw away the weed he had just lighted, but thought better of it. "I will make the descent to-morrow," he said earnestly.

"Could you restrict yourself to three mint-julips, daily?"

"Three! A man couldn't live on three! He'd have to--have to take such poisons as--as cold water into his system."

"Remember, Colonel, I would mix them."

"That settles it! Three goes!" He fervently reached toward her, plainly planning to embrace her.

"Wait, Colonel," she exclaimed, "there is one more condition. Could you, for my sake, promise never to enter another race-track?"

He started back from her in horror. "Never enter another race-tack! I, Colonel Sandusky Doolittle, known everywhere, from Maine to California, as a plunger, give up the absorbing passion of my life!"

"Remember what you said to Frank," said she. "'It's a delusion and a snare.' But, of course, if you think more of a delusion than you do of me--"

"No; hang it!" cried the Colonel, "I think more of you. Twenty years--the longest race on record and a win in sight! I'll not lose by a balk at the finish! I promise you, Miss 'Lethe, on the honor of a Kentuckian."

"Then, Colonel, I must confess, I have loved you, also, for every one of those long twenty years."

"Twenty years!" He turned his head aside and muttered: "What a damned fool I have been!" Then, to her, he said, exultantly: "Aha! A neck ahead!"

It is difficult to say what would have happened, then, if Madge, Holton, Barbara and Frank had not come from the stable, chattering about Queen Bess.

CHAPTER XIV

Joe Lorey, mad with wrath, his heart filled with the lust of killing for revenge, infuriated to the point where he felt need of neither food nor sleep, yet made less rapid time down the rough mountain paths than had the girl. Love-lent wings are swifter than an impulse born of hatred and resentment can be. She had flown upon such wings to save the man who filled her innocent thoughts with longing; Joe had gone clumsily, despite his cunning as a mountaineer, for leaden, murderous thoughts had weighed him down, hampering the quickness of his wit, delaying his fleet feet, confusing the alertness of his watchfulness for faint-limned trails, loose areas perilous of slides upon steep slopes. Indeed, though hate had driven him, Joe Lorey never in his life had made so very slow a journey to the bluegrass as that which he had started on from his wrecked still, with hatred of Frank Layson, who he thought had viciously betrayed him, blazing in his heart.

Hours after the light-footed girl, spurred by her fear for one whom she but dimly guessed that she had learned to love, had arrived at the bluegrass mansion and been welcomed by the owner of Queen Bess, the mountaineer reached the confines of the splendid farm, and lurked there, waiting for night-fall to make his entrance into the house grounds safe.

The rough youth's mental state was pitiable. Tragedy had pursued him, almost from his life's beginning, he reflected, as he furtively awaited opportunity for the revenge which he had planned. The fierce feud of the mountains had robbed him of his parents, and, with them, of the best years of his youth; the rough life of the mountains had robbed his strong young manhood of those opportunities which, he dimly realized, might have made him different and better; when love for sweet Madge Brierly had come to him, Fate had brought up from the bluegrass the young stranger, who, with his superior learning, polished manner and smooth speech, had found the conquest of the girl (Joe bitterly reflected) all too easy; and finally had come the crowning, black disaster--the betrayal of his still to the agents of the government, its destruction and his transformation from a free man of the mountains into a furtive outlaw.

He could not see that life held anything but gloom for him--black, impenetrable, ever thickening. He had but one thing left to live for--a revenge as dark as were the wrongs which he had suffered.

He knew that government agents have shrewd wits, keen eyes, strong arms, and never let a moonshiner escape if, through any strategy, they may bring about his capture; he knew that since the discovery and destruction of his still he was a marked man; so it was nearing dusk when, after intensely cautious and immensely skilful manoeuvering against discovery, he actually entered the Layson grounds.

The long, exciting afternoon, full of Queen Bess, a certain sense of triumph over Barbara Holton, the extent of which she could not guess, countless thrills of gratitude and exultation born of the kindness and consideration shown her by Miss Alathea and the Colonel, had sped away before Madge realized that it had been half-spent. Now, though, the deepening twilight warned her of the flight of time and told her that she must, perforce, perform the task for which she had descended from the mountains.

All the others except Frank had drifted toward the house, and she had hung behind for the express purpose of getting private speech with him, when she had the day's first opportunity.

"Mr. Frank," said she, "afore we go into th' house I got a word to say to you as I don't want nobody but you to hear."

A quick glance at her face showed him that what she had to say was, really, of great importance, for her lovely mouth was serious, her deep eyes were full of worry, her smooth brow was nearer to real frowning than he had ever seen it.

"Why, Madge, what is the matter?"

She put her hand upon his arm, turning her sweet face up to him with a revelation of solicitude which, had she known how plain it was, she would have hidden at all hazard. "It may mean life or death to you," she told him solemnly.

"Life or death to me, little girl? What are you talking of?" said he, almost incredulous.

"Joe Lorey's still were raided by the revenuers after you come down!"

"It can't be possible!"

"It is. It lies in ruins and in ashes an' he is hidin' out among th' mountings, somewhars, in danger, ev'ry minute, of arrest an', then, of prison. 'Twas all he had in th' wide world."

"Poor fellow! I am sorry," said Layson, with quick sympathy. "I'll see what can be done. And you say he's hiding out up in the mountains?"

She hesitated. "I said so, but I reckon it ain't true, exactly. It was that that made me hurry down to speak to you. Some say as how he has come down into th' bluegrass to find th' man as gin th' word. It is a crime as never is forgiven in th' mountings."

As she spoke, unseen, behind them, a dark, slouching, furtive figure slipped across an open space and took a crouching stand behind a tree near by. Had they listened without speech they might have heard the heavy breathing of the very man of whom they spoke, might have heard the sharp click of the lock of his long rifle as he brought its hammer to full cock. Had they turned about they might have seen the blue glint of the day's last light upon that rifle's barrel, which was levelled straight at Layson's heart. But they saw none of these things nor heard a sound.

"Who does he think betrayed him?" Layson asked, with deep interest, but no trace of guilty knowledge, thrilling in his voice.

Madge hesitated. Then she blurted out the truth. "Who?" she repeated, "Why--why you! *YOU*--YOU!"

The rifle barrel steadied to its mark, the finger curled to press upon the trigger.

"Why, Madge," said Layson, earnestly, "I didn't even know he had a still! I swear it!"

There was an honest ring in the youth's voice which could not be mistaken.

"I knowed it warn't your doin'," the girl said with a great sigh of relief.

And as she spoke the rifle barrel slowly fell.

"I knowed it warn't your doin', but Joe'll never believe it. Night an' day you'll have to be close on your guard. There's no tellin' what minute your life may be in danger."

"I don't believe it of Joe Lorey," Layson answered earnestly. "We fought, and he fought fair."

After they had gone, Joe crept out from his hiding place among the shrubbery and looked after them with puzzled, pain-filled eyes, like a great animal's.

"If they'd only knowed that I war standin' in th' shadder there!" he mused. "If he hadn't spoke them words I'd pulled th' trigger, but he spoke up like as ef 't war true an' I jest couldn't do it."

A cautious footstep on the close-knit sward, which would have been inaudible to any ear less keen than his, attracted his attention, suddenly, and he slipped back to his leafy hiding-place. Peering from the covert he saw Holton coming. The man was furtive, apprehensive in his every movement, suspicion breeding. When Joe stepped out from his thicket boldly, to confront him, the ex-slave-dealer fell back, frightened.

"Hello, sir," was Joe's laconic greeting.

"Joe Lorey!" exclaimed Holton.

"That's me," Joe boldly granted. He peered at him so closely that Holton shrank away from him, involuntarily. "And you--why you're the man as gin th' word that Frank Layson had warned th' revenooers of my still."

"I told ye for yer good," said Holton, clearly recognizing that his position was unfortunate. "An' recollect you promised not to tell anyone my name."

Joe nodded gravely. "While I believe ye told th' truth I'll keep my word," he answered. "But I wants to tell you that I heered Frank Layson deny it, hyar, to-night, an' it sounded like he war speakin' th' plain truth. See hyar, sir, you nearly egged me on to doin' murder." He reached forward and seized Holton by the shoulder roughly, with a grasp so powerful that the old man, though he was of sturdy frame and mighty muscle, knew that he was helpless in the grip. "Now look me in th' face. Tell me as you vally your own life--war it truth or lies, you told me?"

"It war th' truth," said Holton, doggedly; "th' truth an' nothin' else."

Joe shook his head incredulously. "I'd like better proof nor your word, stranger, for, some way, your voice it don't ring true, nor yer eye look honest."

"I'll gin ye th' proof," said Holton desperately. "Ye know that I war never near yer still. Layson told me it war in th' wall of a ravine--Hangin' Rock Ravine--an' a big oak stood in front of it an' hid the mouth o' th' cave. Thar, do ye believe me, now?"

Joe nodded, slowly, thoughtfully. "No man as lived up in th' mountings would have told ye." He considered ponderously for a moment. "Yes, I reckon that I'll have to take yer word. 'T was him as done it."

"Of course it war," said Holton, and then, perhaps, a bit too eagerly: "an' you'll make him pay for it?"

"Yes," said Joe, "but I've another score to settle, first, another man to find--Lem Lindsay."

Holton was plainly startled, although Joe could not guess just why he should be. "Lem Lindsay!" he exclaimed.

"Yes; the man as murdered my father. I've had word of him, at last. I've heard as how he war seen, years ago, in New Orleans--he war a nigger-trader, then--an' that he's come up in th' bluegrass country, since, like enough under another name." He looked at Holton eagerly. "I say, sir, you don't know a man like that, do you?"

Holton spoke a little hurriedly. "No, no; there ain't no man like that in these parts."

"It don't make no differ whar he bides," said Joe. "Soon or late our paths'll cross an' bring us face to face. When he struck down my father it war sealed and signed above that he war to fall by my hand; an' there's a feelin' in my heart that that hour air drawin' nigh." He nodded and then turned away. "Good-night, stranger."

Holton was thoroughly alarmed. Many things distressed him. He could plainly see that his daughter's love-affair with Layson had gone wrong, he realized that there was little chance that he could buy Madge Brierly's coal lands at anything but a fair value, and now--to fall by his hand!

"I'll make that false," he muttered, "Why, I've got to do it!"

He moved away among the trees, but stopped in frequent thought as he progressed.

"They'll lay the crime on Lorey," he reflected, after he had laid his plan. "They'll hunt him down and lynch him and I shall be safe. Layson'll be ruined, he'll have to sell Woodlawn, and my gal'll be th' missus there, in spite of him. I've got to do it."

Like a shadow of the night he hurried through the grounds until he reached the stable where Queen Bess was thought to be secure.

"Every window barred, every door is sealed but this!" he cunningly reflected as he paused at the front entrance.

With frantic haste, lest he should be discovered at the work, he piled brush from a near refuse pile against the door and stuffed wisps of grass and hay into the bottom of the heap. Into this tinder pile he thrust a lighted match and disappeared, just as Madge came to the bench where she had paused when she first came to Woodlawn, early in the afternoon.

It was plain enough, from her dejected looks and listless attitude, that the dance had given her no pleasure, but, on the contrary, had filled her with distress.

"I couldn't stand it thar, no longer," she was thinking, bitterly. "I war jest a curiosity, like a wild woman. Miss Barbarous poked fun at me till I war plumb afraid I'd fly at her like a wild-cat, so I jest slipped away. Oh, I see, now, as I never seed afore; the differ that there is 'twixt Mr. Frank an' me! An' I know, now, what 't is air ailin' me. I loves him. Oh, I loves him better nor my life! But it can't never be." She dropped her head into her hands and sobbed. "Good-bye, good, kind, Mr. Frank, good-bye!" She stretched her arms out toward the mansion she had lately left, where lights were twinkling gaily, whence sounds of music now came faintly to her ears. "You'll soon forget the little mounting girl. You'll never know she loved you. I'm goin' back--back to the old mountings."

As she rose an ominous crackling caught her ear and held her at attention, then, in a horrid flash, the fire blazed out among the hay and brush which Holton had piled up against the stable door.

"Oh, oh!" she cried. "Th' stable is burnin'! Fire! Fire! Fire! Neb, are you in there? Don't you hear me, Neb? Th' stable air on fire!"

Neb's voice came from the dim interior, muffled and skeptical. "What dat?" he said. "Don't want no foolishness 'round heah. I's ahmed."

"It's me, Neb, me," she cried. "Th' stable 's burnin', Neb!"

"Gorramighty!" she heard Neb exclaim, now in a voice expressive of great fright. "Dat's so, dat's so! Quick, honey, open up de doah!"

Madge was working at the biggest log which Holton had thrust against the door to feed the blaze. The flames and smoke surged 'round her as she struggled with the unwieldy thing, her hands grasped, more than once, live coals, without making her release her hold. Once or twice the bursting flames, swung hither and swung yon by the light, vagrant breezes of the night and the drafts born of the fire, itself, flared straight toward her face, and, to save her hair, which, once igniting, would, she knew, make further work impossible, she had to draw back for a second; but each time, as she saw another chance, she sprang again to the desperate task. At last, after a dozen efforts, she had thrust the blazing log so far from the already burning door that Neb could push it open. He stumbled out, his old hands held before him, gropingly, half-suffocated.

"Neb, you ain't hurt," said she.

"You go ring dat bell," said he, pointing to a standard bearing at its top an ornamental iron crotch in which a big plantation bell was swung. "Soon's I get my bref from all dat smoke I'll go back an' git Queen Bess."

The girl sprang to the rope and soon the bell was ringing out a wild alarm.

"Hurry, Neb!" she cried. "Oh, hurry! Th' fire's a-gainin', ev'ry second! Hurry!"

Neb dashed back into the stable upon trembling limbs, while, without a pause, the girl kept up the clangor of alarm. Her eyes were ever on the door through which the faithful black had disappeared, watching anxiously to see him come out with the mare.

But second after second--seconds which seemed to her like hours--went by and he did not appear again. Her heart began to beat with frantic fears that Neb, himself, as well as the superb animal which she had already learned to love, had fallen victim to the fire, when, at last, he stumbled from the door.

"'Tain't no use," he said, as he weakly staggered up to her. "It kain't be done. Queen Bess am crazy wid de fiah. She jes' won't come out! I cain't *git* huh to come out." He sobbed. "An' she am all dat Marse Frank hab on earth!" Beside himself he ran off toward the house, shouting for his master wildly.

"All he has on earth!" the girl exclaimed, the bell-rope falling from relaxing hands. An instant she stood there in thought, horrified at the idea of the catastrophe which threatened Layson. Then: "I'll save her! She will follow me!"

Without a second's hesitation, with no thought for her own safety, she drew her skirts about her tightly, wrapped her shawl around her head to save her hair and dashed through the growing flames about the stable-door, into the inferno which now raged within the structure, just as Neb, running with a lurching step, but with a speed remarkable in one so old and stiffened by rheumatic pains, dashed back to the scene of the disaster, in advance of Frank, the Colonel, Holton, Miss Alathea and the other inmates of the house, guests, servants, all.

Without a word, as he approached, Frank pulled off his coat, evidently preparing for a desperate dash through the now roaring flames to rescue his beloved mare. Then, bracing himself for a great spring through the lurid barrier, he cried, "I'll save her!" and would have leaped into the flaming entrance if Neb had not caught his arm with desperate grip.

"No, honey," the old negro cried, "yo' shan't go in!"

The Colonel joined the negro in restraining the half-crazed owner of Queen Bess. "It's no use, Frank," said he. "We'll not let you go in."

They dragged the struggling youth back from the fire just as, to their amazement, an exultant voice rang from the inside of the burning building. "Back! Back!" it cried. "I'm a-comin' with Queen Bess!"

An instant later Madge sprang out through the flames, followed by the mare, about whose head the mountain girl had wrapped her shawl.

"Come, girl! Come, girl!" said Madge, alert of eye, cool-witted, soothing.

As docilely as she had followed her that afternoon, the mare stepped through the blazing door and out into the stable-yard.

CHAPTER XV

Lexington was in a wild state of excitement on the morning of the year's great race, the Ashland Oaks. In a private parlor of the Phoenix Hotel the two men who were, perhaps, most deeply interested of all in it, were weary of their speculations after they had gone, for the thousandth time, over every detail of possible prophecy and speculation. The Colonel sat beside a table upon which stood a "long" glass from which protruded, and in which nestled fragrant mint-leaves. At the bottom of the glass there lingered, yet, the good third of a julep.

"There's one capital thing about a mint-julep," he said comfortably, and smacked appreciative lips. "One always suggests another." He drained his glass and rose. At the other side of the room was the bell-button. His finger was extended and about to touch it when he stopped to think. "No! Great heavens!" said he. "That makes my third, already, and I'm as dry as the desert of Sahara." He sat down again, an air of martyrdom upon his face. "Ah, well, Miss 'Lethe's worth it. I say, Frank, anything new in the extra?"

The youthful owner of Queen Bess, to whom it seemed as if almost life itself were staked on the result of the coming contest at the track, lowered, with a nervous hand, for an instant only, the newspaper he had been poring over.

"Only this," he said, and slowly read: "'Queen Bess is still the favorite for the Ashland Oaks. The report that she was injured in the fire by which her stable was burned, proves to be a canard. Her owner declares her to be unhurt and in fine condition.'"

The Colonel nodded his approval. "That's what I've telegraphed the Dyer brothers. I'm sure they won't refuse to take her when they know the facts in the case. It was a close shave, though. If it hadn't been for that little thoroughbred from the mountains--"

"When she rushed into the flames, last night, wasn't she magnificent!" said Frank, flushing with enthusiasm. "And when she came out, leading Queen Bess to safety, she looked like an angel!"

The Colonel coughed in deprecation. "The simile's off, a little bit, ain't it? Angels are not supposed to come out of the flames."

"At least, Colonel, you'll admit that she's the best and bravest little girl you ever knew."

The Colonel smiled. "Yes; but, my boy, this enthusiasm is alarming." He laughed outright. "It seems to indicate another conflagration, with Cupid as the incendiary."

The youth colored. "Oh, nonsense!"

"Be more careful, Frank," his friend urged, becoming serious. "She's a dear, simple little thing, not used to the ways of the world. Don't let her get too fond of you."

"What do you mean?"

"See here, my boy. I know you young fellows don't want an old fool, like me, interfering with your affairs, but I've taken that little girl right to my heart. I tell you, Frank, she's too brave and true to be trifled with. She's not that kind."

Layson flushed hotly. The intimation, even from the Colonel, was more than he could bear with patience. "Stop!" he cried. "You've said enough. What you mean to insinuate is false!"

The Colonel rose, embarrassed. The youth's earnestness astonished him. Could it be possible that this scion of an ancient bluegrass family, this leader of the younger set in one of the most exclusive circles in Kentucky, could really be thinking seriously of that untutored mountain-girl? "My boy, forgive me!" he exclaimed. "I--I didn't understand. I never dreamed there could be anything--er--serious. I thought, of course--"

Frank paced the floor with nervous tread. Other things than the impending contest for the Ashland Oaks had been worrying him of late. Since he had left the mountains there had scarcely been a moment, waking or sleeping, when the face of the sweet mountain girl who had fascinated him among her rocks and forests, and had come down to the bluegrass to save not only his life but the life of his beloved mare, had not been vividly before him. Untutored she might be, uncouth of speech, unlearned in all those things, in fact, which the women he had known had ever held most valuable, but her compensating virtues had begun to take upon themselves their actual values--values so overwhelming in their magnitude that her few lackings grew to seem continually less important in his mind.

"Never mind, Colonel," he said slowly, "you can't say anything to me but what I've said, over and over again, to myself. I know she's ignorant and uncultured. I know what it would mean if I should marry her. If I were to choose for a wife a fashionable girl, whose life is centered in the luxury which surrounds her, the world would smile approval; but for Madge, with her true, brave heart and noble thoughts, there would be only sneers and insults because she happened to be born up there in the mountains. That is the kind of people we are down here in the blue-grass." He smiled, somewhat bitterly. "And I--well, I'm too much like the rest to need any warning--too much of a coward to think of making her my wife."

He sat, dejectedly, in a chair by the long table, and, with face held between his hands and elbows planted on the board, looked across it, through the open window, out into the thronging street with gloomy eyes. For days he had been fighting battle after battle with himself. He could not make his mind up as to what he ought to do. He knew he loved the mountain-girl, but--but--

"There, there, my boy, I'm sorry," said the Colonel, sympathetically, apologetically. "Let's drop the subject. The ladies will be here, soon. Before they come I'll step over to the office and get the answer from the Dyer Brothers." He rose, looking at his watch. "It's nearly time it was here. They were to wire promptly. I'll bring it to you as soon as it comes." He went to Frank and put his hand upon his shoulder comfortingly. "Don't worry, my boy. It will all come out, all right. Ahem! I mean there's nothing the matter with the mare and the sale will go through."

"I hope so," said Frank, rising without much show of energy. He was clearly on the edge of real discouragement. "If it doesn't--and that assessment to be met--ah, well! What's the use of worrying? It doesn't help the matter any." He walked slowly to the window and looked out. "Here come Madge and Aunt 'Lethe," he announced, "through with their shopping at last. How different Madge looks from the little mountain-girl I first knew!" He turned and faced the Colonel. "Ah, if the world knew her as I do--"

The Colonel left the room, bound for the telegraph-office, just before a shrill scream came from the corridor, without, startling Layson greatly.

"Oh, dellaw!" the frightened voice said. "Le' me out! Le' me out!"

He recognized the voice, at once, as belonging to the girl whom he had been discussing with the Colonel, and it was so full of terror that he rushed quickly to the door, prepared to rescue her from some dire peril.

"What can be the matter?" he thought, frightened.

At the door he met Madge, white of face and startled, coming in.

"Why, Madge! What is it?"

She leaned against the writing-table, gasping. It was plain enough that she had been greatly frightened.

"Wait till I git my breath," she said; and then: "They got us into a little room, and, all of a sudden, we started skallyhootin' fer th' roof--room an' all!"

Frank fell back, relieved, and trying not to show amusement.

"That was the elevator," he explained. "A machine to carry you upstairs and save you the work of climbing."

"Dellaw!" exclaimed the girl, not yet entirely calm. "As if I couldn't walk! Thought we was blowed up by another dynamighty bomb!"

Miss Alathea entered hurriedly, looking about the room, in evident distress. At sight of Madge she gave a great sigh of relief. "My dear, I'm so sorry you were frightened!"

The girl laughed nervously, pulling herself together. "I understand, now, Miss 'Lethe, and I'm as cool as a cucumber."

There was a group of darkies at the door, and, suddenly, they all began to grin. Miss 'Lethe knew the sign.

"The Colonel's coming," she said positively. "Their faces show it. Look at them?"

Her guess proved a true prophecy. The Colonel, plainly busy with absorbing thoughts, was striding along the uneven old brick sidewalk, seeing nothing, hearing nothing, when the crowd of darkies, sure of his good-nature, beneficiaries from past favors, many times, surrounded him, beseeching him for tips upon the coming races. Very different were these city darkies from the respectful negroes of the Kentucky plantations of the time. They swarmed about him in an insistent horde.

"Who gwine win dat race, Marse Cunnel? Who gwine win dat race?" they chorussed.

He stopped and beamed at them good-naturedly.

"Who's going to win?" said he. "Queen Bess, of course."

He joined the group, inside, with a bundle in one hand and an open telegram in the other. "Good morning, ladies. Miss 'Lethe, you're looking fresh and blooming as you used to twenty years ago." He tried to catch himself, but failed. "As fresh and blooming," he corrected, "as usual, Miss 'Lethe." His bow was very courtly and her own no less so.

"Frank, my boy," said he, turning to the youthful owner of Queen Bess, "I've got their answer, and it's all right."

Frank had been acutely worried. There had been some question of the sale of the mare to the Dyer Brothers before the fire; now that this disaster had occurred and stories had been started, as, of course, he knew they must have been, about injuries to her, there might be, he had feared, good reason to expect the celebrated horsemen to withdraw their proposition. The Colonel's news, therefore, was very welcome.

"They take the mare?" he asked, all eagerness."

"N-o," began the Colonel, "but--"

Frank's face fell, instantly, and his shoulders drooped despairingly. "Then it's all wrong."

"Not yet," said the Colonel, "score again." He raised the telegram and read from it: "'Can't take mare without positive proof that she's all right. Let her run in the Ashland Oaks, to-day. If she wins, we take her.'" The Colonel looked up beamingly. "Do you hear? They take her!"

The condition which, now, the Dyer brothers made, when, before this, they had made none, bothered Frank. The telegram did not elate him quite as much as the old horseman had supposed it would. "Ah, if she wins!" said he.

Miss Alathea spoke up, eagerly. "Oh, Frank, of course she'll win."

"She's *got* to win!" exclaimed the Colonel with much emphasis.

Frank was in a pessimistic mood. "I'm not so sure," said he, a little gloomily. The strain of the past days had been a hard trial for the youth. "If that imp of a jockey, Ike, should get in range of a whiskey bottle--however, he has promised not to leave his room."

The Colonel laughed. "Ike leave his room?" he said. "You're right--he won't; but it will not be his promise that will keep him from it. He couldn't leave it if he would."

"Why not?" inquired Miss 'Lethe.

"Because," the Colonel answered, "I have got his clothes!"

"His clothes!" said Frank, astonished.

"Yes--a Napoleonic device. When I went to see him, this morning, I found him in bed. I knew how it might be if he got out, so I saw to it that his meals would reach him promptly, and borrowed the one suit of clothes he brought with him, under pretence of needing them to help me order a new jockey-suit for him to wear in the great race. I've been fair about it, too--I've got the new clothes for him." He pointed to the bundle which he had just brought in. "They're in there--and they'll not disgrace Queen Bess. They're the best I could get."

Frank, less interested in the clothes than in the fact that the jockey, now, was quite secure against temptation, sighed with satisfaction. "Then he's safe," said he.

The Colonel nodded, notably well satisfied with his performance. Miss Alathea, shocked, as she tried to be, by all this business, adjunct of gambling, every bit of it, yet smiled admiringly at the big horseman. Only Madge, learned, through much experience with mountaineers, whose greatest curse is whisky, in the ways of men addicted to its use, was not convinced that all was surely well.

"I'd keep a watch on him, just the same," she said. Now that she understood the vast importance of this race to Layson her whole heart was wrapped up in its fortunes. "When a man wants whisky he gener'ly finds a way to git it."

"You're right, Madge," Frank agreed. "I think I'll go and look after him, now."

He started toward the door just as a knock sounded on it. When he opened it he found Horace Holton standing waiting for admittance. The man seemed to be excited.

"I don't want to intrude, sar," said the ex-merchant in slaves, "but I come to tell you what you'd orter know. Th' news of th' fire, last night, hev set ev'rybody wild. They're lookin' to you, sar, to sw'ar out a warrant for Joe Lorey an' set th' sheriff on his track."

Frank came back into the room with the old man, worried by the news which he had brought. He had been thinking of this very matter and he was not at all convinced that he wished to swear a warrant out for Lorey. Finally, after a few seconds of silent and deep thought, he shook his head. "I want more proof, first," he declared.

Holton was astonished and ill-pleased. "What more proof d' ye want?" he asked. "Ain't it as plain as day that he come down from th' mountings to get even with you for th' raidin' of his still? Who else would 'a' done it?"

Madge was listening with flushed face and frowning brow. She did not, for a second, think Joe Lorey was the culprit. Her suspicions had not wholly crystalized, but she had known the mountain-boy since she had known anyone, and she could not believe that he would fire a building in which was confined a dumb and helpless creature. She knew him to be quite as fond of animals as she was. She believed Holton, also, had some ulterior reason, which she did not fathom, then, for trying to fasten suspicion on the lad. In her earnestness, as she considered these things, she stepped close to the old man, almost truculently. "That's what I mean to find out," she declared. "Who else done it."

Holton was angered by her manner and her opposition. He had not expected to meet any difficulty in the execution of his plan to throw the blame of the outrageous crime at Woodlawn, on the shoulders of the mountaineer. "What have you got to do with it?" he angrily demanded.

She was not impressed by his quick show of temper. "Reckon I've got as much to do with it as you hev," she replied. "Joe Lorey wouldn't never plan to burn a helpless dumb critter. He ain't no such coward."

"Who else had a call to do it?" said the old man, placed, unexpectedly, on the defensive. "Who else war an enemy of Mr. Layson's?"

Madge spoke slowly. She was not sure, at all, whom she was accusing; her suspicions were indefinite, obscure, but they were taking form within her mind. "Thar's one as I knows on," she slowly answered. "It's th' one as told Joe Lorey that Mr. Frank had set th' revenuers onto him." Her conviction strengthened as she spoke, and, as she continued, she looked Holton firmly in the eye and spoke with emphasis. "Show me th' man as told that lie, an' I'll show you th' scoundrel as tried to burn Queen Bess!"

Layson liked the spirit of her warm defense of her old friend, and, himself, knew enough about the moonshiner to make it seem quite reasonable. He knew that Joe was a crude creature, but believed, and had good reason to believe, that he had his code of honor which he would abide by at all cost. It was impossible for him to feel convinced that this would have permitted him to set fire to the stable. "Madge, I believe you're right," said he.

Holton was nonplussed. Things were not going as he had expected and had wished them to, at all. "Oh, shore, it war Joe Lorey," he protested. "It couldn't 'a' been nobody else. I warns you, here an' now, Layson, that ef you don't set th' law after him he'll be lynched before to-morrer night."

Layson was a little angered by the man's persistence. "I'll see that that doesn't happen," he replied, "and I'll leave no stone unturned to find the scoundrel who really did the deed, and have him punished. But I'm not certain that the man will prove to be Joe Lorey."

Holton, angry, baffled and astonished, left the room, with a maddening conviction growing in his mind that things were going wrong and would continue to go wrong. He almost regretted, now, that he had yielded to the impulse to set fire to the stable. If Layson would not let him throw suspicion where he had intended it should fall, then one part of his plan would have failed utterly: he would not have put Joe Lorey, who, at liberty, must ever be a peril to him, from his path; and, furthermore, if they kept on with investigation, in the end they might--they might--but he would not let himself believe that, by any possibility, the real truth could come out. He assured himself as he stepped out into the crowded street that he was safe, whether or not the crime was ever fastened on Joe Lorey.

Layson, after Holton left, looked around upon the party with a worried eye. "I can't take this matter up, yet," he declared. "Until the race is over I can think of nothing else. Colonel, I'll look after Ike, and then we'll be off to the track."

"So we will, my boy," the Colonel answered, "so we will. Ah, what a race it will be!" As Frank went out, the horseman rubbed his hands with keen anticipations of delight.

"Oh, Colonel," exclaimed Madge, brought back by this turn in the conversation to contemplation of the most exciting prospect which had ever been before her, "won't we have fun?"

"Won't we?" said the Colonel, very happily.

But then Miss Alathea spoke. She had listened to all the talk about the fire, the incendiary, the pursuit, and its dreadful possibilities of lynching, with the keenest of distress. Now the Colonel's calm declaration that, presently, they would be off to the race-track which he had sworn forever to taboo, shifted her mind suddenly from those unpleasant topics.

"Colonel!" she exclaimed, in pained astonishment. "Do you forget your promise?"

"Er--er--" the old horseman began and became speechless.

Madge was all excitement. "Mr. Frank has told me all about it," she said gaily. "I kin see it, now--th' grand-stand filled with folks, th' jockeys ridin' in their bright colors, th' horses a-champin' an' a-pullin' at their bits--an' then--th' start!" The girl had dreamed about such scenes before she had so much as guessed that she might ever witness one, and now, when she was actually about to go out to the track, herself, and with her own eyes gaze upon the greatest race which old Kentucky had known for many a year, it seemed too good to be true. Her eyes sparkled as she spoke, her feet danced as if they might be in the stirrups, her hands clutched on imaginary reins. "All off together, a-goin' like th' lightnin'!" she exclaimed. "Queen Bess a-lyin' back an' lettin' th' others do th' runnin', Ike never touchin' her with whip nor spur until th' last, an' then jest liftin' her in as if she had wings!"

"Stop! Stop!" cried the Colonel. "Not another word, or I'll drop dead in my tracks!" Then, cautiously, to Madge: "I say, little one, couldn't you let me have a word alone with Miss 'Lethe?"

The girl nodded wisely. "I understand," said she; and then, with a quick glance at Miss Alathea, who was not attending, and an earnest and imploring look at the poor Colonel: "Whatever you do don't you forget that we are goin' to th' races!" She left the room.

Forget! The Colonel was not likely to forget about those races! He was in deep misery of mind. "Miss 'Lethe?" he said timidly.

"Yes, Colonel," said the charming lady, turning toward him.

"Miss 'Lethe, have you the remotest idea of the agony I'm suffering?"

"Why, Colonel, what's the matter? Aren't you well?" Miss 'Lethe's keen anxiety was instantaneous.

"Yes--yes--I'm well--that is, I am now, but I shouldn't wonder if I'd be dead before night. Miss 'Lethe, when we made our little arrangement, yesterday, I didn't know that the sale of the mare, your twenty-five thousand dollars, the assessment on Frank's stock, everything was going to depend upon this race. I tell you, if I don't see it, I'm liable to an attack of heart-disease."

"Ah, Colonel," said she, sadly, "I see where your heart really is!"

"With you, Miss 'Lethe, always with you," he urgently assured her; but there was pleading in his eyes which really was pitiful.

"Remember your solemn promise."

"But one little race," he begged. "That wouldn't count, would it? And then swear off forever."

"No, Colonel; no," she firmly answered, "for if you yield, this time, I'll know that in the race for your affections the horse is first, the woman second."

The Colonel sank dejectedly into a chair. "I can't permit you to think that," said he. "I'll--keep my promise."

She went to him, delighted. "Ah, I was sure you would," said she. "Now I can go and finish my shopping in peace. It's all for your good, Colonel--for your good." With a happy smile she left him there, alone.

"For my good!" exclaimed the Colonel, ruefully. "That's what the teacher used to say, but the hickory smarted, just the same. Of course Miss 'Lethe is first--but--but--the horse is a strong second!"

To add to the man's agony, Madge, now, returned, dressed and ready for the most exciting moments of her life. "I'm all ready, Colonel," she said eagerly. "Think we'll have good seats? I do hope I'll be whar I kin see!"

He would not, yet, disappoint the child; he would not, yet,--he could not-- admit that he, himself, was to meet with such a bitter disappointment. "You'll see, all right," he told her, "and so will I." But, after a second's thought he added: "I will if I can hire a balloon!"

They heard Neb's excited voice out in the corridor, and, an instant later, the old darkey hurried in. Immediately the Colonel knew, from his appearance, that something had gone seriously wrong.

"What is it, Neb; what is it?" he demanded.

"Fo' de Lawd, sech news!" said Neb. "Sech news!"

"Neb, Neb, what's the matter?" Madge asked, frightened by his manner.

"Somebody," said the negro, "done gone smuggle in a bottle o' whiskey to dat mis'able jockey, Ike, an' he am crazy drunk!"

CHAPTER XVI

D runk!" cried the Colonel, shocked inexpressibly. "And the race this afternoon!"

"Marse Frank said you was to come, suh, an' help sobuh him."

Madge approached the Colonel anxiously. "Yes; sober him, if you have to turn him inside out!"

"'Fraid he's done on bofe sides, missy; drunk cl'ar t'rough," said Neb.

The Colonel grasped his hat. "We'll try, we'll try," he said. "Oh, whisky, whisky! What a pity anyone can get too much of so good a thing!"

"I neber could, suh," Neb replied, "but dat 'ar jockey--"

They hurried out together.

Madge was in intense distress. She knew what this might mean. If Queen Bess could not run--and she could not, certainly, without a jockey--the Dyer Brothers would not buy her, probably; and if she were not sold in time, then Layson would be quite unable to meet the assessment on his stock in the coal-mining company. She was by no means certain what this was, or what the reason for it, but she had heard talk of it and knew that it was very serious. Almost beside herself with her anxiety, she could do nothing save sit there and wait for news. The entrance, even of Barbara Holton, who came in, now, was a relief to her overtaxed nerves.

"Say," said she, admitting Barbara nearer to good-fellowship than she had ever done before, "I reckon you have heered the news--Ike's drunk--dead drunk!"

Barbara regarded her excitement with a careful calm. She, herself, had been excited by the news when it had reached her, but a moment since, but she would not let this girl know that. Her role was to endeavor to force the mountain girl back into what she thought her place, at any cost.

"Yes, I've heard," said she, "and it's too late to get another jockey, so Queen

Bess can't run."

She had formed a plan, deep in her mind, and had sought the mountain-girl with the skilful scheme.

"Then Mr. Frank is goin' to be ruined!" Madge exclaimed, dejectedly.

"Not unless you wish it," Barbara replied, looking straight into her eyes.

"Dellaw! Me wish that? Just you tell me what you mean!"

The bluegrass girl stood looking at the mountain maiden with appraising eye for a few seconds. Then she crossed the room and stood close by her side, while she tapped upon the table nervously with her carefully gloved fingers.

"If this sale fails, as it seems it must," she said, slowly, "it rests with you whether my father will advance the money to pay the assessment on that stock of Mr. Layson's."

"Your father give him the money?" Madge said in astonishment. "Well, I'd never thought o' that! But what have I got to do about it?"

The situation was a hard one, even for the self-possession of the lowlands girl, who had inherited her father's coolness in emergency as well as some other traits less desirable. Her color rose and she tried, earnestly, to gather words which would express the thought she had in mind without including a confession of the weakness of her own position. This she could not, do, however. She walked over to the window, gazed from it, for a moment, at the passing crowds, and then returned to Madge, to tell her bluntly: "I want you to go away from here."

"Me go away? What for?"

It was impossible, Barbara now discovered, to make her meaning wholly clear, without some measure of humiliation. The first thing that was, obviously, necessary was a statement of facts as they were, and this must include confession of her own sore weakness. She hesitated, trying to avoid it, but when she quite decided that it could not be helped, plunged on with a perfect frankness. What she wished was immediately to gain her point. If she must eat a bit of humble pie in order to accomplish this, why, she would eat it, much as she disliked the diet.

"Can't you see that it is you who stand between Frank and me?" she cried. "If it hadn't been for you, I should have been his promised wife! If you will go away and never see him again, I can win him back."

Madge was dumbfounded. The cold and utter selfishness of the girl's proposal was astounding. She looked at Barbara with eyes in which incredulous amazement gave way, slowly, to an expression of chill wonder. "Say, you don't seem to squander many thoughts on other people! S'posin' I happen to love him a little, myself!"

Barbara laughed scornfully. Sprung from low stock, herself, but reared in luxury, she had the most complete contempt for anyone whom circumstances had denied advantages such as she had known. "You--*you* love him!" she exclaimed.

The words had slipped from Madge's lips without forethought, and, instantly, she very much regretted them; but, now that she had uttered them she did not so much as think of trying to recall them or deny their truth. "Yes, and I ain't ashamed of it," said she. "I *do* love him--a thousand times better nor you ever dreamed of."

"What good will it do you?" asked her rival, coldly. "You don't suppose he'll ever think of making you his wife! Why, look at the difference between you and me!"

"Yes," said Madge, sarcastically, "there *is* a powerful sight of differ! You'd be willin' to ruin' him to win him, while I'd be willin' to gin up my happiness to save him!"

Barbara, more in earnest than she ever had been in her life before, took a quick step toward the mountain girl. "Then prove it by going away," said she, "and I will see that my father advances Frank Layson the money he needs." She looked at her eagerly. "Do you promise?"

"No," said Madge, with firm decision. "No; I won't."

"Then it is you who will ruin him."

While they had been talking an idea had sprung to sudden flower in Madge's mind. It was a daring, an unheard of plan that had occurred to her. There were details of it which filled her with shrinking. She knew that if she put it into practice, and it ever became generally known, she would be the talk of Lexington and that not all that talk would be complimentary. She knew that, after she had carried out the plan, even the man for whom she thought of doing it might look at her with scorn. But it was the only plan which her alert and anxious brain could find which promised anything at all. And if it won, perhaps--perhaps--he might not scorn her! At any rate it was a sacrifice, and sacrifice for him was an attractive thought to her.

"Me ruin him?" she said to Barbara. "Don't you be too sure! There is a shorter and a better way nor yours, to save him, an' I'm goin' to try it!"

The bluegrass girl, astonished, would have questioned her, but Madge waited for no questioning. Without another word she hurried from the room, in a mad search for Colonel Doolittle.

＊   ＊   ＊   ＊   ＊

From the country round about for miles the planters had come into Lexington upon their blooded mounts, their wives, daughters, sweethearts, riding in great carriages. Now and then a vehicle, coming from some far-away plantation, was drawn by a gay four-in-hand, and the drivers of such equipages, negroes always, showed a haughty scorn of their black fellow-men who travelled humbly on the backs of mules, or trudged the long and dusty way on foot. Gorgeous were the costumes of the ladies whom the carriages conveyed; elegant the dress of the gay gentlemen who rode beside the vehicles on prancing steeds, gallant escorts of Kentucky's lovely womanhood, prepared, especially, to watch the carriage-horses when the town was reached and guard against disasters due to their encounter with such disturbing and unusual things as crowds, brass-bands and other marvels of a great occasion.

Everywhere upon the sidewalks people swarmed like ants, delighted with the calm perfection of the day, the magnetism of the crowds, the blare of martial music, the novelty of passing strangers, and, above all, by the prospect of the great race which, for weeks, had been the theme of conversation everywhere throughout the section.

In the spacious corridors and big bar-rooms of the city's hostelries the rich men of the section vied with flashily dressed strangers, in magnitude of wagers, and the gambling fever spread from these important centers to the very alleys of the negro quarters. Poor indeed was the old darkey who could not find two-bits to wager on the race; small, indeed, the piccaninny who was not wise enough in the sophisticated ways of games of chance to lay a copper with a comrade or to join a pool by means of which he and his fellows were enabled to participate in more important methods of wooing fickle Fortune.

Here and there and everywhere were the piccaninnies from Woodlawn, the

Layson place, crying the virtues of the mare they worshipped and her owner whom they each and everyone adored, boasting of the wagers they had made, strutting in the consciousness that ere the moment for the great race came "Unc" Neb would gather them together to add zest to the occasion with their brazen instruments and singing. The "Whangdoodles" were the envy of every colored lad in town who was not of their high elect, and created, about noon, a great diversion upon one of the main streets, by gathering, when they were quite certain that their leader could by no means get at them, and singing on a corner for more coppers to be wagered on Queen Bess. The shower of coin which soon rewarded their smooth, well-trained harmonies, burned holes in their pockets, too, until it was invested in the only things which, on this day, the lads thought worth the purchasing--tickets on the race in which the wondrous mare would run.

Through the gay crowd old Neb was wandering, disconsolate, burdened with the melancholy news of the defection of the miserable jockey, looking, everywhere, for Miss Alathea Layson, but without success. He stopped upon a corner, weary of the search and of the woe which weighed him down.

"Marse Frank," he muttered, "say I war to tell Miss 'Lethe de bad news; but he didn't tell me how to find a lady out shoppin'. Needle in a haystack ain't nawthin'! Reckon 'bout de bes' dat I kin do is stand heah on dis cohnuh an' cotch huh when she comes back to de hotel."

He stood there for fully fifteen minutes, peering in an utter desolation of woe, at every passing face, but finding nowhere that one which he sought. Then, at a distance, he saw the Colonel coming. The expression on the horseman's face amazed him and filled him with an instant hope that something had turned up to rob the situation of the horror which had darkened it, for him, ever since he had discovered that the jockey had disgraced himself.

"Dar come Marse Cunnel," he exclaimed, in his astonishment, "*a-lookin' mighty happy*! Dat ain't right, now; dat ain't right, unduh de succumstances."

He hurried to the Colonel, who, instead of seeming sorrowful, discouraged, wroth, beamed at him with a genial eye.

"What's the matter, Neb?" he asked. "You look like a funeral!"

"Dat's de way I feel, suh; wid no jockey fo' Queen Bess an' Marse Frank good as ruined."

"Neb," said the Colonel, coolly, "you don't mean to be a liar, but you are one."

"What?" cried the darkey in delight. "Oh Marse Cunnel, call me anyt'ing ef tain't so about de mare!"

"Of course it isn't," said the Colonel happily. "I have found a jockey, Neb; a jockey."

"Praise de Lawd!" cried the old negro.

"One of the best," the Colonel went on, gaily. "Just come in from the--from the east. I engaged him at once, so you get word to Frank. In five minutes we'll be on our way out to the track."

Neb's spirits had instantly revived. Six inches droop was gone from his old shoulders. "It'll be de grandest race eber run in ol' Kentucky! Lawsy, Cunnel, won't it tickle you to death to see Queen Bess romp in a winnuh?"

Instantly the Colonel's high elation faded. More than the droop which had been in Neb's shoulders now oppressed the horseman's. His face clouded. "There *he* goes, too!" he cried. "Neb, another word like that and I shall brain you! Do you hear me? I--I shan't be there!"

"Not be dar!" Neb exclaimed. "Kain't swaller dat, suh. Ef you should miss dat race, why, you'd drop daid."

"I believe you, Neb--believe you. I say, Neb, look here. I have promised on the honor of a Kentuckian, never to enter another race-track. I must keep my word; but, for the Lord's sake, isn't there a knot-hole, that you know of, somewhere in the fence, which would let me see the race without going inside?"

Neb knew that race-track as he knew the plot of hard-trodden ground before the little cabin where he had been born back of the big house out at Woodlawn. Many a race had he seen surreptitiously when he had not funds to buy admission to the track. He grinned, remembering talk which he had heard between the Colonel and Miss 'Lethe, and understanding, now. He laughed. "Oh, I yi!" he cried. "Marse Cunnel, dar ain't nobody'll git ahead of you! You bet dar is a knot-hole, not fur off frum de gran'-stan', neither, an' a tree, too, you could climb, stan's mighty handy."

The Colonel groaned. "I climb a tree to peek above a race-track fence!" said he. "No; never. They'd think I was trying to save my admission fee! The knot-hole will have to do for me, Neb. You've saved me. Heaven bless you! Have a cigar--they're good."

"T'ankee, suh," said Neb, reaching for the weed the Colonel now held toward him. "Lawsy, ain't dat jus' a whoppuh? Whah you-all git sech mon'sous big cigahs as dat?"

"I'm only smoking half as many, now, so I get 'em double size," the Colonel answered, sighing but not wholly miserable.

Neb did not see the humor of this detail. He was thinking of the race and of Queen Bess. "Hooray fo' de Cunnel!" he exclaimed, irrelevantly, to a little group of colored men who had been gathering. "Whatever he says yo' kin gamble on. Lawsy, ain't I glad I's got my money on Queen Bess? Golly, won't Marse Holton jes' feel cheap when he done heahs dis news? Seen him down dar in de pool-room, not so long ago, a-puttin' up his money plumb against Queen Bess. Goin' to lose it, suah, he will." He went off, muttering, and shaking his old head. "Somehow I jes' feels it in mah bones dat he ain't true to Marse Frank, yessuh. If I evah fin's it out fo' suah, I'll jes' *paralyse* him!"

He had quite forgotten that he had come out to find Miss Alathea, and was not looking for her when he actually stumbled into her.

"Why, Neb, what are you doing?" she said, recoiling.

"Pahdon, pahdon, please, Miss 'Lethe," said the negro. "I was thinkin' of de sweet bimeby an' waitin' fo' to tell de news to you--fust dat Ike got drunk an' Marse Frank war gwine hab to scratch de mare--"

"Oh, dear! Oh, dear! Then Frank--why, he'll lose everything!"

"Hol' on, Miss 'Lethe; dat de fust half, only. Secon' half am dat Marse Cunnel found a jockey an' Queen Bess am gwine ter run."

"Bless his heart!" she cried. "I wonder if it's wrong for me to pray that that jockey will win." She looked, almost embarrassed at the aged negro for a moment, and then, mustering up courage, said: "Neb, look here. I'm ashamed to acknowledge so much interest in a horse-race, but it seems as if I can't wait to hear of the result."

"Lawsy, I don't blame you, none; feel dat way mahse'f."

"I must know the result the instant the race is decided."

"Send yo' wuhd right off, Miss 'Lethe."

"Oh, I can't wait for that. Neb, I never did such a thing before and never will again, and, even now, I won't enter a race-track; but, Neb, isn't there some place outside the fence where I could watch the race without actually going in?"

Neb doubled up in silent laughter. The old negro was enjoying life, exceedingly, on this, the day, which, for a time, had seemed so full of gloom. The white folks were quite at his mercy. "You bet dar is," said he, "a knot-hole not fur f'm de gran'-stan', an' a tree what you could climb, right handy."

Miss Alathea was not favorable to the thought of climbing trees, and said so. "No, no; the knot-hole will be far better for me."

"But, Miss 'Lethe, why, de Cunnel--"

She did not let him make his explanation. "Sh! Sh!" she hissed. "Not a word of this to him, or anyone! Will you show me, when the time comes?"

"Oh, I'll show you," Neb replied, and before he had a chance to add a word she had hurried off into the crowd.

"I war gwine to tell her dat de Cunnel'd be dar, too, but she wouldn't wait to heah. Wal, I reckon she'll jes' fin' 'im when she git dar."

Down the street his piccaninny band came straggling, looking for him.

"Hol' on, chillun; hol' on," he cried, and joined them. "Now yo' lissen. Yo' is not to make a squawk until the end of de Ashlan' Oaks. Yo's to sabe yo' bref to honuh ouah Queen Bess. If she wins, yo' staht in playin' 'Dixie' as yo' nevuh played afo'. If she loses yo's to play, real slow an' mo'nful, 'Massa's in de Col', Col', Groun'.'"

In the meantime the Colonel, in a quiet spot, had joined the jockey who had been discovered to take the place of drunken Ike. The unknown rider was wrapped closely in an ulster, from beneath which riding boots, unusually small, peeped, now and then, as the feet within them moved somewhat nervously about.

"All right, are you?" he inquired.

"I ain't afeared," the jockey answered, "but I'm powerful nervous. Never had on clo'es like these before, an'--don't you look at me!"

Strange talk, this was, for the jockey who was soon to ride Queen Bess for the capture of the Ashland Oaks and the salvation of the fortune of the house of Layson!

"Don't look at you!" said the Colonel, in expostulation, and, in the next sentence, revealed a secret which he was guarding carefully from everyone. "See here, little girl, you've got to face thousands and not wince, and you can't ride in that overcoat, either."

But the jockey wrapped the coat still tighter. "Oh, sho! That can't make no differ--just a little coat!"

"I tell you it's impossible. It would give the game away at once. Come, take it off. Practice up on me."

The jockey shivered nervously. "Reckon I will hev to. Say, turn your back till I am ready."

The Colonel turned his back, somewhat impatiently. The time was getting short. "All right, but hurry up."

The jockey pulled the long coat partly off, then, in a panic, shrugged it on again. "Oh, now, you're lookin'!"

"Not a wink," declared the Colonel.

"Wal, here goes!" This time the coat came wholly off and the jockey who had been discovered to take the place of drunken Ike stood quite revealed. The voice which warned the Colonel of this was a faint and faltering one. "Now," it said timidly.

The Colonel turned. "Hurrah!"

The jockey held the coat up in a panic.

"See here, now--none o' that!" the Colonel warned. "Give it to me." He reached his hand out for the coat, and, reluctantly, the jockey let him take it.

There stood the trimmest and most graceful figure ever garbed in racing blouse, knickers, boots and cap, with flushed face, dilating, frightened eyes and hands not a little tremulous. The girl who had told Barbara Holton that she would not hesitate to make a sacrifice to save the man she loved was making one--a very great one--the sacrifice of what, her whole life long, she had considered fitting woman's modesty. Queen Bess must win and there was no one else to ride her. The mountain-girl shrank from the thought of going, thus, before a multitude, as shyly as would the most highly educated and most socially precise girl in the grand-stand, near, which, now, was filling with the gallantry and beauty of Kentucky; but she did not let her nervous tremors conquer her. There was no other way to save the day for Layson, and, somehow, the day must certainly be saved.

The Colonel, now, spoke very seriously as she stood there, shrinking from his gaze. There was not a smile upon his face. It was plain that he regarded the whole matter with the utmost gravity.

"Now, little one, you begin to realize what this means," said he. "Or--no, you don't and I've got to be square with you if it spoils the prettiest horse-race ever seen in old Kentucky. I tell you, my dear child, we're mighty particular about our women, down here in the bluegrass. We'd think it an eternal shame and a disgrace forever for one of them to ride a public race in a costume like the one that you have on, and it would mean not less than social ruin to the man that married her. If anyone should find it out, what you are going to do might stand between you and your happiness. I'm warning you because I know I ought to. Think it over and then tell me if you're willing to face it--willing to take all the risks."

"I don't need to think it over," Madge said firmly. "I said as I'd gin up my happiness to save him, an' I will. Colonel, I've got on my uniform, I've enlisted for th' war, an' I am goin' to fight it through!"

"A thoroughbred!" he cried. "A thoroughbred, and I always said it of you. Come on, little one."

CHAPTER XVII

Brilliant as a garden of flowers was the grand-stand where the fairest of old Kentucky's wondrous women were as numerous as were her gallant men; full of handsome figures were the lawns, where old Kentucky's youth and manhood strolled and smoked and gossipped of the day's great race to come; like an ebon sea in storm was the great crowd of blacks which in certain well-defined limits crowded to the rail about the track. The blare of the band kept the air a-tremble almost constantly, the confused, uneven murmur of a great crowd filled the pauses between brazen outbursts. Everywhere was life and gayety, intense excitement, as the moment for the starting of the famous Ashland Oaks approached. The cries of the book-makers rose, strident, from the betting-ring; on the tracks the jockeys, exercising or trying out their mounts, were, each after his own kind, preparing for the struggle of their lives; stable-boys, and the hundred other species of race-track hangers-on which swarm at such times to the front, were everywhere in evidence; touts with shifty eyes slipped, here and there, among the sightseers, looking for some credulous one who might be willing to pay well for doubtful information. Every minute amidst the throng the words "Queen Bess" might be heard at any chosen point, as the crowd gossipped eagerly about the horse which had been looked on as the favorite, but which, many positively now declared, had been so injured in the fire that she would run but poorly in the race which, it had been thought, would be the most sensational effort of her life.

Frank, nervous and excited, stood in the paddock, watch in hand, with old Neb by his side.

"Why doesn't that jockey come?" he asked, for the hundredth time, almost beside himself with worry as the moments slipped away.

"He'll come, Marse Frank," said Neb. "You kin gamble on de Cunnel."

"If I only knew what kind of a jockey he is!" Then, as Horace Holton came up, smiling greetings: "Holton, how's the betting?"

"Can't you hear?" said Holton, as a vagrant breeze brought to their ears bits of the vocal tumult from the betting-ring.

"Ten to nine against Queen Bess," Frank heard a voice call loudly, although the crowd's great murmur made the words come indistinctly to his ears. "Even on Catalpa," was the next penetrating cry, and then: "Two to one, Evangeline!"

The young owner shuddered. Could it be possible that Neb was right and that the Colonel's jockey would appear on time, or were the dire predictions of defeat which, he knew, were being made everywhere around him, true prophecies? Tales of all but fatal injuries to the handsome mare had been freely circulated, and, despite denials in the newspapers, were still alive, and these he knew to be quite false; but he knew of the other dire disaster--the defection of his jockey--of which the crowd was also well aware. He had not the slightest doubt that if Queen Bess should run at all she would do all that her best friends expected of her and more; but it seemed to him a possibility that he would find it necessary, at the last minute, to withdraw her from the race entirely, for sheer lack of a rider.

Again the breeze brought from the betting-ring the loud shouts of the bookmakers. The message that they told was most depressing to the worried owner.

"Why, this morning she was the favorite," he said, "and now the odds are all against her!"

Holton nodded. "On the strength o' this jockey as nobody knows. Got any money on, yourself, Layson?"

"Not a cent. I've enough at stake, already."

Holton smiled unpleasantly, intimating that Frank's lack of betting on his horse was proof positive that the worst tales told were true. "That settles it. The bookies are right. Th' mare's no chance with a new jockey, an' you know it."

"If I were betting," said Frank angrily, "I'd back her with every dollar that I have on earth."

Holton smiled at him unpleasantly. "I say she can't win and you know it." He waited for some answer from the anxious owner, but received none. Then, taking out his check-book: "See here--I'll bet you five-thousand even against her!"

Frank, annoyed but helpless, shook his head. "I haven't the money," he admitted.

"You ain't got the sand!" said Holton, aggravatingly.

Frank turned from him angrily, and old Neb, who had listened, stepped quickly up to him. "Marse Frank," he pleaded, "don' yo' let dat white-trash bluff yo'!" The old darkey's voice was tremulous, his eyes were moist with feeling for his humiliated master. A great resolve thrilled through him. "See heah, honey, I's be'n sabin' all mah life. I's got a pile o' money in de bank. Take it all, now, honey, an' bet it on Queen Bess."

Frank shook his head, but smiled at the old darkey, touched alike by his devotion to himself and confidence in the mare they both loved. "No, no, Neb; not your money," he replied. He stood in deep thought, for a moment, tapping the ground nervously with worried foot. "But I'll back the mare for all *I'm* worth!" he finally declared. "If she loses, I'm a ruined man, anyway." He turned, now, to Holton. "Holton," he said, "I've got just three thousand dollars in the bank. I'll put it all on Queen Bess against your five-thousand."

It seemed, almost, as if Holton had been waiting for this offer, for his smile broadened as he found that he had goaded Layson into making it. "I'll take it," he said quickly, and then, turning to the crowd about them, among which were some of the state's best citizens, he added: "Gentlemen, you're witnesses. Three-thousand against five-thousand on Queen Bess."

They nodded, and not one of them but looked at Layson with commiseration, as at a man foredoomed to bitter disappointment.

Neb, however, grinned at Holton impishly. "Yes; you'll look mighty sick when yo' hab to pay it, too."

From the judge's stand rang out the silvery notes of a quavering bugle-call, and Holton smiled unpleasantly.

"The call to th' post," said he, "an' whar's your jockey?"

"He'll be here on time," said Frank, voicing a confidence which it was hard for him to feel. He turned, then, to the darkey. "Neb, bring out Queen Bess."

The excitement, all around them, was intensifying, every minute. Jockeys, now, were mounting their horses, and riding off for the short canter to the judges' stand. As each appeared in view of the great crowd in and about the grand-stand a mighty shout arose.

Holton's smile was broadening. "If that jockey doesn't show up mighty quick," he sneered, "you're out of the race."

Just as he spoke old Neb returned, with the superb mare behind him, saddled, bridled, ready for the race, fretting at her bit, impatient of the crowds and noise.

"Who knows whether he's coming, at all?" said Holton, a bit dashed at sight of the fine mare's superb condition, but still sneering. "Nobody's seen him."

Neb looked off toward the weighing-room. "Yo' 're wrong," he shouted, capering with amazing spryness for one whose limbs were old and stiff, "fo' heah he comes!"

Every member of the party turned, in haste, to look in the direction whence Neb pointed.

They saw a slight, graceful figure, dressed in the brilliant colors of the Layson stable, which, without so much as glancing at them, ran to Queen Bess and took a place upon the far side of the mare, where, stooping as if to look carefully to the saddle-girths, its face was quickly hidden. But, even as the jockey stooped, one of his hands held out to Frank, across the saddle, a little folded paper.

Without paying much attention to the jockey, Layson took this note and hastily unfolded it. "It's from the Colonel," he announced. "I knew he'd never fail me."

Then he read, aloud, so all might hear:

"This will be handed to you by a jockey I have just engaged. He comes from the east and is highly recommended. I know his endorser. Regretting that the promise of a Kentuckian prevents me from being with you, I am yours regretfully, on the outside, SANDUSKY DOOLITTLE."

"It's all right!" Frank shouted, gleefully, and then, to the strange jockey: "Quick, on the mare and off to the post!"

Without a word, without a second's pause, Madge, for the unknown jockey was, of course, the little mountain girl, jumped upon Queen Bess and hastily rode off, to be greeted, with a mighty outburst of cheering and applause as the favorite appeared before the waiting crowds in unmistakably fine condition and mounted by a rider whose every movement showed a perfect knowledge of the work and complete sympathy with the beautiful animal he rode.

*   *   *   *   *

Doomed by his promise on the honor of a gentleman to Miss Alathea, to witnessing the race from the outside, if he witnessed it at all, Colonel Sandusky Doolittle, fully aware of the unusual interest of the moments, some account of which has just been made, was sunk in melancholy after he had sent Madge through the magic portals, with explicit instructions as to exactly what to do when once she was safe inside. He was breathing hard from the mere exertion of preventing his unruly feet from running to the gate, of keeping his unruly hand from diving deep into his pocket for the entrance fee. These preventions he accomplished, though, without once really weakening, and was safe at a good distance from the tempting gate when the crowd within began to shout as the horses were brought out.

"There, they're bringing out the horses!" he exclaimed, unhappily. He set his jaws as might one who, with a great effort, abstains from food when famishing. "I didn't go in!" he muttered. "I've kept my word, though it has nearly finished me!"

Anxiously, if hurriedly, he searched along the fence for the knot-hole Neb had told him of. Twice, in his great eagerness, he passed it by, but, on the third inspection he discovered it, and placed his eye to it. In a moment he backed away, dejectedly. "I can't see worth a cent!" he bitterly complained. "It's not hole enough for me!" Lost, in his disappointment, even to shame for the wretched pun, he straightened up, surveying his immediate surroundings.

Close by was the tree which Neb had also spoken of. He examined it with an appraising eye, then looked about to see what spectators were near. No one was in sight save a pair of piccaninnies, down the fence a hundred yards or so, with eyes glued to other knot-holes or to cracks.

"To the deuce with dignity!" he cried. "I'll just inspect that tree."

He was doing this with care, when, breathless and eager, a lady hurried toward him. As the tree intervened between them he did not see her coming, nor did she note his presence. It would have been quite plain to anyone who had observed her that she was engaged upon a quest much like that which he had pursued, for she carefully inspected each plank in the high fence, as, slowly and cautiously lest she should pass unheeded that which she was seeking eagerly, she made her way in his direction.

"Everybody's at the races," she thought, comforting herself. "I'm perfectly safe. No one in the world will see me.... But where *is* that blessed knot-hole?"

Suddenly her eye chanced on it, and, an instant later, was applied to it, the while the Colonel paused, with his back to her, still anxiously inspecting the tree.

"Ah!" said Miss Alathea, aloud, as she caught a glimpse of something interesting inside the fence.

Instantly the Colonel turned and looked down at her, startled. Then: "A woman!" he exclaimed, beneath his breath. "A woman at my knot-hole!"

Firmly determined to maintain his right he sternly approached her.

"Madam!" he exclaimed, as incensed by her usurpation of the knot-hole as he would have been, at ordinary times, by theft of watch or pocket-book, and tapped her lightly on the shoulder.

She shrank back from the knot-hole, startled and indignant. "Sir!" she cried, and then, as he recognized her, she turned and saw who had addressed her.

"Colonel Sandusky Doolittle!" she exclaimed, amazed.

"Miss Alathea Layson!" cried the Colonel, equally amazed, at first, but winding up his gesture of surprise with a low and courtly bow.

"Colonel, what are you doing here?"

"Madame," he countered, "what are *you* doing here?"

Miss Alathea's dignity forsook her. "Colonel," she confessed, "I couldn't wait to hear the result."

"No more could I," he somewhat sheepishly admitted.

"But I didn't enter the race-track," she explained in haste.

"I was equally firm."

"And Neb told me of this knot-hole."

"The rascal--he told me of it, too."

"Colonel," she said, smiling, "we must forgive each other. If you really must look, there is the knot-hole."

"No, Miss 'Lethe," he said gallantly, "*I* resign the knot-hole to you. I shall climb the tree." Without delay (for sounds from the barrier's far side hinted to his practiced ear that matters of much moment were progressing, there) he scrambled with much more difficulty than dignity into the spreading crotch.

"Oh, be careful Colonel!" Miss Alathea cried, alarmed. "Don't break your neck!" But she added, as an afterthought: "But be sure to get where you can see."

"Ah, what a gallant sight!" he cried as he found himself in a position whence he could command a view of the exciting scene within the barrier. "There's Catalpa ... and Evangeline ... and ... yes, there is Queen Bess!"

A burst of cheering rose from the crowd within.

Miss Alathea was on tip-toe with excitement. "What's that?" she begged.

"A false start," he answered, scarcely even glancing down at her. "They'll make it this time, though," he added, and she could see his knuckles whiten with the strain as he gripped a rough limb of the tree with vise-like fingers.

A moment later and the shouting became a very tempest of sound.

"They're off!" he cried, staring through his field glasses in an excitement which promised, if he did not curb it, to send him tumbling from his shaky foothold. "Oh, what a splendid start!"

"Who's ahead?" inquired Miss Alathea, very much excited. "Colonel, who's ahead?"

"Catalpa sets the pace, the others lying well back."

"Why doesn't Queen Bess come to the front?" Miss Alathea cried, as if he were to blame for the disquieting news he had reported to her. "Oh," she exclaimed, to the Colonel's great astonishment, "if I were only on that mare!"

"At the half," the Colonel shouted, beside himself with worry, "Evangeline takes the lead ... Catalpa next ... the rest are bunched."

Miss Alathea, at the moment, was trying to see satisfactorily, through the very knot-hole which the Colonel had abandoned. She sprang from it hastily, however, and to the foot of the tree which acted as his pedestal, when he exclaimed:

"Oh, great heavens! There's a fall ... a jam ... and Queen Bess is left behind three lengths!" He leaned so far out that he heard the limb beneath him crack, and, in hastening to a firmer footing, almost lost his balance. This startled him, and, for an instant, took his eager gaze away from the struggling horses on the track within, but he quickly regained poise. "She hasn't the ghost of a show!" he cried, disheartened. "Look! Look!"

Miss Alathea hugged the tree and looked, not at the horses, for that was quite impossible, but up at him with wide, imploring eyes.

"She's at it again, though, now!" he cried. "It's beyond anything mortal, but she's gaining ... gaining!"

Miss Alathea's excitement now was every bit as great as his. She had never seen a race in all her life, yet, now, she performed there at the foot of the great tree, a series of evolution not unlike those of many a "rooter" at the track within. She jumped up and down upon her toe's, clenched her hands and cried: "Oh, keep it up! Keep it up!"

"At the three-quarters she's only five lengths behind the leader and still gaming!" cried the Colonel, in excited optimism.

Miss Alathea could no longer endure the agony of waiting on the ground for his reports. Instead she tried to scramble to his side, but, failing, utterly, to accomplish this unaided, held her hands up to him, crying: "Oh, pull, pull! I can't stand it! I've just got to see!"

The Colonel turned upon his perch and looked down at her, smiling. "Coming up, Miss 'Lethe?" he inquired. "All right, don't break your neck, but get where you can see." Hastily he gave her such assistance as his absorbed attention to the events within the fence permitted, and, with a wild scramble, she found herself close by his side, holding half to him, half to a curving branch.

"Look! Look!" he cried, again. "In the stretch! Her head is at Catalpa's crupper ... now at her saddle-bow ... but she can't gain another inch. Still ... yes ... yes ... she lifts her! See!... See!... Great God! She wins!"

Within the fence wild pandemonium broke loose. The crowd went mad with shouting. Hats, handkerchiefs, canes, umbrellas, flew into the air as if blown upward by the mad explosion of the crowd's enthusiasm. The band was playing "Dixie."

Frank and Neb rushed forward to lift from the winner the victorious jockey, who by such superb riding as that track had never seen before, had snatched victory from defeat after the mare had been delayed in the bad pocket which, from his distant point of survey, had alarmed the Colonel. The jockey eluded them, however and, with face averted, hurried with the splendid mare back to the paddock, and there disappeared, disregarding the crowd's wild shouts of acclamation.

Holton stood near Frank, white-faced and angry. Old Neb, as he ran beside Queen Bess, looked back at him and grinned.

CHAPTER XVIII

Miss Alathea, on the day after the great race, sat waiting for the Colonel in the handsome old library of Woodlawn, worrying about her unconventionalities of the preceding day. When she heard his voice, out in the hall, telling Neb to carry certain bundles into the library and knew, of course, that he would follow after them almost immediately, her heart throbbed fiercely in her bosom. She shrank back into a window recess, too embarrassed to face him without first pausing to gather up her courage.

"Put 'em there, Neb," said the Colonel, pointing to the table, and then, after the packages had been arranged to suit him: "Here, take this, and drink to the jockey that rode Queen Bess."

"T'ankee, Marse Cunnel, t'ankee," Neb replied, pocketing the tip. "Oh, warn't it gran'? An' yo' climbed de tree, arter all!"

"Sh! Clear out, you rascal!"

Neb did not go at once, but, with the boldness of an old and privileged retainer, stood there, chuckling. "Climbed de tree!" he gurgled. "An' so did Miss 'Lethe!"

With this he slapped his knee, and, laughing boisterously, left the room as the embarrassed lady of the house stepped out of her concealment.

"Ah, Miss 'Lethe," said the Colonel, "good morning."

"I expected you back from Lexington last night, Colonel." She looked at him reproachfully.

"Stayed over to celebrate, my dear," the Colonel answered. "Stayed to celebrate the victory." With a beaming face he advanced upon the lady, plainly planning an embrace.

But she eluded him. "Wait a moment, Colonel. On what did you celebrate?"

The Colonel laughed. "Oh, I didn't forget. I celebrated on ginger-ale and soda-pop."

Miss Alathea smiled with happy satisfaction. She eluded him no longer, but, herself, went to him and bestowed the kiss.

"I doubt if my stomach ever recovers from the insult," said the Colonel, delighted by the kiss but remembering the mildness of the beverages which had marked his jubilation. "Miss 'Lethe, a julep--a mint-julep--before I perish."

With a smile she crossed the room to where, upon the side-board (a side-board is an adjunct of all well-regulated libraries in old Kentucky), a snowy damask cloth concealed glorious somethings. With a graceful sweep she took it from them and revealed three juleps in their glory of green-crowns. "Look, Colonel!"

"Three! Great heavens!" the Colonel cried, delighted. He took one and disposed of it in haste.

"I mixed them myself," Miss 'Lethe said.

The Colonel drank another, but less rapidly.

"Remember," she said, warningly, "three and no more!"

"Yes, yes," he granted. "I must save the other one." It was difficult to sip it, for Miss Alathea's juleps were like nectar to his thirsty palate, but he restrained himself and drank of this last ambrosial glass with great deliberation, trying to make it last as long as possible.

"What are all those bundles, Colonel?" asked Miss Alathea, pointing to the packages which old Neb had brought in.

"They're for Madge. She bought them yesterday." He sighed. "Ah, will you ever forget yesterday?"

"Oh, don't speak of it!"

"Can't help it." The Colonel waxed enthusiastic at the mere memory of the great occasion. "Whoopee!" he cried. "What a race it was!"

"To think," said Miss Alathea, "that I--*I*--should enter a race-track!"

"To think that *I*--should stay out of one!"

"It was all your fault, Colonel," said Miss Alathea. "In your excitement after the race you grasped my hand and I was compelled to follow."

"How strange!" exclaimed the Colonel, slowly, with a slight smile tickling at the corners of his mouth. "At times I fancied you were in the lead, I following."

"Colonel," said the lady slowly, "perhaps I might as well confess. I've made a discovery. The sin isn't so much in looking at the horses run--it's in betting on them. That's where souls are lost."

"And likewise money," said the Colonel, nodding, gravely.

"So, Colonel, if you'll promise not to bet, I've no objection to your attending the races in moderation."

In delighted amazement the Colonel forgot that that last julep could be brought to a quick end by hurried management and took a hasty and a mammoth swallow. "What!" he cried. "Can I believe it? Miss 'Lethe, you're an angel! It's the last drop in my cup of happiness!"

Miss Alathea shyly smiled--smiled, indeed, a bit shame-facedly. "There's one condition, Colonel--that you take me along--yes, to watch over you."

"Take you with me?" said the Colonel. He paused in puzzled contemplation of her for an instant. "Oh, I catch on. You'll go with the children to see the animals!" He laughed. "You rather like it." He became enthusiastic. "No more knot-holes or trees for us! At last--two souls with but a single thought, two hearts that beat when Queen Bess won! Here's to our future happiness!"

He raised the glass and would have drunk from it, but, now, alas! the glass was empty. It surprised and grieved him, but, when Miss Alathea held her hand out, quietly, for the vessel which had held the final julep but which now held it no longer, he yielded it up gracefully nor asked her to refill it.

As Miss Alathea placed the empty glass upon the side-board Madge entered from the hallway. She ran up to the Colonel. "I heard you'd come," she said, "an' couldn't wait. Say, air it all fixed about Queen Bess?"

"Fixed?" cried the gallant horseman. "Well I should remark! Queen Bess is sold and paid for and a draft for the assessment forwarded to the Company. Inside of a year Frank will have the income of a prince."

"All," said Miss Alathea, "owing to that mysterious jockey who disappeared immediately after the race. Oh, I'd like to kiss that boy!"

"If you did, I should not be jealous," said the Colonel with an air of generosity.

"Miss 'Lethe, kiss me. Won't I do as well?" Madge asked, going to her.

Miss Alathea kissed her, but was still thinking of the unknown jockey, who, in the nick of time, had come from nowhere, materialized from nothing, to save the day for Frank by riding Queen Bess to victory. "I feel as if I must know his name," she said. "Madge, help me persuade the Colonel to tell us." She went to him and petted him. "Colonel, you will not refuse me!"

Madge looked at him apprehensively, warningly. "An' I reckon you won't refuse me, Colonel." Then, going close to him, she whispered: "Remember, mum's the word!"

"Away, you tempters, away!" the Colonel cried, and waved them from him. "It's a professional secret, and I've promised to keep it on the honor of a Kentucky gentleman--just as I promised you, Miss 'Lethe."

"As you promised me? That's enough, Colonel--not another word!"

Madge nodded, smilingly. "That's right, Colonel. Mustn't break your word." Just then she caught sight of the bundles which the Colonel had had Neb bring in. "Oh, are them my bundles, Colonel?"

"Every one of them."

The girl hurried to the mysteriously fascinating packages and began investigation of their contents. "Thank ye, thank ye!" she exclaimed, while she was busy with the wrappings. "Awful good of you to bring 'em." Then, to Miss Alathea in explanation: "Things I bought yesterday, Miss 'Lethe, all by myself. Jus' went wild. Reckon I'll let you an' th' Colonel see 'em." She took a large, dressed doll out of its wrappings. "Look at that!"

"What a beauty!" cried the Colonel.

"Can talk, too." Madge pressed the wondrous puppet's shirred silk chest. "Ma-ma," it cried. "Ma-ma."

"Never had nothin' but a rag-doll, myself," the girl went on, delighted by their approval of this automatic wonder. "'Tain't for me. It's for a little girl as lives up in th' mountings."

From the doll she turned to an amazing jumping-jack, the next treasure taken from the packages. She pulled the toy's animating strings and watched its antics with delight. "Mos' as lively as a Kentucky Colonel climbin' a tree," said she, and laughed roguishly at the horseman. "Oh, I heard of it; I heard of it."

The Colonel tried in vain to protest, Madge's laughter kept up merrily, as she took an old-fashioned carpet-sack from quite the biggest of the bundles and began to pack her purchases in it, until the Colonel and Miss Alathea left the room, gaily protesting at her ridicule.

Instantly all of the signs of high elation vanished from the girl's face. She drooped. Left alone, it quickly became plain that her recent animation had been forced, unreal. "Well I guess I'd better not open up th' other bundles," she said listlessly. "I'll pack 'em as they be. It's time I started too. I'm goin' back to the mountings." Softly she hummed the air the darkies had been singing when she came into the room.

"Weep no more, my lady, oh, weep no more to-day,   I will sing one song of my old Kentucky home,   Then my old Kentucky home, good-night!"

There was infinite pathos in her half-unconscious rendition of the plaintive, darkey melody. To the mountain girl the moment was full of sadness. She had come down from her mountains to save the man she loved from the assassin's bullet and had saved him, not from that alone, but from a crushing blow to hope and fortune. Her work was done. All that now was left to her was to go back to her little cabin, hiding the secret of her love for him in her sore heart, enshrining, there, the memory of every minute she had ever passed with him as holy memories to comfort her in days to come. Melancholy thoughts pressed on her hard.

Frank entered.

He stopped short in the doorway, looking with amazement at her work of packing for departure.

"Why, Madge!" said he. "What does this mean? Packing up! Surely you're not going away!" There was a thrill of real distress in his pleasant, vibrant voice which comforted her.

"Yes, I'm going back to th' mountings. I was ... goin' afore, but I couldn't miss that hoss-race."

"Madge," he cried impulsively, "you must not and you shall not go. I cannot bear to think of you wasting your life in the lonely mountains. Madge, your land will make you rich, and with your brightness you could study and learn. Education will make you an ornament to any society."

She shook her head. "As fur as I can see," said she, "society ain't what it is cracked up to be. I don't seem to have no hankerin' after it. Oh, o' course, I'd like to have all this softness an' pootiness around me, always; I'd like to go out in th' world an' see th' wonders as I've heard of; but I don't think that 'u'd satisfy me. I'd still be hankerin' an' thirstin' arter somethin' that I couldn't have. There's been a feelin' in my heart, ever sence I come here, that'll take th' air o' th' mountings to cl'ar away. Like enough, up there among th' wild things that love me, amongst th' rocks an' hills, I'll find th' rest an' peace I ain't had since I come away."

The youth looked at her with wide, worried eyes. He had not thought the situation out in any very careful detail; but he had, at no time, contemplated her immediate departure. Now that it seemed imminent it brought his feelings to a focus, showed him, instantly, that he could not bear to have this mountain maiden who had done so much for him thus vanish from his life. A realization that he loved her deeply, tenderly, unchangeably rushed over him. That she was a child of nature, uneducated and unaccustomed to the world he knew became a matter of but small importance to him as he stood there watching her, while, sadly but deliberately, she kept on with her work of packing in the carpet-bag her small possessions and the many gifts which she had purchased in the city for the children of her "mountings." That the world which he had ever thought his world might laugh at her and ridicule him if he married her he knew, but, suddenly, this seemed of little consequence. The errors in her education could be readily corrected and her heart and instincts were more nearly right, already, than those of any lowland girl whom he had ever known.

"Madge," he cried, "I cannot give you up! I love you!"

The girl's hands stopped their busy work among the bundles. Her cheeks paled and her lips parted to a gasping little intake of breath. It had not, once, occurred to her modest, self-sacrificing mind that, even as the bluegrass gentleman had found her heart and taken it forever and forever to be his own, no matter where she was or how great might be the distance be which separated them, so, also, had his heart really and forever passed to her, the simple, unlettered and untrained little maiden of the wilderness. It seemed impossible, incredible.

"You love me!"

"Yes, I love you as I never have, as I never can love any other woman. Madge, dearest, I want you for my wife!"

The great desire, the certainty that if he did not win her then all other triumphs would be empty, meaningless, had come suddenly upon him, but it had come with overwhelming force. His voice was vibrant with a passion which surprised himself.

"No, no; it can never be!" she said tremulously. Her heart was in a turmoil, her hands trembled with excitement. Ah, it was hard for her to put away from her the brilliant vista which had opened there before her startled eyes! But she was sure that she must do it; that if she loved this man she must forswear him for his own dear sake. What right had she, a mountain-girl, to come down there to the bluegrass to shame him in the face of friends and foes by her ignorance and awkwardness? Her heart yearned toward him with a warmth and fervor which she had not known as possible to human longings, but--no, no, for his sake she must give him up, as, for his sake, she had made the long, desperate journey from the mountains to save him from Joe Lorey's bullet, as, for his sake, shrinking and dismayed, conscious that in doing it she might very well be sacrificing his respect for her, she had donned the blouse and breeches of a jockey, yesterday, to ride his mare to victory when none other had been there to save the day for him. That had been a sacrifice almost beyond the power of words to tell--a sacrifice of modesty; now came an even greater one, but one which, none the less, must certainly be made. "No, no," said she again, "it can never, never be!"

"But I want you--just as you are! What do I care for the world, without you, or for what it says, so long as you are mine?"

A flood of bitterness rushed to her heart. Ah, why, why, had fate made it so necessary that, to save him, she must do what, yesterday, she had been forced to do!

"You're thinkin' of my ignorance, an' such," she said, with sad eyes bent upon the gifts which, now, although she looked at them, she did not see and had forgotten. "But there's more nor that as stands between us, Mr. Frank."

"You mean you don't love me?"

"No, no; oh, what air th' use o' denyin' it? I love you! It's that--it's that that drives me from you, an' that breaks--my--heart!"

He went close to her and tried to take her hands in his. "Madge, dear," he said softly, "I want you to listen to me. I tell you I shall not let any foolish pride or any fears for the future stand in the way of our happiness. When I thought, a moment ago, that I might lose you forever, I saw what my life would be without you; and, now that I know you love me, nothing shall come between us. Madge, dear heart, I want you to put your hand in mine."

She drew away, but it was plain that she was sorely tempted. "Ah, if I only dared!" said she.

"Come, Madge, darling!" he said fervently, opening his arms to fold her to his heart.

"No, no," she said, "it wouldn't be right." The Colonel's words: "We'd think it an eternal shame and a disgrace for one of our women to ride a race in a costume such as you have on," rang in her mind and filled her with despair. "The Colonel said--" she began, weakly.

"Oh, damn the Colonel!" Frank cried angrily, wondering why any one should meddle with his heart-affairs.

And as he spoke the Colonel entered hurriedly, evidently bearing news of import.

Startled by the young man's earnest words, he stopped short in astonishment. "Why--what's that, sir?" he exclaimed amazed, and then, seeing clearly that he had broken in upon a fervent sentimental situation and unwilling to believe that Frank could really have meant him when he had been so emphatic, turned his thoughts, again, to the news which had brought him in such haste.

"I say," he said, excitedly, "I've been cross-examining that rascal, Ike, and I've found out who smuggled the whiskey to him."

"Who was it?" Madge and Frank cried almost in unison.

"That double-distilled, three-ply scoundrel, Horace Holton," said the Colonel, angrily.

"Holton!" Frank exclaimed. "I wouldn't have believed it!"

"I would," Madge commented.

"I'll find him and settle with him for it!" Frank angrily exclaimed.

"I'm afraid that's easier said than done," the Colonel answered, "but I'm with you, and we'll do our best."

Through the windows came the noise of baying hounds. It instantly attracted their attention, as it ever will that of Kentuckians. "What's that? A fox-hunt?"

Frank had hurried to the window and was looking out. "No," he answered, in incredulous amazement, "it's Holton and his gang. They're hunting Joe Lorey with dogs!"

Madge hurried to his side, distressed beyond the power of words to tell. "Oh, oh!" she cried. "They're coming this way, and--and--who's that?"

As she spoke Joe Lorey dashed up, breathless to the window.

CHAPTER XIX

The moonshiner stood there, pathetic in his beaten strength before them. "They're huntin' me with dogs!" he said. "They're goin' to string me up without justice or mercy!"

Madge hurried to his side. "Joe, they shan't do it!" she exclaimed, and took his hand.

"It'll take more nor you to save me, little one," he said, and smiled down at her pitifully. "There's no hope for me, now. That's why I've come hyar, to say to you all, afore I die, that I am innocent o' firin' th' stable." He threw back his shoulders and stood before them, impressive and convincing. "Afore God, I am innocent!"

Frank looked at him with eyes which, as they gazed, altered their expression. He had thought the man quite possibly guilty of a vicious act--a foul attempt to burn a helpless animal in order to obtain revenge upon the man who owned her. But as he gazed he could not doubt that he was speaking simple truth. "Joe," he said impulsively, "I believe you!"

Joe turned to him with gratitude plain upon his face. "You believe me--arter all that's passed?" He looked straight into the eyes of the young man he had hated, with a searching, earnest gaze. "Then," he said, after a second's pause, "I believe as what you said, that night, war true. It war never you as ruined me." He held his hand out to the man whom, not so long ago, he had wished, with all his heart, to kill.

Frank grasped it with a hearty grip, just as the terrifying baying of the hounds approached the house.

"Frank, they're coming here!" the Colonel cried, excited.

Joe turned away from Frank, looking here and there like a hunted animal. "Oh, it's hard to die afore I've met Lem Lindsay!" he said hopelessly. It was quite plain that he considered his fate sealed.

Even as he spoke Holton and half-a-dozen others sprang to the broad gallery which fronted the whole room. Holton was plainly the leader of the party, for when he motioned all the others back, they obeyed his signal without protest, while he, himself, peered eagerly in through a wide, open window.

Frank, angered beyond measure by this bold intrusion, would have sprung toward him, to attack him, had not the Colonel waved him back.

"Frank, my boy," said he, "keep cool, keep cool!"

As he spoke, without apology, Holton stepped through the window into the room, itself.

"Layson," he said curtly, "I'm a committee o' one to ask if you'll turn over that man, an' make no trouble." He jerked a thumb toward Joe.

Layson was wrathful at the man's intrusion; he had been impressed by what the fugitive had said. "No," he answered, hotly. "Joe Lorey's in my house, under my protection, and, by the eternal, you shan't lay a hand on him!"

The Colonel smiled, delighted. "Kentucky blood!" he cried. "I'll back you to a finish!"

He ranged himself by Frank, and Madge, as belligerent as either of them, hurried, also, to his side.

"I'm with you, Colonel," she exclaimed, with the spirit of the mountain-bred, "and we'll win ag'in, as we did once before!"

Joe saw this with distress. Layson's generosity had softened him. He knew, perfectly, by this time, that Madge was not for him, and her spirit in joining his defenders--the very men whom he had thought his enemies--touched him deeply. The realization came to him with a quick rush that he had wronged the bluegrass folk whom he had hated with such bitterness. He looked first at those who wished to take him prisoner and make him suffer for a crime of which he was not guilty, and then at his defenders, who had every reason to doubt him, but still, without a question, had accepted his own plea of innocence. He had already made these people trouble. Now was his opportunity to save them from an awkward situation and, perhaps, a perilous one. There might be shooting if he offered to resist or let these good friends attempt to defend him. That would endanger them, and, worse, endanger Madge. "I'll go. I don't want to make no trouble," he said hastily.

Holton nodded with approval. He wished to take the man as quickly and as simply as he could. Every complication which could be avoided would make less probable discovery of the fact that he, himself, and not the fugitive young mountaineer, was the real culprit.

"That's sensible," he said, "for them men, out thar, are bound to hev you, by fair means or foul."

"Those men will listen to reason," Frank said with a determination which disconcerted the ex-slave dealer. "They shall hear me!" He stepped toward the open window. "Colonel, come with me." Without waiting for him he stepped to the gallery outside.

The Colonel started to go also, but, seeing that Holton, too, was about to hurry out, paused long enough to go up to him threateningly. "Don't you dare to follow!" he warned him. "We'll play this hand alone." The man fell back and the Colonel kept his eyes on him as, slowly, he joined Frank on the gallery.

Holton's discomfiture lasted but a moment. As soon as the Colonel had passed out of sight he got his wits back and looked threateningly at Madge and the mountaineer. "We'll see about that," he declared viciously, and, making a movement of his hand which indicated that he must be armed, although he had not shown a weapon, so far, moved toward another window which also opened on the gallery.

But he had not counted on old Neb. The darkey found in this emergency the opportunity for which he had been waiting many years. Lapse of time had never dulled his keen resentment of the blow the man had struck him; now it was with keen delight that he stepped out of the shadow just outside the window, with a carelessly held pistol in his hand, which somehow appeared to cover Holton. "De Cunnel said you'd please stay heah, suh," he said placidly; but the pistol gave his words an emphasis which could not be mistaken.

Holton paled with rage, but did not take another forward step.

As he fell back Joe Lorey spoke. The murmur of the mob outside, incited, he well knew, to hunger for his life, and the loud voices of the Colonel and of Frank, raised in expostulation, made an accompaniment for what he had to say to Holton, and that he still was in grave danger made his attitude more menacing, his words more impressive.

"Yes," he said to Holton, while Madge gazed, spellbound, "you hold on. I've a word to say to you."

"Say it, then, and say it quick," said Holton, trying to make his tone contemptuous.

"I'll say it quick, and I'll say it plain. You know as it war never me as fired that stable. You war there an' saw me leave afore th' fire. It's yer place to cl'ar me. Why air you a-houndin' me to my death?"

Holton was uncomfortable. "Them men out thar believe ye guilty. It ain't my work," he said.

The mountaineer was not deceived. He knew this man to be his enemy, although he knew no reason for his hatred. "It's you as air settin' 'em on," he said, "as you set me on Frank Layson when you told me that lie ag'in him in th' mountings."

Madge had listened, speechless, during this dramatic scene, but stood watching it, alert and ready to lend aid to her friend, if opportunity arose. Now, at Joe's words, she started forward.

"Was it him as told you?" she inquired, amazed.

Joe did not answer her, but continued to face Holton and address him. "I believed you," he went on, "because I thought you couldn't a-knowed o' th' still except through him; but since he never told you, it air proof to me that you have been in these here mountings, sometime, afore." Strange suspicions were glittering from his hostile eyes as he faced the now thoroughly alarmed man who, a moment since, had been the blustering bully.

"I tell you I were never thar!" said Holton hurriedly.

"Then how did you know of th' cave an' the oak?" said Joe, accusingly. The glitter of suspicion in his eyes was growing brighter every second. "It's plain to me as how you've passed many a day thar in them mountings. Thar's somethin' bound up in yer past as has egged you on ag'in me. I wants to know what that thing is--I wants to know just who an' what ye air!"

"It's easy enough to show who Horace Holton is," the man said, blustering, but he was very ill at ease. "What do I care what you want?" And then he made a slip. "You can't bring no proof--" he began, but caught himself.

Madge had been watching him with new intentness. The excitement of the moment may have sharpened the girl's wits, or, possibly, its hint of peril may have brought to Holton's face some detail of expression, which, during recent weeks, had not before appeared upon it.

"But I kin," she said, slowly. "I war right in what I thought when I first saw you in th' mountings. I *had* seen your face afore!"

"Don't you dare say that!" cried Holton, stepping toward her angrily. The man who had been the accuser, was, strangely, now, quite plainly, half at bay.

"That look ag'in!" the girl said, studying his face. "That look war printed on my baby brain!"

"Silence, I say!" cried Holton, now badly frightened. He had not counted on this recognition.

"Never!" the girl said boldly. She was certain, now, as she looked at him, that the suspicion which had flashed into her mind was accurate. Her cheeks paled and she stepped toward him with set face, clenched hands. Every fibre in her thrilled with horror of him, every drop of blood in her young body cried for vengeance on him. "I'll rouse th' world ag'in ye!" she exclaimed, so tensely that even Lorey looked at her with alarmed amazement. "I'll rouse th' world ag'in ye, for I'm standin' face to face with my own father's murderer--Lem Lindsay!"

"Lem Lindsay!" said Joe, wonderingly, and then, with the expression on his face of a wild-beast about to spring upon his prey: "At last!"

Holton shrank away from them in terror which he could not hide. His bravado was all gone. He was, no longer, the accuser, but, with the mention of that name, had changed places with Joe Lorey and become the fugitive, shrinking, alarmed.

"'Sh! Don't speak that name!" he pleaded. He made no effort at denial. There was that in the girl's eyes which told him that her recognition had been absolute. "I've been hidin' it for years." He spoke pleadingly. "Look hyar. I've got everythin' that heart can wish. Joe Lorey, I'll save you from them men. I'll sw'ar I saw you leave the stable afore th' fire begun." He moved his eyes from one of the accusing faces to the other, terrified. "I'll make ye both rich if you'll never speak that name ag'in!"

"Your weight in gold would make no differ!" Joe cried menacingly. "Lem Lindsay, it air Heaven's work that's given you into my hands!" He went toward him slowly, menacingly, with his strong fingers working with desire to clutch his shrinking throat. "It air Heaven's will as you should meet your fall through Ben Lorey's son!"

Holton, desperate, gathered courage for a last effort to escape from the net which he had woven to his own undoing. With a quick movement he drew from his belt, where his long coat had concealed its presence, hitherto, a gleaming knife, and, with it upraised, rushed at Joe viciously. "I'm a free man, yet," he cried, "an' I'm a-goin' to stay free!"

Joe, alert, calm-eyed, cool-witted, waited for him with a hand upraised to catch his wrist, with muscles braced to meet the fierce attack.

Madge rushed to the window, calling loudly: "Colonel! Mr. Frank!"

But Holton and Joe Lorey were, by that time, locked in a desperate grip and struggling with the energy of men battling for their lives. Twisting and straining, each striving with the last ounce of energy within him to get the better of the other, they plunged across the room and out into the hall.

Just as Frank and the Colonel hurried in, a shot was heard and then a heavy fall. An instant later Joe came to the door.

"Heaven's will are done!" he said, quite simply.

Layson rushed toward him, but paused, aghast, looking off through the open door. "Joe, you've killed him!" he exclaimed.

"An' I had a right!" said Joe, now strangely calm. "When he killed my father it were ordained that he should fall by my hands. I ain't afeared to stand my trial."

"The men outside have promised," Layson said, dismayed by this new and terrible complication, "that you shall have a fair trial on the other charge. They've gone, now, for the sheriff. But this charge," he looked toward the door which led into the hall, "will be more serious!"

"I can clear him of 'em both," said Madge. "I'll sw'ar th' killin' was in self-defense; I'll sw'ar that Holton owned, before me, that he saw Joe leave th' stable afore th' fire."

"He saw him!" exclaimed Frank, astonished. "What was Holton doing there?"

"Oh, don't you see?" said Madge. "He war your enemy--th' man as told Joe th' lie ag'in you in th' mountings, th' man as tried to burn Queen Bess."

The Colonel had entered, quickly, from the gallery, and stood listening, amazed and fascinated. Now, after a moment's pause to think the matter out, he advanced to Joe with outstretched hand. For the man who had been guilty of that vile mischief he felt no regret, for the man who had, in a fair fight and with good reason, shot him down, he felt full sympathy. "Tried to burn Queen Bess!" he cried. "Joe, the jury'll clear you without leaving their seats! Come, my boy--the sheriff's here, and you will have to go with him; but don't you worry. I'll see you through."

Joe stood, thinking, with bowed head and frowning brow. Suddenly he looked up and cast his eyes about upon the company. "Before I goes, I wants to say a word to Madge," said he, and turned to her with an impressive earnestness. "Little one, don't you never fret about me, no more." He took her hand and she gave it to him gladly. "I see, now, as you was never made for me." He took a step toward Frank and led her to him. "I see whar your heart is, an' I puts your hand in his." With bowed head he relinquished the brown hand of the mountain-girl whom he had loved since childhood, to the outstretched hand of the young "foreigner," whom he no longer looked at with the hatred which had so long thrilled his heart. "And--now I says good-bye. God bless you both!"

He went out, slowly, with the Colonel.

"Madge, he's right," said Frank, "this little hand is mine."

He would have clasped her in his arms, but, finally, she held him off.

"No, no," said she, "not till you know my secret. It was I who rode Queen Bess,"

"You rode Queen Bess!"

The Colonel was re-entering the room. "But the world will never know it," he said gallantly, "on the honor of a Kentuckian."

Frank's smile was radiant. "If it did, I should say: 'Here, Madge, in my arms, is your shelter from the world.'" He drew her to him gently. "Madge, my little wife!"

The Codes Of Hammurabi And Moses
W. W. Davies

QTY

The discovery of the Hammurabi Code is one of the greatest achievements of archaeology, and is of paramount interest, not only to the student of the Bible, but also to all those interested in ancient history...

Religion   ISBN: *1-59462-338-4*   **Pages:132**

MSRP $12.95

The Theory of Moral Sentiments
Adam Smith

QTY

This work from 1749. contains original theories of conscience amd moral judgment and it is the foundation for systemof morals.

Philosophy ISBN: *1-59462-777-0*   **Pages:536**

MSRP $19.95

Jessica's First Prayer
Hesba Stretton

QTY

In a screened and secluded corner of one of the many railway-bridges which span the streets of London there could be seen a few years ago, from five o'clock every morning until half past eight, a tidily set-out coffee-stall, consisting of a trestle and board, upon which stood two large tin cans, with a small fire of charcoal burning under each so as to keep the coffee boiling during the early hours of the morning when the work-people were thronging into the city on their way to their daily toil...

Childrens   ISBN: *1-59462-373-2*   **Pages:84**

MSRP $9.95

My Life and Work
Henry Ford

QTY

Henry Ford revolutionized the world with his implementation of mass production for the Model T automobile. Gain valuable business insight into his life and work with his own auto-biography... "We have only started on our development of our country we have not as yet, with all our talk of wonderful progress, done more than scratch the surface. The progress has been wonderful enough but..."

Biographies/ ISBN: *1-59462-198-5*   **Pages:300**

MSRP $21.95

The Art of Cross-Examination
Francis Wellman

QTY

I presume it is the experience of every author, after his first book is published upon an important subject, to be almost overwhelmed with a wealth of ideas and illustrations which could readily have been included in his book, and which to his own mind, at least, seem to make a second edition inevitable. Such certainly was the case with me; and when the first edition had reached its sixth impression in five months, I rejoiced to learn that it seemed to my publishers that the book had met with a sufficiently favorable reception to justify a second and considerably enlarged edition. ..

Pages:412

Reference   **ISBN: *1-59462-647-2***   *MSRP $19.95*

On the Duty of Civil Disobedience
Henry David Thoreau

QTY

Thoreau wrote his famous essay, On the Duty of Civil Disobedience, as a protest against an unjust but popular war and the immoral but popular institution of slave-owning. He did more than write—he declined to pay his taxes, and was hauled off to gaol in consequence. Who can say how much this refusal of his hastened the end of the war and of slavery ?

Law   **ISBN: *1-59462-747-9***   **Pages:48**

MSRP $7.45

Dream Psychology Psychoanalysis for Beginners
Sigmund Freud

QTY

Sigmund Freud, born Sigismund Schlomo Freud (May 6, 1856 - September 23, 1939), was a Jewish-Austrian neurologist and psychiatrist who co-founded the psychoanalytic school of psychology. Freud is best known for his theories of the unconscious mind, especially involving the mechanism of repression; his redefinition of sexual desire as mobile and directed towards a wide variety of objects; and his therapeutic techniques, especially his understanding of transference in the therapeutic relationship and the presumed value of dreams as sources of insight into unconscious desires.

Pages:196

Psychology   **ISBN: *1-59462-905-6***   *MSRP $15.45*

The Miracle of Right Thought
Orison Swett Marden

QTY

Believe with all of your heart that you will do what you were made to do. When the mind has once formed the habit of holding cheerful, happy, prosperous pictures, it will not be easy to form the opposite habit. It does not matter how improbable or how far away this realization may see, or how dark the prospects may be, if we visualize them as best we can, as vividly as possible, hold tenaciously to them and vigorously struggle to attain them, they will gradually become actualized, realized in the life. But a desire, a longing without endeavor, a yearning abandoned or held indifferently will vanish without realization.

Pages:360

Self Help   **ISBN: *1-59462-644-8***   *MSRP $25.45*

☐ **The Rosicrucian Cosmo-Conception Mystic Christianity** *by Max Heindel*   ISBN: *1-59462-188-8*   **$38.95**
The Rosicrucian Cosmo-conception is not dogmatic, neither does it appeal to any other authority than the reason of the student. It is: not controversial, but is: sent forth in the, hope that it may help to clear...   New Age/Religion Pages 646

☐ **Abandonment To Divine Providence** *by Jean-Pierre de Caussade*   ISBN: *1-59462-228-0*   **$25.95**
"The Rev. Jean Pierre de Caussade was one of the most remarkable spiritual writers of the Society of Jesus in France in the 18th Century. His death took place at Toulouse in 1751. His works have gone through many editions and have been republished...   Inspirational/Religion Pages 400

☐ **Mental Chemistry** *by Charles Haanel*   ISBN: *1-59462-192-6*   **$23.95**
Mental Chemistry allows the change of material conditions by combining and appropriately utilizing the power of the mind. Much like applied chemistry creates something new and unique out of careful combinations of chemicals the mastery of mental chemistry...   New Age Pages 354

☐ **The Letters of Robert Browning and Elizabeth Barret Barrett 1845-1846 vol II**   ISBN: *1-59462-193-4*   **$35.95**
by Robert Browning and Elizabeth Barrett   Biographies Pages 596

☐ **Gleanings In Genesis (volume I)** *by Arthur W. Pink*   ISBN: *1-59462-130-6*   **$27.45**
Appropriately has Genesis been termed "the seed plot of the Bible" for in it we have, in germ form, almost all of the great doctrines which are afterwards fully developed in the books of Scripture which follow...   Religion/Inspirational Pages 420

☐ **The Master Key** *by L. W. de Laurence*   ISBN: *1-59462-001-6*   **$30.95**
In no branch of human knowledge has there been a more lively increase of the spirit of research during the past few years than in the study of Psychology, Concentration and Mental Discipline. The requests for authentic lessons in Thought Control, Mental Discipline and...   New Age/Business Pages 422

☐ **The Lesser Key Of Solomon Goetia** *by L. W. de Laurence*   ISBN: *1-59462-092-X*   **$9.95**
This translation of the first book of the "Lemegton" which is now for the first time made accessible to students of Talismanic Magic was done, after careful collation and edition, from numerous Ancient Manuscripts in Hebrew, Latin, and French...   New Age/Occult Pages 92

☐ **Rubaiyat Of Omar Khayyam** *by Edward Fitzgerald*   ISBN:*1-59462-332-5*   **$13.95**
Edward Fitzgerald, whom the world has already learned, in spite of his own efforts to remain within the shadow of anonymity, to look upon as one of the rarest poets of the century, was born at Bredfield, in Suffolk, on the 31st of March, 1809. He was the third son of John Purcell...   Music Pages 172

☐ **Ancient Law** *by Henry Maine*   ISBN: *1-59462-128-4*   **$29.95**
The chief object of the following pages is to indicate some of the earliest ideas of mankind, as they are reflected in Ancient Law, and to point out the relation of those ideas to modern thought.   Religiom/History Pages 452

☐ **Far-Away Stories** *by William J. Locke*   ISBN: *1-59462-129-2*   **$19.45**
"Good wine needs no bush, but a collection of mixed vintages does. And this book is just such a collection. Some of the stories I do not want to remain buried for ever in the museum files of dead magazine-numbers an author's not unpardonable vanity..."   Fiction Pages 272

☐ **Life of David Crockett** *by David Crockett*   ISBN: *1-59462-250-7*   **$27.45**
"Colonel David Crockett was one of the most remarkable men of the times in which he lived. Born in humble life, but gifted with a strong will, an indomitable courage, and unremitting perseverance...   Biographies/New Age Pages 424

☐ **Lip-Reading** *by Edward Nitchie*   ISBN: *1-59462-206-X*   **$25.95**
Edward B. Nitchie, founder of the New York School for the Hard of Hearing, now the Nitchie School of Lip-Reading, Inc, wrote "LIP-READING Principles and Practice". The development and perfecting of this meritorious work on lip-reading was an undertaking...   How-to Pages 400

☐ **A Handbook of Suggestive Therapeutics, Applied Hypnotism, Psychic Science**   ISBN: *1-59462-214-0*   **$24.95**
by Henry Munro   Health/New Age/Health/Self-help Pages 376

☐ **A Doll's House: and Two Other Plays** *by Henrik Ibsen*   ISBN: *1-59462-112-8*   **$19.95**
Henrik Ibsen created this classic when in revolutionary 1848 Rome. Introducing some striking concepts in playwriting for the realist genre, this play has been studied the world over.   Fiction/Classics/Plays 308

☐ **The Light of Asia** *by sir Edwin Arnold*   ISBN: *1-59462-204-3*   **$13.95**
In this poetic masterpiece, Edwin Arnold describes the life and teachings of Buddha. The man who was to become known as Buddha to the world was born as Prince Gautama of India but he rejected the worldly riches and abandoned the reigns of power when...   Religion/History/Biographies Pages 170

☐ **The Complete Works of Guy de Maupassant** *by Guy de Maupassant*   ISBN: *1-59462-157-8*   **$16.95**
"For days and days, nights and nights, I had dreamed of that first kiss which was to consecrate our engagement, and I knew not on what spot I should put my lips..."   Fiction/Classics Pages 240

☐ **The Art of Cross-Examination** *by Francis L. Wellman*   ISBN: *1-59462-309-0*   **$26.95**
Written by a renowned trial lawyer, Wellman imparts his experience and uses case studies to explain how to use psychology to extract desired information through questioning.   How-to/Science/Reference Pages 408

☐ **Answered or Unanswered?** *by Louisa Vaughan*   ISBN: *1-59462-248-5*   **$10.95**
Miracles of Faith in China   Religion Pages 112

☐ **The Edinburgh Lectures on Mental Science (1909)** *by Thomas*   ISBN: *1-59462-008-3*   **$11.95**
This book contains the substance of a course of lectures recently given by the writer in the Queen Street Hall, Edinburgh. Its purpose is to indicate the Natural Principles governing the relation between Mental Action and Material Conditions...   New Age/Psychology Pages 148

☐ **Ayesha** *by H. Rider Haggard*   ISBN: *1-59462-301-5*   **$24.95**
Verily and indeed it is the unexpected that happens! Probably if there was one person upon the earth from whom the Editor of this, and of a certain previous history, did not expect to hear again...   Classics Pages 380

☐ **Ayala's Angel** *by Anthony Trollope*   ISBN: *1-59462-352-X*   **$29.95**
The two girls were both pretty, but Lucy who was twenty-one who supposed to be simple and comparatively unattractive, whereas Ayala was credited, as her Bombwhat romantic name might show, with poetic charm and a taste for romance. Ayala when her father died was nineteen...   Fiction Pages 484

☐ **The American Commonwealth** *by James Bryce*   ISBN: *1-59462-286-8*   **$34.45**
An interpretation of American democratic political theory. It examines political mechanics and society from the perspective of Scotsman James Bryce   Politics Pages 572

☐ **Stories of the Pilgrims** *by Margaret P. Pumphrey*   ISBN: *1-59462-116-0*   **$17.95**
This book explores pilgrims religious oppression in England as well as their escape to Holland and eventual crossing to America on the Mayflower, and their early days in New England...   History Pages 268

QTY

The Fasting Cure *by Sinclair Upton*   ISBN: *1-59462-222-1* $13.95

In the Cosmopolitan Magazine for May, 1910, and in the Contemporary Review (London) for April, 1910, I published an article dealing with my experiences in fasting. I have written a great many magazine articles, but never one which attracted so much attention... New Age/Self Help/Health Pages 164

Hebrew Astrology *by Sepharial*   ISBN: *1-59462-308-2* $13.45

In these days of advanced thinking it is a matter of common observation that we have left many of the old landmarks behind and that we are now pressing forward to greater heights and to a wider horizon than that which represented the mind-content of our progenitors... Astrology Pages 144

Thought Vibration or The Law of Attraction in the Thought World   ISBN: *1-59462-127-6* $12.95

by William Walker Atkinson   Psychology/Religion Pages 144

Optimism *by Helen Keller*   ISBN: *1-59462-108-X* $15.95

Helen Keller was blind, deaf, and mute since 19 months old, yet famously learned how to overcome these handicaps, communicate with the world, and spread her lectures promoting optimism. An inspiring read for everyone... Biographies/Inspirational Pages 84

Sara Crewe *by Frances Burnett*   ISBN: *1-59462-360-0* $9.45

In the first place, Miss Minchin lived in London. Her home was a large, dull, tall one, in a large, dull square, where all the houses were alike, and all the sparrows were alike, and where all the door-knockers made the same heavy sound... Childrens/Classic Pages 88

The Autobiography of Benjamin Franklin *by Benjamin Franklin*   ISBN: *1-59462-135-7* $24.95

The Autobiography of Benjamin Franklin has probably been more extensively read than any other American historical work, and no other book of its kind has had such ups and downs of fortune. Franklin lived for many years in England, where he was agent... Biographies/History Pages 332

Name	
Email	
Telephone	
Address	
City, State ZIP	

☐ **Credit Card**   ☐ **Check / Money Order**

Credit Card Number	
Expiration Date	
Signature	

Please Mail to: Book Jungle
PO Box 2226
Champaign, IL 61825
or Fax to: 630-214-0564

ORDERING INFORMATION

web*: www.bookjungle.com*
email*: sales@bookjungle.com*
fax*: 630-214-0564*
mail*: Book Jungle PO Box 2226 Champaign, IL 61825*
or PayPal *to sales@bookjungle.com*

Please contact us for bulk discounts

DIRECT-ORDER TERMS

**20% Discount if You Order
Two or More Books**
Free Domestic Shipping!
Accepted: Master Card, Visa,
Discover, American Express